CLAIMED BY
THE MOUNTAIN MAN

GEMMA WEIR

CW01496993

Claimed by the Mountain Man

Montana Mountain Men #4

Copyright © 2021 Gemma Weir

Published by Hudson Indie Ink

www.hudsonindieink.com

This book is licensed for your personal enjoyment only.

This book may not be re-sold or given away to other people. If you would like to share this book with another person, please purchase an additional copy for each recipient. If you're reading this book and did not purchase it, or it wasn't purchased for your use only, then please return to your favourite book retailer and purchase your own copy. Thank you for respecting the hard work of this author.

All rights reserved.

This is a work of fiction. Names, characters, places, brands, media, and incidents are either the product of the authors imagination or are used fictitiously. The author acknowledges the trademark status and trademark owners of various products referred to in this work of fiction, which have been used without permission. The publication/use of these trademarks is not authorised, associated with, or sponsored by the trademark owners.

Claimed by the Mountain Man/Gemma Weir – 1st ed.

ISBN-13 - 978-1-913769-74-1

Megan,

One mountain man is great, but seven is sooo much better. Also, I was crazy pregnant when I wrote this, so sorry... but not really.

#claimedbyPen

WARNING

This book contains an over the top, jealous, unreasonable, possessive asshole.

If you consider unapologetic alphaholes unacceptable, or feel their behavior is in some way abusive, then this isn't the book or series for you.

If you're a nay sayer who thinks what I write is romanticizing domestic violence and abuse then please, please stop reading now.

This book isn't a guide to dysfunctional relationships, it's fiction. My books are fantasy, this isn't real life, it's a romance novel and should be read as such.

We all know in the real world throwing a woman over your shoulder, messing with her birth control or stalking her and letting yourself into her home is a one-way ticket to either a restraining order or the mental hospital. But I'd like to think that in fiction it's okay to agree that these things are incredibly sexy. Please do not kink shame me or my enthusiastic readers for finding these extreme alphahole behaviors hot, maybe if you read this book with the pinch of romantic salt it was intended to come with, you might like it too.

So if, like me, you love a guy who is so obsessively in love with his girl that he will snarl, demand, punish and fuck her until she gives herself to him completely, then read on and welcome to the world of my Montana Mountain Men.

CLAIMED BY THE MOUNTAIN MAN

GEMMA WEIR

ONE

PENN

I want what my brothers have. I don't think that's too much to ask. Beau, Huck and Granger have all found their women and they're balls deep in their happily ever afters with wedding rings and babies and all that shit; now it's my turn.

I know most guys are happy fucking about until they're dragged kicking and screaming into a relationship, where they're forced to settle down and stop being jackasses, but I'm not like them. At least not anymore. I've had my fair share of pussy, probably more than my fair share, but I'm done with that now. I want *my* woman, the one I own, the one that's so indisputably mine they repel other guys

9

because the smell of my cum leaches from their pores. I want to own her in a way that's almost too fucked up to confess, even to myself, but that's the truth, so fuck it, why should I lie?

Women fall at my feet, I'm hot and I know it. But I don't want easy, I want the fight, I want someone to tell me no. Then I want to watch as they learn that I don't take no for an answer.

Now all I need is to find her, because not just any woman will do, it has to be *my* woman and she needs to hurry the fuck up and get here, because I'm done waiting. I've watched my brothers fall and now it's time for me to claim my own prize.

TWO

LULU

Jesus, how can the traffic be this ridiculous in a town this small? At this rate I'll be late for my first day at my new job. Because what I need is to make a bad first impression, especially given that the only reason I have this job is because my new landlady, who also happens to be my godmother, basically forced Janet, my new boss, to give it to me.

Rockhead Point shouldn't have this many cars, I mean, Christ, it's in the mountains in the middle of nowhere, how many people can really live here?

I've been in town exactly a week and I'm already craving the hustle and bustle of Chicago. I'd never really considered myself a city girl, until I got here and realized how much I took for granted the constantly fast-moving pace of living among the masses.

Exhaling slowly, I remind myself why I'm here and my frustration ebbs. This is the right place for me to be. After everything that happened back home, staying in the city wasn't an option, neither was moving anywhere else. I'm here because of Aunt Chloe, because she loves me and because she's the only one of my family who has unwaveringly supported the decisions I've made over the last year.

When everything went to shit, she was there for me, she didn't say I told you so, or sneer at me and tell me there was an easy solution to the situation I found myself in. Instead, she calmly helped me sort through my options, then when it became clear to me that there was only one way forward, she offered me help, a place to stay and constant, unending love.

The bottle neck of cars moves and I slowly edge forward, the neat, inoffensive store front of the lawyer's office where I start work today appearing in front of me. I'm definitely not as early as I'd like to be as I guide my car into a space in the parking lot and grab my purse from the seat beside me, but I'm not late and for now, I'm going to call that a win.

Back in Chicago, I was right in the middle of prep to

take the bar when my life changed, I never got around to taking the test, instead I took my paralegal certificate online and now here I am, not following the meticulously plotted ten-year plan that would have seen me in a Prada suit taking the legal world by storm. But it's okay, because this life was my choice, my decision, and I don't regret it. My career might be the dark blight on my horizon, but everything else is blindingly glorious sunshine.

Slipping my feet into my nude pumps I kicked off to drive, I open my door and slide out, locking my car and smoothing down my skirt as I make my way out of the lot and onto the sidewalk.

Today is a good day. New town, new job, new life.

My cell beeps in my purse and I reach for it, a surge of panic tumbling through me in case something's wrong. I'm so intent on finding it that I don't notice the person in front of me until I walk straight into them. Bouncing off the rock-hard chest of an immovable object I startle back, my heel twisting beneath me as my knees buckle and I prepare to hit the ground.

Only instead of hitting the hard sidewalk, a huge hand wraps around my wrist, his grip tight, bordering on painful as my backward momentum is stopped and instead, I'm slowly pulled upright. My breath bursts out of me in a shocked exhale and I lift my head, looking up into the face of my savior.

Hard, black eyes. An angel's face, with the aura of a devil. Dark hair, strong cheekbones, an austere roman nose and full lips stare back at me. My savior is much taller than me, but I'm barely five feet two, so most everyone seems tall to me. His shoulders are broad, his arms thick, his hand is huge; thick fingers grip my arm like he's making sure I don't run.

Intensity is rolling off him in waves and I can't help the shudder of fear that ripples across my skin. Neither of us has spoken and it's either been a millisecond or an hour since he stopped me from falling, but somehow time has no place here.

"It's you," he rasps, his voice, low, rough and full of warning.

I blink, because I don't know this man. He's the kind of guy you eye fuck in a club, then run away from because he's so sexy and quintessentially male that you know he'll break your heart with nothing more than a kiss. "I'm sorry?" My words are intended as a question, but somehow, they sound more like an apology.

"Come."

The single word is all he says and he turns, not releasing his hold on me as he starts to move, dragging me along with him. I take two steps before I question my behavior. What the hell am I doing? Who is this guy and why am I letting him take me somewhere? Snatching my arm, I plant my feet and attempt to free myself from the sexy psycho's grip, but he's strong and apparently pretty intent on taking me wherever he plans to go.

"Hey," I shout, trying to pry his fingers free with my other hand as I stumble along behind him.

Exhaling, like me not wanting to be dragged to some unknown location is an incredibly big inconvenience to him, he slows to a stop and turns to face me. "What?"

"Err, you need to let me go."

"No," he says nonchalantly.

"What? You can't just say no. I don't know you, you're not a cop and I need to go to work," I say, attempting to sound calm in response to his strange behavior.

"Quit, you don't need to work."

"What the actual fuck is happening here? I don't know you and of course I need to work," I shriek confusedly.

"No you don't, I take care of what's mine, I don't want you to work."

"Yours? Who are you? What the hell is going on? Let go of me, you asshole, or I'll scream so fucking loud the entire town will hear."

He moves so fast I barely even have time to blink before his hand is around my throat and his lips are on mine. He's kissing me. He's kissing me? I don't react, too scared and shocked and bewildered to respond, but he doesn't seem to care as his lips stroke against mine, his

15

tongue making its way into my mouth and exploring.

I try to wiggle away, all my muscles tense and in escape mode, but the hand at my throat tightens and I immediately still, aware of the danger this stranger could represent, this huge mountain of a man who's assaulting me right out in the open on the street.

After a long moment he pulls way, a tiny reluctant sound falling from him as he presses a soft kiss to my lips and stares down at me, his hateful black stare sparkling with something that I don't recognize.

"I've been waiting for you."

"Who the fuck are you?" I snarl.

"Mouth. Normally I like a woman who curses, but I don't like it on your lips."

"Fuck you," I hiss back, unable to stop the words from slipping out, even in the face of this madman.

His chuckle is pure sin, "Oh my little kitty has claws."

"Let me go."

"Never," he laughs again.

Forcing myself to relax, I instruct my muscles to go limp and just like I expected, his grip on me loosens. Sensing my chance, I rip myself free of his hold and without thought, turn and run, bursting through the door and into the lawyer's office as if the devil himself is chasing me down.

My breathing is ragged and I'm shaking as I stumble

over to the receptionist's desk, wide eyed and manic.

"Goodness me, are you okay? What happened to you?" Annette, the receptionist I met last week when Chloe dragged me down here exclaims.

"I was just attacked on the street," I pant out, my one hand pressed against my racing heart.

"Oh, good lord," Annette cries, jumping up from her seat and circling her desk to come to my side just as the door opens and my attacker saunters in, a wide grin etched across his lips.

"Oh Penn, thank goodness you're here, Lulu was just attacked out on the street, can you call the sheriff and tell him he needs to get on down here," Annette says, addressing my pursuer like he's not a madman who just tried to kidnap me.

"It was h…him," I stutter out, lifting my finger to point at him.

"What, dear?" Annette says, her palm rubbing soothingly up and down my arm.

"He… he was the one who attacked me."

"Penn?" she asks confusedly.

"He grabbed me and tried to drag me down the sidewalk, then he assaulted me," I cry out, my voice getting stronger as I push down the panic and force myself to calm.

"Penn attacked you?" her words come out on a

squeak, like she can barely understand the things I'm saying.

"Morning Annette, how're Herb and the kids?" the psycho asks so cordially I feel my mouth fall open.

"They're fine, thank you, Penn. But what's all this about you attacking our new employee?"

He chuckles and I stare incredulously between the two of them. What the hell kind of town is this? Chicago might have its faults but if I burst into a building and said someone had assaulted me I'm fairly sure my attacker would get more than a smile and a scolding look.

"She's mine," he answers succinctly.

Annette's eyes widen comically and she slowly turns to face me. "Oh dear."

THREE

PENN

M ine.

That's the first thought that crosses my mind when the tiny woman who just walked straight into me looks up at me from beneath dark, long eyelashes. She's tiny, curvy and beautiful. Her hair is curled into bouncy twirls, hitting just below her chin, a deep mahogany color, almost brown until the light hits it and shows the red. Rich brown eyes peak out from her pixie like features, with full plump lips that I want to make puffy and swollen with my kisses and my dick.

Her body is a fucking playground. Wide hips, full tits, an hourglass shape that begs me to wrap my hands around her waist and hold her still while I fuck her from beneath, forcing my dick into her until she's screaming or crying. I've never been into skinny woman; I want an ass to slap and something to hold onto while I watch their tits bounce as I drive my dick into them. I bet her nipples are big too, round and pink and waiting to be sucked.

She's perfection, every sexual fantasy come to life, and all fucking mine.

My dick's rock hard and I need to be inside her now, like right this fucking second. I want to feel her heat around my cock; and she's mine, so why the fuck should I wait? My hands are still on her from where I stopped her from falling, so I turn and head toward my car, trying to decide if I can last long enough to get her home, or if I should just take her to the apartment above the shop. It's where I normally take women I fuck, but this woman is mine, so I should probably take her home, right?

It takes me a moment to realize she's not totally on board with my plans to go fuck her brains out, but then I haven't actually told her them yet. I know I spoke, but I don't know what I said, my head and my dick are too consumed with the fact that she's here, my woman is fucking here.

Nails pry at my fingers and she shouts at me, her pouty lips twisting into a grimace as she tries to pull herself free, but instead of letting her go I drag her to me and kiss her. Her lips taste like toothpaste and I hate it. I've got nothing against mint per-se, but I want to know what she tastes like, maybe from now on I'll feed her my dick after she brushes her teeth so she tastes like my cum. Yeah, I like that idea, so does my cock.

Reluctantly, I pull my lips from hers and she curses at me. "Mouth. Normally I like a woman who curses, but I don't like it on your lips."

Her mouth falls open and she gawps at me like she can't believe what I'm saying. When she relaxes, her muscles unclenching beneath my touch, my dick twitches excitedly at the way she's reacting. Then the little vixen yanks herself free from my hold and bolts for the door of Taylor James's law office.

A chuckle falls from my lips as I watch her throw open the door and disappear inside. It's funny that she thinks she can run from me, that I'll let her go, that I won't chase.

Adjusting my dick in my pants so it's not quite so fucking obvious that I'm sporting a hard-on the size of my fucking arm, I wait a moment before I follow her into the building. She's at Annette's, desk, her cheeks pale, her chest heaving up and down.

Annette speaks, asking me something that I don't pay any attention to.

"It was h...him," my woman stutters out, lifting her finger to point at me.

"What, dear?" Annette asks as she rubs her palm soothingly up and down her arm.

"He… he was the one who attacked me."

"Penn?" Annette asks confusedly, her eyes looking to me for an explanation.

"He grabbed me and tried to drag me down the sidewalk, then he assaulted me," she cries out.

Assault? I definitely kissed her, but I didn't hurt her. Although maybe the hand at her throat might have been a bit much considering we just met, but the women in this town would line up to kiss me and she's calling it an attack. What the fuck?

"Penn attacked you?" Annette squeaks, her eyes wide as she implores me to explain this.

"Morning Annette, how're Herb and the kids?" I ask cordially, smiling widely.

"They're fine, thank you, Penn. But what's all this about you attacking our new employee?"

New employee? She's working for Taylor? I don't want her to work, I want her at home waiting for me; preferably naked. Annette's still waiting for me to explain, so I turn to the woman I've known my whole life and say simply. "She's mine."

Since Beau fell for Bonnie over a year ago, our family legacy has become somewhat of an urban legend in town. Whispers of how we know our woman on sight have been circling for months, with girls I've known my entire life throwing themselves into the path of me and my remaining single brothers, in the hope that we'll suddenly realize they're ours. So it's no surprise that Annette's eyes widen comically large, her lips falling open as she looks to my woman at her side and says, "Oh dear."

"Oh dear?" my woman shrieks. "Oh fucking dear?! What the fuck? Call the cops!"

"Mouth," I warn again, lifting my finger and pointing it at her.

"Fuck you. You attacked me, you assaulted me. I'll say whatever the fuck I want."

"Penn, what did you do to the poor girl?" Annette asks.

Annette is Taylor's eldest daughter, she's older than Beau, maybe later forties, with a husband and brood of kids at home. We're not exactly friends, but her youngest brother Carl is a good buddy, so I suppose you could say we're friendly by default.

"I just kissed her, Annie," I cajole, using the pet name her brother called her when we were kids and sneaking beer or cigarettes.

Her expression softens as she purses her lips and turns to my woman. "Lulu, honey, did the neanderthal bother to introduce himself before he went all caveman on you?"

"Lulu?" I say. "Your name is Lulu?" I ask my girl.

Annette tuts. "Really, Penn, you didn't even ask her name before you planted one on her, no wonder the poor girl is saying you attacked her, you've probably scared her half to death."

"What the fuck is going on here?" Lulu asks, incredulity lacing each word that comes from her sharp mouth.

"Honey, this here is Penn Barnett, he's an idiot, but I swear he's not dangerous." Annette looks up at me, arching her brows. "You want to explain before she calls the sheriff?"

"You're mine," I say, locking eyes with Lulu and forcing her to hold my gaze.

"Really, Penn?" Annette scolds again. "Honey, Penn is one of seven brothers, their daddy Hannigan, he met their mama and knew the moment he set eyes on her that she was meant to be his wife. From what I've been told, he married her less than a week after meeting her, they had seven boys, and lived blissfully in love until he passed away."

"Okay," Lulu says, eying me warily as I take a step closer to her.

"Well apparently his sons fall in love the same way as their daddy did, they find their woman and know immediately that she's the one for them."

"You've got to be shitting me," Lulu says, her face twisting into an expression of disbelief and… repulsion?

"I know it sounds ridiculous, like something out of a romance film. But it's happened that way for three of the seven boys so far," Annette says with a wistful, girly sigh.

"So what the fuck does that have to do with me? And why the hell—after this asshole put his hands on me, tried to kidnap me and then sexually assaulted me—are you trying to explain some stupid story about love at first sight instead of helping me get his ass into a cell?"

"Kitten, I stopped you from falling, then I kissed you, I'm not sure you could find a judge in the country who'd arrest me for that," I say with a smirk, as I close the distance between us and rest my hands on either side of her on the desk, not touching her, but caging her in. "I'm a Barnett, and you're mine."

"Like hell I am," she snaps, placing one palm flat against my chest and pushing.

I don't move. Hell, I don't even sway, not when her second palm lands on my chest and she leans into her arms, trying to physically move me away. "Not going to happen, Kitten, look at the size of me, then the size of you, a tiny little kitty like you isn't going to move me unless I decide to move."

"You're in my personal space, I'd like you to leave."

I can tell by the tone of her voice that's she's trying to force herself to be calm and stow all the fire and anger that's bubbling just below the surface, she's fucking adorable. "Let me take you out."

"No."

"Only way I'm moving from here is with your phone number on my cell and an agreement to let me take you out. I'm not a fucking patient man and considering what I really want to do is throw you over my shoulder, take you back to my place and claim that hot, wet little pussy, I think your number and dinner is a pretty good compromise," I whisper against her ear.

"Oh my god, who the fuck says stuff like that to a stranger? I'm calling the cops."

Smirking down at her, I arch my brow and dare her to do it. I can see by the look in her eyes that she's expecting me to back down, to move away; hell, maybe she thinks I'm going to leave. But I'm not. She's mine now and I'm not going anywhere.

Her eyes are half on me, half on her purse as she starts to root around inside the deep purple leather bag that's so big I've seen smaller suitcases. Triumph flares in her gaze when she finds her cell and dials what I'm guessing is 911. "I'm not kidding, I just dialed the cops," she warns, lifting the cell to her ear.

Annette clears her throat behind us. "Honey, I'm not—"

"It's fine, Annette," I say, glancing at her over my shoulder and flashing her a smile. "Is she working with

26

Taylor or Janet?"

"She's Janet's new paralegal."

I cringe a little at that, Janet Hallsworth is a grade A bitch. She's Taylor's niece, but she didn't grow up in Rockhead Point like most people in town. Janet grew up in New York and she's got the attitude that comes with being a big city girl. I don't really remember the details of the scandal that brought her from her high-rise office in a big law firm, to working with her uncle here in Montana, but even five years later she's still pretty sore about being here. She hit on Beau right back when she first moved to town, and when he turned her down, she decided that all Barnett men were assholes and nothing's swayed her opinion of us so far.

"Could you let your dad know what's going on and ask him to speak to Janet? You know she'll only cause a fuss if I try to talk to her."

Annette nods and scurries away to the offices at the back of the building. Focusing my attention on Lulu, I wait for her to start to speak to the 911 dispatcher, who is probably Carrie Flanagan, Cora's brother's on-again-off-again girlfriend. But instead of telling them about all my crimes, she says. "Sorry I called by mistake, I'm fine," then slowly ends the call, glaring at me. "If you don't leave, I'll call the cops back."

"Rockhead Point has a sheriff's department not a PD,"

I tell her calmly.

"Whatever, asshole. Either way, if you don't go, you're going to get arrested."

The smile that spreads across my lips is indulgent and she blinks in response. "You're not from a small town, are you?"

"Where I'm from is none of your god-damn business."

"That mouth of yours is looking to get you in trouble, Kitten, I think I'm going to spend a lot of time washing that filthy language off your tongue with my dick."

Her pupils dilate, even as she forces her lips into a frown. "Never going to happen, dickweed, but maybe you can use that thought to take your mind off being used as some guy's bitch in jail."

A chuckle bursts free from my lips. "You're a fiery little thing aren't you. I'm going to enjoy taming you. I like you all spicy like this, but I want to see you purring like the little kitten you are."

Shaking her head, she looks away from me, a disgusted expression laced across her fuckable lips. "I'm not sorry for kissing you, I couldn't help myself, but maybe I should have at least introduced myself first. I'm Penn."

"I think you should leave."

"If I could, maybe I would, but now I've found you I'm not sure I'm going to be able to walk away from you ever again."

"Look, I'm sure this love at first sight bullshit works on some women, but I'm not interested."

"Is Lulu your real name or a nickname?"

"That's none of your business," she says, but the fight has gone from her voice.

I allow her a little breathing room, leaning back as a reward for her calming down. "Tell me and I'll leave."

Her sigh is defeated. I don't like it. I want her to bite back so I'll have an excuse to force her to calm down. "My real name is Lucile, but I hate it, so… Lulu."

The urge to reach out and kiss her again is so fucking strong I almost do it, almost. My dick is rock hard and if I didn't think she really might call 911 again, I'd drag her into my arms and fuck her mouth with my tongue. Instead, I smile at her. "Lulu, sweet, cute, it's perfect for you."

"I told you my name, now it's time for you to go."

"I'll go on one condition."

"What?"

"Give me your cell number."

"No."

"You don't get it yet, but I wasn't kidding when I said you were mine. The only way I'm going to be able to walk away like you want me to right now, is if I have a way of getting in touch with you. Otherwise, I'm going to park my ass in a chair and sit here for the rest of the day so I know you're okay."

"You planning to add stalking to your rap sheet?" she barbs, and I can't help the smile that slips free.

"Maybe I'll just have a really long visit with Annette, I've known her most of my life, that's the great thing about small towns, everyone, knows everyone else."

"Whatever, waste your day, I have to get to work."

With that she turns and I let her go, watching as she marches her fat, juicy ass down the corridor and away from me. Smiling, I sit down on the waiting room couch, pull out my cell and type out a message in our family group chat.

Me

I found her. Her name's Lulu and she started work today at Taylor's lawyer's office. She's mine, but she's not exactly amenable at the minute so I might need your help.

The replies come through thick and fast and I smile, glad that my family is just as crazy as me.

Bonnie

Poor girl.

Bay

Congrats bro, I take it you won't be coming to work today

Cody

Another one bites the dust

Granger

Awesome news, my record is five hours, reckon you can beat that?

Alice

I'm happy for you, Penn. Granger, you basically kidnapped me.

Granger

You loved it.

Huck

Cora says congrats and that she's planning a girls' night out to welcome the newbie as soon as this baby pops.

Beau

Happy for you, brother.

Teddy

How can we help?

FOUR

LULU

Pushing through the door into the office that's now mine, I close it behind me and exhale shakily. Penn Barnett is a force of nature and it took almost everything I had not to melt into his huge, dominating, infuriating arms. I'm still angry about him kissing me, following me and all the "mine" bullshit, but Jesus, he is one seriously sexy man. When he whispered those naughty things in my ear, the urge to allow him to overwhelm me was almost unbearable.

Since I was a teenager and really started noticing boys, I learned I had a type. I wish I could say that I liked the sweet nerdy guys who bring you flowers and carry your books, but the truth is those ones were never the stars of my dirty teenage fantasies. Nope, I crave the assholes. The jocks, the overbearing meatheads who have a tendency to bully their way into getting whatever and whoever they want in life.

Alphaholes are my catnip. Unfortunately, that means that my dating history mainly consists of assholes who cheat on me, or those who want to fuck me in private, loving my curves, but pretend I don't exist in real life. My last serious boyfriend, Eric, was a total meathead, he was on the college football team, big, built, sexy and totally into me. We dated for most of my junior and senior years at the university of Chicago and I really thought he was the one, until I found him in bed with a stick thin cheerleader named Muffy.

He really enjoyed telling me how my curves and my career aspirations were cute, but that if the NFL was going to come calling, he needed to have the right kind of woman on his arm. At the time, I was more angry than hurt, but it taught me a valuable lesson. Guys like that are assholes. I've been single ever since, choosing to focus on law school and passing the bar. Well, at least until my life changed almost eighteen months ago.

Still, I'm not immune to hot guys, and Penn Barnett with his huge body and his gravelly "Mine" is the worst kind of temptation for me.

Inhaling, I force myself to slow my breathing until I'm relatively calm. The office I'm standing in acts as mix of waiting room, storage room, and antechamber. Janet, my new boss's office is through a door at the far end. Her door is shut and I'm grateful as I take a moment to pull myself together.

Crossing the room, I lower myself into my seat, place my purse beneath my desk at my feet and move the mouse to bring my computer to life. Taylor, the founding partner and senior lawyer here, gave me all the user names and passwords to access the computer system last week, so I confidently log on and open my email. There're ten unread emails sitting in my inbox, all from Janet.

I had planned to go and make both myself and her a coffee before I got started, but as an eleventh email pings into my inbox, I decide against that plan and get straight to work. Janet made it very clear when I met with her last week that she doesn't like me, doesn't want me here and is only entertaining my presence because Taylor, her uncle, employed me as a favor to my godmother Chloe.

Apparently it doesn't matter that I graduated from Harvard Law, or that I only need to take the bar to become a practicing lawyer, she doesn't care. To her, I'm nothing but an inconvenient nuisance. I'm determined to change her mind. I might only be a paralegal, but I'll be the best damn paralegal she's ever met and when I do take the bar, I'll be her equal and she can take her disdain and shove it up her ass.

I don't leave my desk for the next two hours, forcing everything but my list of tasks from my mind. It's obvious that some of the things Janet has requested I do are intended to piss me off, like researching ancient out of date precedent that I very much doubt she would ever need in a small-town lawyer's office. But I do it all without question, emailing back everything she's asked for one by one.

By the time my stomach starts to growl, it's after two and I've still yet to even see Janet today. I'm assuming she's in her office, but there's been no proof of life, so I tentatively tap on her door.

"Come."

Pushing it open just wide enough for me to peer around the gap, I smile. "I'm just going to grab some lunch; did you want me to get you anything?" It's totally not my job to get her food, but I'm nice and it's my first day. I don't want to give her any excuse to be any more unpleasant to me.

"No thank you," she says curtly, not even bothering to lift her gaze from her computer monitor.

"Okay then." It's obvious she has no intention of speaking further, so I close the door behind me, grab my purse and head over to Taylor's office that mirrors mine and Janet's on the other side of the corridor.

Taylor is a robust, white-haired man that looks far too much like the KFC colonel. Unlike his niece, he is by far one of the nicest men I've ever met. He has a sunny, playful disposition and a manner that makes you want to hug him. His paralegal is a man named Dave, who seems to have an equally sunny outlook, and he immediately lifts his head and smiles widely at me the moment I step inside.

"Well good afternoon, Lulu, how's your first day going? I've been listening out for the yelling so I could come on over and rescue you, but it's been mighty quiet over there."

"So far, so good," I say, not wanting to bitch about my new boss's frosty nature on my first day.

"I'm glad to hear it, you've already lasted longer than the last two paralegals, if you make it the full week it'll be a record," Dave laughs.

"How many paralegals has she had?" The question slips out before I can stop it.

"You're number twelve."

"Twelve! In how long?"

"That's just in the last three months," he says with a smirk.

My eyes widen and suddenly I'm wondering if Taylor wasn't just being nice when he offered me this job. "Err, wow. Okay, I actually came to ask if you wanted me to grab you anything while I'm getting lunch?"

"No thank you, sweetie, I always bring something from home. I'm vegan and, well, Rockhead Point hasn't caught up with the rest of the modern world about veganism just yet."

I smile. "Is Taylor in, has he eaten?"

"He is and he has. Mama June always packs him a brown bag. She has him on a low-fat diet and she doesn't trust him not to gorge himself on fried chicken if he has to go out and buy something."

Less than five minutes in Dave's company and I already feel better. There's something about him that's infectiously happy, and after everything that's happened this morning, a little ray of sunshine is exactly what I need. With a smile and a wave, I leave his office and head toward the exit, only to stumble when I spot the local psycho, Penn Barnett sitting on the waiting room couch, his feet propped up on the table, a wide smile on his face.

"Kitten, I was wondering when you'd be coming out for lunch. What do you fancy? Granny Annie's food is great or there's Wake Up and Go Go if you need a caffeine fix."

He's here, and his body language is screaming comfortable, lusty comradery. What the actual hell? "What are you doing?"

"Taking you for lunch." He smiles, unfurling himself

from his seat on the couch and revealing his intimidating height as he towers over me.

"No thanks. But I meant what are you doing *here*?" I do a weird, spinney finger gesture.

"I told you I wasn't going anywhere until you gave me your number and agreed to go out with me."

"You've been here the whole time?" I furrow my brow, turning to Annette who is sitting behind her desk. She nods, smiling sheepishly before looking away, pointedly focusing her attention on her computer screen. "Why?" I ask, turning back to eye him suspiciously.

"Because you're mine and I'm not just going to walk away."

Something about the tone of his voice and the way his whole body is tense makes me want to throw myself at him, almost as much as it makes me want to turn tail and run in the opposite direction. Penn Barnett is kind of annoyingly perfect, he's a hot, dominant asshole. If my life was different, I'd be on him like white on rice. But my life isn't different, and right now I'm not in the position to indulge some alphahole who thinks I'm his property within minutes of meeting me.

"Yeah, no. That's not going to work for me," I say, wrinkling my nose dismissively and striding past him. "Annette, you need anything for lunch?" I call over my shoulder.

"No thanks, sweetie," she calls back. I don't acknowledge her, I can't look behind me because if he's looking at me with all that intense want and need, I'll falter. So instead I throw open the door and leave.

He's beside me a moment later, his arm dropping around my shoulders. "Get your arm off me. I don't know you and I don't want you touching me."

"I think we both know that's a lie, you like it when I touch you."

"Err nope, strange men don't do it for me," I quip, still striding on. I'm not exactly sure where I'm going, I vaguely remember there being a café or coffee shop in this direction when Chloe showed me around town, but really, I could be headed in the totally wrong direction. Either way, I can't stop now, not with my stalker in tow.

"I'm not a strange man, I'm your man, so you can admit you like me touching you. If anyone else touches you we're going have a problem though," he growls.

"Wow." I stop walking and turn to look at him, dislodging his arm from around me as I do. "Do you actually hear the shit coming out of your mouth right now? I have a boyfriend, and he's going to have a problem with you kissing and manhandling me, so hands off," I cry.

"No you don't."

"Excuse me?"

"You don't have a boyfriend."

"What? Yes I do."

"What's his name."

Fuck. "Tony," I say quickly.

"Tony," Penn repeats back to me, a smirk etched across his plump full lips. "And where is Tony?"

"At work."

"What does he do?"

"Lawyer."

"Where does he live?"

Oh crap, he's got me here. Obviously, fictional Tony doesn't live here in this tiny town where everyone knows everyone. "Chicago."

"So he's not your boyfriend. If he was any kind of a man he wouldn't let his woman live on the other side of the country from him."

"Oh my god, do you hear yourself? He's not a caveman and I can live wherever I choose."

"No, Kitten, he's not a man. You obviously made him up, has anyone ever told you you're a terrible liar?"

He's smirking again. God, he's good looking, why is he so good looking? And yes, many people have told me I'm a terrible liar, but I've been working on it and I really thought I was getting better. After all, you can't be a good lawyer unless you have a great poker face.

"Whatever, I'm still not yours to touch, so keep your hands to yourself." I try for an imperious tone as I turn and start marching down the street again, but I think I probably sound more peevish, not a great look on a grown ass woman.

His quiet chuckle follows me, then the weight of his arm settles over my shoulder again, his fingers drawing circles on my bare skin. "If you don't like it, then why are your nipples hard?" he drawls smugly.

I try to shrug his arm off but he keeps it fixed in place and after the third failed attempt to remove him, I give up, keeping my body tense to ward myself against the tingles that his fingers are creating. It isn't until I spot the coffee shop ahead of us that I start to relax, I pretty much know he's going to insist on joining me, but at least I can put a table between us and maybe convince him I'm not interested in him.

The bell above the door jingles when I push it open and he immediately presses his palm against it above my head, holding it open for me while I step inside. A pretty brunette is serving behind the counter, and the place is reasonably quiet. There're only a handful of people ahead of me and about half the tables filled. Penn is ominously quiet beside me, but his arm is still hanging possessively over my shoulder, keeping me with him and silently marking me as his.

"Welcome to Wake Up... Oh hey, Penn," the girl says when she looks up from the counter. Her smile freezes a little when her eyes go from me to the arm that's around me. Shit, is this girl Penn's ex? Am I about to be stuck in the middle of some messed up relationship drama because this guy won't take no for an answer and walk away?

"Hey Bonnie, I'd like you to meet Lulu, she's mine," Penn announces loudly.

"Yours," Bonnie says softly. Her eyes widen as a slightly manic expression appears on her face, right before she bounds around the counter and throws her arms around me, hugging me tightly.

I am not a hugger.

Frozen, I keep my arms by my side, my purse still gripped tightly in one hand while the second stranger of the day invades my personal space.

"Oh my goodness, I'm so happy for you guys," the girl gushes. She's young, maybe late teens, or early twenties. Eventually she releases me completely and takes a step back.

"Lulu, this is my sister Bonnie," Penn explains with a chuckle.

His sister, this is his sister. I'm inadvertently meeting his family and he just told her I'm his. Fuck my life. I've entered the twilight zone, that really is the only explanation for this entirely too messed up day.

"I'm not his," I hiss, then turn to Penn, "I'm not yours."

"Oh sweetie, resistance is futile, but I've been where you are. We should swap numbers, trust me you're going to need someone to talk you through how to deal with a Barnett man," Bonnie says sweetly.

"That's nice of you, but I have no interest in dealing with him, so I'm good. I'd love a large latte and one of those yummy looking bagels though please."

"Err," Bonnie looks at me and then to Penn beside me. He must give her some kind of nod or whatever, because she steps back and heads behind the counter.

"I'll take a large black coffee, a pecan banana muffin and pastrami on rye if you have it please," Penn says.

"You guys eating in?" Bonnie asks.

"Yes," Penn says at the same time I say "No."

Her eyes stay wide as she looks between us again.

"Takeaway please, Bonnie, I have to get back to work," I tell her, trying to be as polite as possible. Just because I'm pissed at her annoying and boundary ignoring brother, doesn't mean I need to be rude to her.

"Takeaway then apparently," Penn says, a slightly huffy tone to his voice.

I consider arguing and telling her he's eating in and I'll be leaving, but it's not worth the argument, so instead I reach into my purse to grab some money. Penn's handed her some cash before I get a chance, but not to be deterred I still hold money for my own food over the counter.

Her laugh is loud and full of amusement. "Let him pay, a free lunch is a free lunch." Ringing up the food and drinks she passes him his change, then rolls her eyes as he pushes it all into the tip jar beside the cash register.

Penn plays with the ends of my hair as we wait, I can feel him watching me, but I stare ahead, forcing my attention to stay on Bonnie as she scurries around making drinks and toasting sandwiches.

"You can't ignore me forever, Kitten," he whispers against my ear, pushing my hair out of the way so I can feel his hot breath against my skin.

"I can try," I mutter.

"But why bother? You're mine and I'm yours, there's no point fighting the inevitable. Let me take you to dinner, then after I can show you how good it is to be owned by me. I'll make your little kitty drool for me. I'll make her sore and swollen with my fat dick, then lick her better with my tongue. I'll make you drunk on the pleasure I can give you."

"No thanks," I force out, my voice shakier than I'd like as I fight the full body shudder that tries to escape in reaction to his lust drenched words.

Pulling me a little closer into him, his fingers slide from my shoulder and along my collarbone until they wrap loosely around my throat. I've never experimented with breath play but he's not trying to restrict my breathing, his touch is purely possessive and I hate how much I like it. How is it possible that this guy, this stranger is hitting all of my buttons, like he's reading how to turn me on straight out of my own personalized user manual?

"I don't want you to touch me," I say, making a half-hearted attempt to remove myself from his control.

"Liar. Your pupils are dilated, your breaths are ragged and your nipples are hard. I'd lay money on the fact that your little kitty is wet and your panties are all sticky and coated in want. You might not like how much you want me right now, but it's a lie to say that you don't. I bet you're standing there wondering how I know exactly what to do to make you all needy and horny. It's because you're mine, every cell and molecule in your body and mind was made especially for me. You were made for me and I was made for you. My dick will stretch you out in the perfect way, my fingers will know exactly how to stroke you, how to fuck your kitty to make you squirt your want all over me, and my tongue will know exactly how to lick you to make you all clean again. Fight it all you want, run, scratch, bite, but ultimately you'll be beneath me, your legs parted and my dick slamming inside of you while you beg me for more."

Oh my god. Swallowing past the heavy, thick lump of desire that's lodged in my throat I shake my head, needing to deny his words, even though they're entirely true.

"That's okay, Kitten, I know this is a lot to take in. I'll take it easy on you, let you get used to being mine. But make no mistake, you belong to me, you're mine and I plan to claim you in every way possible."

I sink my teeth down into my bottom lip, trying to stem the tide that's rising inside of me and threatening to burst forth in a moan of want. I'm grateful when Bonnie reappears with our food and drinks. She takes in my appearance and the way Penn's fingers are still spread around my neck, and smirks.

"Take this and give me a call later," she says, handing me a slip of paper with her cell number on. Oh, and welcome to the family." Winking at me, she smiles widely as Penn releases me and picks up our food, holding it in one hand while he guides me out the shop with his free hand planted on the base of my spine.

Neither of us speaks as we make the short walk back to my building, where he opens the door for me and follows me inside. Wordlessly he follows me to my office, then sinks into the chair in front of my desk, pulling our food out of the bag and placing mine in front of me as I sit behind my computer. The wood between us should make me feel better, but somehow his penetrating gaze and knowing eyes seem to be more impactful with the slight distance separating us.

"What's your surname, Lulu?"

"Sullivan," I offer, lifting my coffee to my lips and taking a drink.

"How old are you?"

"How old are you?" I throw back at him.

"Thirty-two."

"I'm twenty-four," I admit reluctantly.

"Where do you live?"

As if I'm going to tell my stalker where I live. Rolling my eyes, I scoff lightly. "In a house."

"I can find out on my own, it just makes more sense for you to tell me." He smiles, taking a bite of his sandwich, his piercing eyes assessing me.

"My mama always told me not to talk to strangers."

"I'm not a stranger, I'm your man. But if you don't want to tell me your address that's fine, you'll be moving in with me anyway."

I laugh, I can't help it. Who the fuck is this guy? I've never met anyone so confident and self-assured in my life. "Yeah, no. That's not going to be happening."

"It is. I'd like you in my bed tonight, but I can see that's probably not going to happen. That's okay, we can stay at your place for a couple of days."

"I like you better when you're not talking, the shit that comes out of your mouth pisses me off but when you're silent I can just look at the pretty. Go back to silent."

A laugh bursts from his lips as he throws his head

back, the sound warm and full of joy. I can feel my resolve softening toward him, even though I shouldn't even be contemplating this ridiculousness with him.

The door to Janet's office bursts open and she storms into the room in a cloud of Chanel perfume and expensive clothes. Her eyes quickly assess the room, taking in me behind my desk and a laughing Penn in the chair in front of it.

"Mr. Barnett," she says, her lips tightly pressed together in an angry, flat line.

"Miss Janet, how are you today?" Penn asks, managing to sound cordial, despite Janet's icy demeanor.

"Good thank you. You've met my new paralegal, Lucile."

I explained to Janet when I briefly met her that I go by Lulu, so the fact that she's using my real name speaks volumes about how much she dislikes me already.

"I have, Lulu's my girlfriend. I hope you don't mind that I decided to join her for lunch."

Penn's being painfully polite, I don't know what's between them, but there's obviously history of some kind.

"Of course, enjoy your lunch. Lucile, I've emailed you with more tasks that I need completing before the end of the day." Janet turns on her heel and storms back into her office, closing the door with an ominous thud.

"An ex?" I ask curiously. Although I don't think she is,

48

because the tension between them doesn't feel sexual, more distasteful.

"Hell no. She was pretty hung up on my eldest brother a while back, she made a pass and he turned her down. Since then, she decided to hate on our entire family. She doesn't seem like your greatest fan either."

"I only met her once briefly before today, but apparently I'm her twelfth paralegal in the last three months, so I don't think it's personal."

"I should probably let you get back to work, you ready to give me your number yet?"

"No," I say with an exasperated smile.

"Okay, I'll be waiting."

With that, he grabs the rest of his food and leaves my office without a backward glance. Who the hell is this guy? He's sweet one minute, an asshole the next, and seems to genuinely believe that I'm his now and that all this love at first sight crap is true.

I'll never say it out loud, but I don't hate the way it feels when he puts his arm around my shoulder. I can still feel phantom tingles from his palm on the base of my spine and wrapped possessively around my throat. I'd totally fuck him and I'd enjoy it. But sex with random strangers isn't a part of my life, at least not for a while.

I've never been exactly promiscuous, but girls have needs too. After I swore off relationships in college, I've been known to indulge in a little late-night bootie with guys in bars and clubs, but it's always been careful fun with no one getting any expectations or their feelings hurt.

In a town this small, with a guy like Penn, a no strings hook-up is a seriously bad idea. I don't have the time or the capacity to deal with him, especially when my life has to be all about the most important thing, the only thing that matters.

Swiping my mouse across the desk, I bring my computer back to life, click into my email and peruse the huge to do list Janet has sent me. Sighing, I roll my eyes. Most of the stuff she's asked me to do are menial tasks like copying and filing, apart from the last ten items, all of which have been emailed across since she stomped back into her office. It's clear that she's trying to either get me to quit, punish me for having a Barnett in my office, or testing my mettle. Either way I need this job, so I take a bite of my bagel, a sip of my coffee, and get to work.

By the time Dave pokes his head through the office door, my eyes are swimming from exhaustion, but I've finished all of Janet's tasks and emailed her the research she requested and will never, ever use.

"Hey sweetie, it's five thirty, you 'bout finished?"

"Yep, all done, I'm just closing down my computer."

"I didn't hear any shouting, does that mean you're

coming back tomorrow?" he asks hopefully.

I laugh. "I'm coming back, although based on the stuff she had me do today, I have a feeling it might be an interesting first week."

"Let me guess, she had you doing virtually impossible research and tasks that aren't your responsibility and you're far too over qualified to do?"

I smile and nod, then shrug. "It's fine, I need this job."

"I heard Taylor say you went to Harvard Law, what the hell are you doing here as a paralegal?"

"I was studying for the bar exam when something unexpected happened. I'll take the bar eventually, but for now I got my paralegal certificate and here I am."

"Well, I for one am glad to have you. Let's go before she tries to get you to stay late waxing her legs or something." Dave shudders, then chuckles.

Grabbing my purse, I cross the room to the door and follow Dave out, stumbling to a stop when I see Penn waiting by the door, a broad smile on his face, his arms crossed across his huge chest.

"You done for the day, Kitten?"

"How are you *still* here, don't you have a job?"

"Course I have a job; I co-own the best garage in town with my brother."

"And he doesn't care that you wasted the day being my stalker?" I quip.

"Nope, he offered to come keep me company," he winks.

Blinking, I stare at his smug, amused expression. "Wow. Okay, er, whatever, I need to get going. It's been… well it's been weird being stalked by you today, have a nice life."

Dave snickers as I march toward the door, ducking underneath Penn's arm as he holds it open for me. Not looking back, I walk around the building and out to the parking lot at the rear, stalling when I reach my car to root through my purse for the keys. Normally I have them ready to go, but Penn's presence has thrown me for a loop.

I'm half expecting him to turn up at the passenger door, or to be standing behind me when I turn around. Only he's not, and a part of me is a little disappointed. How messed up is that? I'm disappointed that the guy who's been stalking me all day has stopped. Shaking my head at myself I climb into my car, start the engine, and reverse out of the space and off the lot.

Chloe's house is in a pretty suburb about ten minutes out of town, I could probably walk, but I'm lazy and I hate walking in heels, so commuting it is. Unlike this morning I don't hit any traffic, the small town is quiet, with a handful of people milling around the streets. It's March and the tourists who were in the mountains for the snow have all left, and the ones who come for the pretty mountain lakes and views are yet to arrive.

After the constant bustle of Chicago, I quite like the slower pace of life that exists here, I'm not sure I'll want to stay forever, but for now this is the right place for me to be. Chloe's cute craftsman style house sits on a small plot, with neighbors on either side. Her gardens are her pride and joy and mature trees and bushes cover the small front yard. She's the envy of her not quite so green-fingered neighbors and even though I've only been living here for a week, this house is already starting to feel like home.

Chloe is my mom's best friend, they met in college and lived together for three years in New York once they graduated. From the stories I've heard, they were quite the cosmopolitan girls about town.

They stayed close after Mom met my dad, and they remained that way when my parents got married and years later had me. Chloe is my godmother but she's as close as an auntie would be if I had any. She moved out of the city when she met her husband Wade, they have two kids Roxanne and James. They moved to Rockhead Point when I was a child after Chloe's mom died and left her the house in her will. She's lived here ever since, although her and Wade divorced and he now lives with his twenty-two-year-old secretary in Wyoming.

Roxanne is a couple of years older than me and despite

how close I am with her mom, me and her have never really gotten on. She's one of those pretty girls, who thinks all other women are a threat. From what I understand, her entire focus in life is finding a rich husband and being taken care of. We don't exactly have a lot in common.

James, on the other hand, is an absolute sweetheart. He's six months older than me and even though we haven't seen that much of each other in the last few years, we speak on the phone at least once a week. He's living in England, doing his doctorate at Oxford University, he's a total geek, but I still love him.

Pulling my car onto the driveway behind Chloe's, I exhale and try to leave all the stress of my weird day behind me. Since my life changed, I've had to shake off the shackles of living to work and try to refocus on the important things. It's been an adjustment I wasn't expecting, but I wouldn't change the outcome.

I don't notice the car on the other side of the street until I'm closing my door behind me and locking my car.

"You're living with Chloe?"

I spin around and see Penn crossing the street, mounting the sidewalk as he closes the distance between us in long, confident strides.

"Did you follow me home?" I shriek.

"You didn't really think I was just going to walk away, did you?" His expression is amused, like him not stalking me is a ridiculous notion.

"You need to go, this is really getting to be a bit much now," I exhale, a tendril of fear curving up from my toes and working its way upwards.

"I wasn't stalking per-se, I wanted to make sure you got home okay, with you being new to town and all. But you haven't answered my question, you're living with Chloe Mason?"

"You know her?" I ask, then roll my eyes at myself. "Of course you know her."

The front door opens and my breath catches in my lungs as I hear the sweet voice of my godmother. She's cooing and talking in low whispers as she steps out of the front door and toward us.

"Look who's home," she sings as she steps beside me.

I reach out without thought and take the squirming baby from her arms. Chubby hands instantly reach for my face, and I giggle and I pretend to nip at the tiny fingers.

"Penn?" Chloe asks confusedly.

"Hey Mrs. Mason, whose is the baby?"

He must have figured it out by now, but I turn anyway, smiling down at the world's most perfect baby in my arms. "This is my daughter, Poppy."

FIVE

PENN

"This is my daughter, Poppy."

The words start to play on repeat in my head. Lulu has a kid. A baby no less, a tiny baby girl who right now is staring up at her mama like the word stops and starts with her, which I suppose it does.

I'm not good with kids, I've no idea how old she is. She's a baby, so little, but not tiny. Maybe six months or a year, or hell I don't know. Cora and Huck's kid is two weeks overdue, and Cora is about ready to kill Huck if it doesn't show up soon, and I don't know anyone else with a kid... or at least not well enough to spend too much time around them. My buddies that are wifed up and have a brood, I only see at the bar when they're allowed out. I'm not the friend that's going to turn up at your kid's birthday party.

I'm staring, I know I am, but fuck, what the hell do I do? My woman. *My* fucking woman has a kid by someone else. Maybe that boyfriend she mentioned earlier was real. Is he the dad? Is this his kid? She's still mine, I know that with a certainty, but what the fuck do I do about the fact that the little girl in her arms makes her at least partially someone else's too? Can I learn to share her with some other asshole who has a claim on her through the baby they made?

"Penn, I think you should go," Lulu says quietly.

She's staring at me now, not at the baby, and there's a sadness in her eyes that I want to eradicate. How has today gone from so amazing to so unbelievably fucked up? I thought it was bad when she pulled into Chloe Mason's drive. Her daughter Roxanne is my ex fuck-buddy, only she thought it was much more serious that I did. Even went so far as to poke holes into condoms to try and get pregnant from me. I ended things with her after a showdown last year, but still, that alone would have been a big enough hurdle.

I'm not sure how Chloe and Lulu know each other, but even though Chloe knows exactly how much of a viper her daughter can be, I doubt she'll be extoling my virtues to Lulu if she asks. Fuck! What the hell do I do? I can't walk away, but I need to figure out what my options are here.

"Why don't I take you all out for dinner instead?" I suggest.

"Poppy has a routine, it's bath and bed time soon, I don't like to keep her out late because it messes with her body clock and she'll be awake all night."

"Let me order us a takeout then. I could help you with Poppy then we can all eat and talk." God, I sound desperate, but I am. I can't just leave. I can't just drive home and forget that my woman is here and I'm not.

"I don't—" Lulu starts.

"That sounds lovely, why don't we all go on inside," Chloe announces, cutting off Lulu's rejection and giving me an in. I don't know why she does it, but I flash her a grateful smile and gesture for the ladies to lead the way.

Chloe moves first and Lulu reluctantly follows. I switch between staring at my woman and her daughter. She's a pretty baby, with dark hair and bright blue eyes, she looks like her mama. Unlike my brothers I'm not desperate to be a dad. Mine was great, but he's been gone so long that I'm not sure I remember what that parental care feels like. After he passed, we all stepped up to parent one another, but if I barely remember what having a dad feels like, how will I know if I'm capable of being a good one to my own kids?

Swallowing thickly I follow Lulu into the house, pausing to glance at the warm, comfortable décor. Unlike her daughter, Chloe is sweet, kind and always smiling. I'm not sure where Roxanne gets her mean, manipulative streak from but I doubt it's from her mom. The floorplan seems pretty open with the living space blending easily into the kitchen and dining room. There's baby crap everywhere, a crib on one side of the couch, baby toys and packs of diapers stacked in a caddy against the wall. Everything looks brand new, so I'm assuming Lulu bought all of this with her when she moved here.

I can't help but search the space for any hint of masculinity but I can't find anything. Chloe and her husband split up when Roxanne and her brother were in high school. I vaguely remember him moving out of state, but honestly, I didn't care enough about Roxanne back then nor when we were hooking up to bother to find out the details. Now I'm desperately trying to figure out if Poppy's dad is staying here too.

The urge to blurt it out rolls along my tongue, but I force the words down. There's no way I can just demand to know who this guy is, no matter how much I want to know. I'm hoping that Chloe inviting me in and Lulu not mentioning a guy other than the obviously fake boyfriend means he isn't in the picture.

But what will I do when he shows up to see his kid?

Can I learn to tolerate a guy who's fucked my woman being near her? Will it kill me to watch Poppy grow up and call someone else daddy?

Shit, my mind is a mess and until I ask some questions all I'm doing is driving myself insane with unknowns. "What do you guys fancy to eat?"

"I was telling Lulu about how good the Chinese food is at Chang's the other day, we haven't had a chance to try it since she moved here," Chloe says, breaking the stilted silence that's filled the room since we got in here.

"Sounds good. Any preferences or shall I just order us a selection?" I suggest, forcing a smile to my lips.

"A selection sounds perfect."

Turning, I glance at Lulu, she's sitting on the couch, a wriggling Poppy on her lap as she makes a doll dance for her, the baby's eyes lighting up with glee as she tries to take the toy from her mama's hands. "Poppy's too little for real food, right?"

"Yeah," Lulu says, a hint of a smile crossing her lips, even though she doesn't look at me.

"Cool, err, okay, I'll go call the order in." Stepping into the hallway, I exhale a shaky breath. Fuck, I don't get flustered, it's not in my nature. I'm confident, calm and controlled, but this is unexpected and I need a moment to get myself under control. Calling through the food order, I slide my cell back into my pocket and lift my hands to my head, raking my fingers through my hair as I inhale slowly.

This isn't what I was expecting, but none of this makes Lulu any less mine. Poppy is a part of Lulu so that makes her mine too. That realization makes everything click into place and suddenly it's obvious. My woman has a kid, so I have a kid too. Right now, I think Poppy is going to be easier for me to win over than her mama, but it doesn't matter. I'm a Barnett, and we don't take no for an answer when it comes to finding and keeping the women that are meant to be ours.

It's time to make Lulu understand what it means to be claimed by me.

SIX

LULU

Penn steps out into the hallway and the low sound of his voice blends into the background.

"Penn Barnett?" Chloe asks with a raised eyebrow and a smirk. "That was quick."

"He literally followed me home like an annoying stray dog," I hiss, ignoring the amusement flashing in her eyes.

"So when did you meet him? The Barnett boys are kind of infamous in this town."

"I literally walked into him this morning and I haven't been able to get rid of him since. He told me I was his, kissed the shit out of me then followed me to work and refused to leave. He's been sitting in reception all day, waiting for me to agree to go out with him and telling anyone who would listen that I was his. When I left for the day and he didn't try to get in my car with me I thought he'd given up. But apparently he just followed me home. You came out with Poppy and you know the rest."

"He told you, you were his?" Chloe says slowly.

"Jesus," I roll my eyes, "Don't tell me you've bought into this love at first sight legend too?"

Chloe's laugh is so loud it makes Poppy jump, her eyes going wide as tears fill them. "It's okay, babycakes, Auntie Chloe is being too loud isn't she," I coo to my daughter. Poppy stares back at me, fat tears rolling down her cheeks as she looks up at me. I wait for the wail, but it doesn't come and instead she flops forward and buries her face into my boobs. This tiny baby is my entire world. I never planned to be a mom in my early twenties, but now she's here I wouldn't change a thing. No matter the circumstances that lead to her conception.

"It's not just a legend, three of the Barnett boys have fallen that way. I've seen it with my own two eyes, those boys go from the consummate bachelor to head over heels in love in a millisecond and the way they love is, well… phew, it's enough to make me a little hot under the collar." Chloe fans herself with her hand and I roll my eyes.

"He's crazy."

"Quite possibly," she snickers.

"He keeps telling me I'm his, it's ridiculous. Although I'm sure this," I nod to Poppy, "will change his mind and he can go and stalk someone else instead."

"I wouldn't be so sure, honey. He could have run a mile at the first sight of that precious little girl, but instead he offered to help you get her ready for bed while we wait for the takeout dinner he just ordered."

Groaning, I lean forward and press my face against Poppy's tiny head. I have no idea why babies smell so good, but I inhale deeply, filling my lungs with her awesome baby smell. "I don't have enough room in my life for a man shaped complication."

"I don't plan on being a complication," a deep voice announces.

Squeezing my eyes shut I try to hide from him, but given his tenacity so far today, I get the feeling he won't just disappear... no matter how much I'd like him to.

"Penn," I start, lifting my head and preparing myself to dole out the speech about why my baby has to be my priority, and how I don't have the capacity to worry about anything but her. But he cuts me off when he strides over to me and scoops her out of my arms. I immediately bristle. I don't know him, who the hell does he think he is touching my daughter? But instead of protesting, Poppy immediately nestles into him, resting her cheek against his shoulder as he holds out a hand for me.

"Let's go get this one ready for bed, then we can talk." His attention is split between me and Poppy, and the sight of him holding my daughter in one arm while he reaches for me with the other is sexy as fuck. I don't know him, I certainly don't trust him, but somehow not placing my hand in his feels impossible. There's a pull to him that I just don't understand. His alphahole personality is exactly what I crave, and he's hot, like thermonuclear hot, but I don't want or need a man in mine and Poppy's lives. The man who provided the other half of her DNA has never even laid eyes on her, I doubt he ever will, but that doesn't mean I should be trying to fill the gap with a random stalker I only met this morning.

I allow him to gently pull me from my seat on the couch and guide me toward the stairs as Chloe stands by and watches, a sly smile etched across her lips.

"Where are we going, Kitten?" he asks as he guides me up the stairs, still carefully holding my content daughter to his chest.

"I need to get the bath started." We reach the landing and I point in the direction of the family bathroom. He follows me in, then hands Poppy to me.

"You have the princess and I'll get things ready. How warm and how much water? Does she like bubbles?"

His interest and questions throw me for a loop as he

turns on the faucet, running the water until he's happy with the temperature before allowing the tub to fill. He asks question after question. Where are the cloths, the shampoo, the diapers, her jammies and anything else she might need? He's not just showing an interest, he's actively learning how to take care of her and honestly, that freaks me the fuck out.

"Why are you doing this?" I blurt.

"What do you mean?"

"This," I throw my arm out to encapsulate the room. "Running the bath, helping, all of it."

Instead of speaking, he closes the short distance between us and lifts his hand to gently cup my cheek. There's none of the intense possession from earlier, his fingers aren't around my throat and he's not telling me all the dirty things he wants to do to me, instead he's soft and sweet. "You're mine, she's yours, so she's mine too. I take good care of the things that belong to me."

My lips part and my mouth falls open. Who is this guy?

"Now, come check this water and then show me how to take care of our princess."

Our Princess. Why the hell do those words make me want to burst into tears? No one but me has ever claimed this little girl, and now this man I hardly know is swooping in here like a knight in shining armor. It's too good to be true, it has to be. But surely someone would have warned me. Annette, or Dave or Chloe would have told me to keep my distance, to run away from his dirty words and sweet touches and possessive claims. Only they haven't. Chloe is my biggest champion, mine and Poppy's fiercest protector. Yet she invited him in to our home, backed up this ridiculous love at first sight rubbish, then let him hold my daughter without even a moment of reservation.

I might not trust him yet, but I do trust her. She would never allow someone who was going to hurt us into our lives.

Grabbing the changing pad, I drop it to the floor then kneel down and carefully lie Poppy onto it. I strip her out of her cute dress, leggings and diaper and then carry her over to the tub. Just like I told him, there's only a couple of inches of water in the bottom and I check the temperature, keeping a protective grip on her arm as I place her in the bath seat Chloe bought.

Her baby giggle is so adorable I barely notice that Penn has kneeled beside me, watching me carefully as I squeeze soap onto a soft wash cloth and start to bathe her. He doesn't attempt to help, other than pushing bath toys toward Poppy when she kicks them away, scooping up handfuls of bubbles and blowing them in her direction as she giggles and squeals with joy.

This should feel awkward, doing this task with a guy I barely know, but oddly it doesn't, nor does it feel weird when he leans over and presses a kiss to my shoulder. It's the only touch he offers me, while he talks sweetly to Poppy.

"Hey Princess, do you like the bubbles?" he asks, scooping another handful and blowing them at her. One gets stuck to her nose and she shrieks with joy as she slaps her wet hand against her face to get at it. Suddenly wet and shocked, fat tears fill her eyes again and she glares at Penn in the way babies do when the game they've been playing isn't so fun anymore. I glance at the man at my side just in time to witness a flash of sheer panic cross his features.

"Naughty bubbles, they need a spanking don't they," he coos at her, reaching past me to gently slap the bubbly water.

The tears sit on the edges of Poppy's lids as she watches Penn with fascination, then reaches out to the water and copies him, slapping the bubbles in front of her and laughing. A game of splashing commences, with her kicking her legs and coordinatingly patting her hands into the water while I wash her hair.

By the time I'm done, most of the bubbles have gone and we're all a little damp. "You want me to grab you a towel, Kitten?" Penn asks, jumping up from his spot beside me on the floor.

"Thanks."

He reappears beside me a moment later as I pluck a wiggling, slippery Poppy from the water. Holding out the towel for her, he wraps her in the fabric, then lifts her to his chest as I clamber up from the floor. Since we got to Rockhead Point a little over a week ago, Chloe has helped me to care for Poppy, but before that I'd been completely alone taking care of my baby, so having someone I barely know so effortlessly offer to help is confusing.

"Where are we going?" he asks, cuddling Poppy to his chest.

Leaning over, I pull the plug from the tub and the water starts to drain. "Over there," I say, leading him to the room Poppy and I share. A white changing console is against the wall and I motion for him to place her down on it while I grab her pink jammies from the dresser.

He steps aside once I reach her, only taking his hand from her when I'm close enough to take his place. I quickly dry her, put on a clean diaper and get her into her bunny jammies as Penn stands at my shoulders watching me.

"Would you mind going downstairs and grabbing her formula? Chloe will have made her a bottle," I say quietly, scooping Poppy into my arms and walking to the overstuffed armchair next to her crib.

"Sure," he says, disappearing out of the room, returning a moment later with a baby bottle gripped in his massive hand. Settling Poppy against my chest, I reach out and take the bottle from him, pushing it into Poppy's mouth and humming a lullaby as she drinks. I missed her today. I miss her everyday; but at least here she's with Chloe, not in day care with strangers. That was a massive reason for moving here, Chloe retired a few years back and with no grandchildren of her own yet, she was excited to have a baby to look after. I'm not sure what I'd have done without her support this last year.

Penn moves to the bed and sits quietly on the edge, watching as I feed my daughter, running a finger over her tiny scrunched forehead and down between her eyes as she slowly falls asleep in my arms. I love this time of day with her, when she's sleepy and relaxed. I could hold her like this forever, feeling her tiny fluttery heart beating against mine. This tiny little creature owns me and now that I have her, I have no idea how I thought I was truly living without her.

I expect him to get bored, or leave, but the entire time I cuddle with Poppy, he sits quietly, his eyes on me, watching us. I hold her long after she's fallen asleep, but eventually I know I need to put her down. So I hold her to me, stand up and cross to the crib, placing her carefully down on the mattress and covering her with the blanket. Switching on the baby monitor, I grab the parent unit and tiptoe to the door. Penn follows me and I close it behind us and head downstairs.

"Oh shoot, I left the bottle," I say, sighing and turning.

"I got it," he says, lifting it into the air to show me.

I smile weakly. "Oh, thanks."

Moving to take it, I'm surprised when he pulls it back out of my reach, curling his arm around my back and pulling me into his chest. "Watching you with her, it's fucking beautiful," he purrs, his breath against my ear making me shudder.

"Penn," I sigh.

"You're both mine."

"You can't just decide that."

"Yes, I can. You were meant for me and I was meant for you. Doesn't matter what came before I found you, but now you're here, I'm claiming you. My dick has never been so fucking hard, I can't wait to get inside of you."

"I don't believe in love at first sight." I push at his chest but he just tightens his grip, sliding his free hand around my neck and squeezing my throat gently.

"How about want at first sight. Your nipples are hard, you're fucking panting and I'm willing to bet your cunt is dripping for me. I dare you to let me find out." His fingers on my neck release and he slowly slides his hand down the center of my body, between my breasts, across my squishy belly and beneath the waist of my skirt. He's giving me time to stop him, but even as I part my lips, no words come out.

He doesn't breach my panties to start off, he cups my pussy over the fabric, feeling the heat pouring from my core. "So hot, Kitten, how long do you think it would take me to make this little kitty purr. Does she want it gentle or rough?"

Closing my eyes, I swallow thickly.

"I think my kitten likes it rough. I don't think you want me to be gentle, I think you'll like it when I hold you down and force my fingers deep inside of you. You don't want to be wooed; you want to be owned."

I try to deny his words, but he's right, I've never enjoyed it when a guy is all sweet and nice. I don't want him to ask permission. Pushing my panties to the side I feel a single blunt fingertip stroking along my sex before thrusting inside of me, he pulls out and pushes two fingers into me, roughly finger fucking me, right here in the hallway.

"Spread your legs."

I do as I'm told, spreading my legs wider as he fills me again and again. A third finger pushes into me and I whimper, the pleasure and pain of being stretched almost too much.

"Fuck, Kitten, I can barely get three fingers into you, you're going to scream when I force my fat cock into your cunt. I can't wait. My dick is going to ruin you."

His words are crass and vulgar and so inappropriate from a man I met this morning, but I can't help the arousal that weeps from me.

"That's it, soak my hand, I want to lick all that sweetness off my fingers."

His fingers move relentlessly, fucking me in short, hard thrusts that make my eyes roll back with pleasure. His thumb finds my clit and he presses down, rubbing as he fucks me with his hand until I'm gripping his shoulders, holding on as an orgasm barrels down on me.

"Come for me, Kitten, and bite down so no one can hear. All your sounds are for me only, no one gets to share in the pleasure I give you."

Burying my face in his chest I do as he says, clamping my teeth into the skin on his bicep as an orgasm explodes from my core, ricocheting through my limbs until I'm a whimpering, shaking mess.

"Fucking perfect," Penn rasps, pulling his fingers out of me and lifting his hand up to show me how wet it is. "All this is you; this is how wet you got just from a small taste of how I'll claim your body."

Lifting his hand he paints my lips with my own arousal, pushing his fingers into my mouth and forcing me to taste myself on him. Dragging them free, he pushes them between his own lips and sucks heartily on them, before he dips his head down and kisses me.

I don't resist, I couldn't right now even if I wanted to. In this moment I truly am his and so I let him own me, moving with him, parting my lips and stroking his tongue back as he invades my mouth. For a big, dominant guy, he doesn't try to make me submit to him, he simply kisses me in the same forceful way that he seems to do everything else.

"You taste fucking delicious," he growls, his voice rough and gravelly.

The doorbell ringing shatters the illusion he's woven around us and I rush to the door, throwing it open as my chest heaves.

"Here," Penn snaps, handing a handful of bills to the delivery guy and taking the box of takeout from him, before unceremoniously slamming the door in his face.

"That was rude," I glare.

"Don't give a fuck, not having another man see you looking all cum-drunk. He's lucky I didn't gouge his fucking eyes out."

"Penn," I gasp. "I'm not yours."

"Tell that to your sopping wet cunt, Kitten." He chuckles, grabbing my hand, and towing me back into the kitchen. Depositing me at the dining table, he moves around Chloe's kitchen like he owns it, washing his hands then pulling out plates, glasses and silverware.

"Something smells good," Chloe says loudly before she steps into the kitchen and plops down in the seat opposite mine at the table. "There's soda, beers and a bottle of wine in the refrigerator," she tells Penn, not getting up herself as he moves around the space.

Narrowing my eyes at her, I glare, but she just smiles, looking incredibly smug. I don't really know what's gotten into her but apparently she's firmly team Penn, even though she knows I only want to focus on Poppy right now. "Traitor," I mouth.

She laughs, then brings her fingers together to make a heart shape, placing them over chest and pouting.

Rolling my eyes, I ignore her, forcing my face into a neutral expression as Penn places a glass of wine I didn't ask for in front of me, another in front of Chloe and a glass of soda at the place setting next to mine.

"I hope you're not a vegetarian, I didn't think to ask and pretty much everything I've ordered has got meat in it."

"She's not," Chloe answers for me, before I can tell him I am.

"Good. Chopsticks or forks?" He holds out three of each and I reach for the chopsticks as Chloe does the same. I expect him to take a fork, caveman that he is, but he follows suit and rips open the packet, snapping them in half.

It's not that I'm assuming he'll behave like an animal or have no manners, but I'm still shocked when he serves both me and then Chloe before he adds food to his own plate and expertly uses the chopsticks to devour the tangy orange chicken, spicy szechuan pork and crispy broccoli florets that are drowned in something I don't recognize, but just became my new favorite.

We eat in comfortable silence with Chloe mainly filling the void with town gossip about people I don't know. I perk up when she starts to talk about James and London and before long, I'm chatting happily about my favorite pseudo cousin and the exciting life he's living on the other side of the world.

When the food is all gone and my wine glass is empty, Chloe excuses herself to go take a bath and I'm left alone with Penn and this cloud of indecision that's floating above me. If I didn't have Poppy, if I hadn't just moved half way across the country for a fresh start, I'd be flinging myself into his lap and begging to ride what I'm guessing is going to be an impressively large cock. Penn exudes big dick energy and I'd be surprised if it was all bravado.

But the thing is, I do have Poppy and she has to be my focus. I don't have room, time or energy for a guy like Penn. He's the type that wants to consume you and I can't allow that to happen, no matter how much I might want him to.

"Look," I start.

"No."

"What?"

"No, I'm not going to back off. No, I don't agree that we can't be together. No, I don't care that we just met. No, I don't think I've imagined this thing between us," he growls, placing his hands on my hips and boldly lifting me into his lap.

"Penn, my life is kind of complicated right now."

"That's okay, we don't need to be complicated, in fact, we're simple as fuck. You're mine and I'm yours. See? Simple," he drawls, his tone slow and sexy.

"And what about Poppy?"

"I already told you, she's mine too."

"You can't just claim me and my daughter." I sigh.

"Why not?"

"Because that's not real life."

"Life's as real as we make it. I know you're it for me, I won't find anyone else, I'll never want anyone else. You're mine, my woman, my life, my fucking happy ever after. This right here, being with you, touching you, this is as easy as breathing to me. Since I saw you this morning I felt something settle inside my chest, like you're the missing piece of me." He grabs my hand and places it on his chest over his heart. I can feel the constant, steady beat and it calms me.

"Penn."

"Who's Poppy's dad?"

"That's none of your business."

"Course it's my fucking business if he's going to be in your life, our life." His grip on me tightens and his jaw clenches.

"He's not a part of mine or Poppy's life."

"That might change."

"It won't, he signed over full parental rights to Poppy before she was born."

"Asshole."

"It's a complicated situation," I say slowly, not really wanting to get into the circumstances of Poppy's conception right now.

"Complicated how?" Penn asks.

"That's not something I want to get into with a stranger," I quip, a hint of anger lacing my words. I don't want to discuss how Poppy came to be, or why I'm here and not in Chicago, especially with someone I met this morning.

His growl is pure frustration, his muscles tensing beneath me. "I don't like that you don't want to confide in me."

"I don't know you," I cry, my voice incredulous.

"So get to know me. What do you want to know?"

"I don't know. How do I get you to leave me alone?"

His laugh is rough and full of menace. "You don't want that. If you did, you wouldn't have come all over my fingers earlier."

"Sex has nothing to do with it. I can be sexually attracted to you without wanting to be with you."

"True, but this is more than just sex, this is intimacy at its basic form, it's my core calling out to your core and claiming it. You can try to deny it, you can even fucking fight it, but it'll still be true and we'll both be missing out on happiness until you accept that you belong to me now."

He sounds so certain and I don't even know what to do. How do I fight someone who feels so strongly that they're right?

"Kiss me," he demands.

"No." I shake my head.

Strong fingers grab my chin in a firm hold. "I said, kiss me."

Swallowing thickly, I try to shake my head but his grip tightens.

"Kiss me, or I'll strip you naked, flip you till your ass is in the air and your cunt is open and dripping for me, and I'll fuck you right here on this couch. It's not the way I envisaged claiming you for the first time, but if I have to prove a point and punish you for ignoring me, I will." His lips skim over my cheek. "But if I do, if I slam my fat dick into you as a punishment, you don't get to come, no matter how much you beg for it."

A moan slips from my lips. Fuck, I shouldn't be turned

on, I shouldn't like threats of sexual punishment, but I do and the sound I just made was like a ten-page confession.

"Oh, Kitten, you're fucking perfect. Now kiss me."

Leaning down I offer him my lips and he takes them, kissing me deeply and possessively until I'm squirming in his lap, my pussy swollen and needy.

"Where's your cell?"

"What?" I ask, dazed.

"Your cell, where is it?"

"In my purse," I say, pointing roughly in the direction of the couch.

"Go get it."

"Why?"

"Because I told you to." He kisses me again and I groan into his mouth, burying my fingers in his hair and holding him to me.

"Go," he smirks, lifting me off his lap and turning me toward the couch.

On shaky legs I pad over to my purse, find my cell and carry it back toward him. He reaches for me the moment I'm close enough, taking my cell from my hands and holding it up to my face when the facial recognition app kicks in. The moment it's open his fingers move across the screen, then a noise sounds from beneath him and he pulls out his own cell, checks the screen, then smiles. He messes with my cell for a few more seconds then hands it back to me.

"Now I have your cell number and you have mine. I should go, you have work in the morning? Do you start at the same time every day?"

"I nod, yeah, 8.30."

"Do you have to take Poppy to day care first?"

"No, Chloe is taking care of her while I work."

"Okay, I'll pick you up in the morning." Lifting me from his lap he places me on my feet, then stands up behind me, towering over me once again.

"What? No, I can drive myself to work," I cry

"I know you can, but I can pick you up, so I'll see you in the morning." Dipping down he kisses me again, one hand wrapping around my neck, while the other rests against my spine, holding me to him. "Night Kitten."

"Night Penn," I reply almost on autopilot as he presses a soft, sweet peck to my lips before he turns and leaves, closing the front door behind him.

SEVEN

PENN

I'm barely aware of the drive home, my mind running in circles at a hundred miles an hour. So much has fucking happened today and I don't even know what to think about first. I wanted this. I've been looking forward to finding my woman since I watched Granger fall for Alice and for the first time in my life, I truly understood what jealousy felt like and I didn't like it.

I didn't want their women. Bonnie, Cora and Alice are great, but it wasn't them I wanted, it was the relationship, the contentment, the sense of ownership. The knowledge that my woman is indisputably mine.

Seeing Lulu today was like being hit by lightning and

then driven over by a truck all at the same time. She's everything I've ever fucking wanted in a woman. She's sexy, her body is curvy and plush and fucking gorgeous. She's feisty and won't take my shit, but I saw the look in her eyes when I growled and told her what to do. She's strong enough to allow herself to be weak for me and I love it. I can't wait to get her beneath me. My dick has been rock fucking hard since she walked into me this morning and until I get inside of her, I can't see it getting soft any time soon.

I groan when I remember what it felt like to touch her. Her pussy was hot and wet and I had to stretch her out to get all three fingers inside of her. I wasn't talking shit when I told her I had a big dick—I do. Most women are a bit intimidated when they see it and I usually have to do a shit load of foreplay so I don't hurt them. Playing with a pussy isn't exactly a chore, but when all I want is to get off, it's frustrating that I have to put in the time. It's different with Lulu, I can't wait to eat her out and get her ready for me, but I know she'll enjoy the bite of pain if sometimes I just decide to slam straight into her.

Seeing Poppy was a shock, but now that I know her biological dad isn't in the picture, she's just as much mine as her mama is. I hadn't exactly expected to get a ready-made family, but that doesn't necessarily make it a bad thing. Watching my woman with her daughter made my heart actually hurt. I can already tell she's an amazing Mama, and that's sexier than I ever expected it to be. I wish I'd met her before she had her, I wish I'd gotten a chance to watch her belly grow with the baby inside of it. I wish Poppy was mine, so I'd never have to think about anyone else sharing that amazing bond with her.

But at the end of the day, every little thing doesn't have to be instantly perfect. We're not teenagers and with age comes baggage. I'm sure as shit not looking forward to telling Lulu that the daughter of the woman she's living with used to be my fuck buddy, but I will, because if Chloe and Lulu are as close as they seem, it's only a matter of time before she finds out anyway.

Pulling into the driveway, I kill my car engine and inhale a long slow breath. Normally driving my Shelby Mustang GT is like an instant mood enhancer, but today it's not having its usual affect. I feel adrift. Leaving Lulu was hard tonight, but it's not like I could drag her home with me, or invade her bed when Poppy's crib is right next to it.

Being anywhere she isn't just feels wrong and as I throw open my car door and make my way to the house, the need to be close to her only increases with each step further away I take. Pushing open the front door, I wait for the wave of homeliness to wash over me the way it normally does whenever I step inside my house, but today it feels muted. Technically I live with my brothers; but last year we started a renovation project on the house we grew up in, so that we could all continue to live here even as our family expanded. Now we each have a mini wing that leads off the main living space and gives us two bedrooms, a living room, kitchen and dining space for when we're not looking to be together.

Weirdly, we all still seem to end up eating together in the original house, but now we have the option not to. I know Beau and Bonnie, Huck and Cora, and Granger and Alice appreciate having the extra privacy and the rest of us enjoy the soundproofing that was installed so we don't have to listen to our siblings fucking.

We all agreed a long time ago that we wouldn't bring women home, unless they were *our* women and therefore a part of the family. Until Beau brought Bonnie home, none of us had ever felt like we'd found our one, but now I have three sisters and our family home does at times sport a bit of a commune feel.

The living room is full of people when I step inside and a palpable sense of excitement fills the air as my brothers and sisters peer around me, obviously searching for the woman I haven't been able to bring home.

"You alone?" Beau asks incredulously.

"Yep," I nod, my feet dragging as I walk past them all into the kitchen, grabbing myself a beer from the refrigerator, not bothering to offer to get anyone else anything before I pad back into the living room and flop down onto the couch.

"Are you okay?" Alice asks.

Alice is my newest sister. Granger met her back in November last year and moved her into our home the same day. She's quiet, due to some fucked up stuff that happened when she was a kid, but she's starting to come out of her shell more every day, and her making the effort to check on me instantly makes my chest swell.

"Yeah, I'm good, it's just been a long ass day."

"What's happened?" Beau asks.

"She has a kid," I blurt out, not planning to make it sound as dramatic as it does.

"Fuck. Is she still with the dad? She's not married, is she?" Cora babbles.

I shake my head. "She says the dad's not in the picture. Poppy, her daughter is a baby, cutest little thing I've ever fucking seen and Lulu with her, fuck, I never…" I trail off, struggling to explain how it made me feel. "They're both mine, but I had to fucking leave her there, I couldn't just throw her over my shoulder and kidnap her when she has the princess to think about."

Someone's hand lands on my shoulder and I look up to find Bay has moved beside me, his huge palm squeezing me lightly. "You'll work it out, her and Poppy will both move in, it's just going to take a little more time that's all," he says, obviously trying to reassure me.

I nod, but now that I'm home and alone I feel almost shellshocked. "I didn't like having to leave them there, without me."

"Where's she living?" Beau asks.

A dry, scoffing laugh falls from my lips. "With Chloe Mason."

"Roxanne's mom?" Huck chokes.

"Yep. I haven't figured out how they know each other yet, but they're close."

"Who's Roxanne?" Alice asks quietly.

Rubbing my face with my palm I cringe. "My ex-fuck buddy who lost her shit and stabbed holes in the condoms to try and get pregnant with my kid."

"Oh," Alice says, her lips forming a perfect circle as she tries not to show how fucked I am.

"Yeah, I ended things with her way back last year, but I'm not looking forward to explaining that one to Lulu," I say with a sigh.

"So what's the plan? What can we do to help?" Teddy asks.

For a moment I'm stunned silent as I glance up and look at my amazing family. "I fucking love you guys. I know I don't say it enough and I know I'm being a fucking pussy because I found my woman today. But I really do, I love you all and I can't wait for you all to meet her and the princess, you're going to love them both."

I spend the next hour talking them through everything that happened today, from her literally crashing head first into my life, to the moment I had to leave Chloe's house and come home. The only thing I left out was how I made her come on my fingers. Between my brothers I could see the sympathy in Bay, Teddy and Cody's faces and the knowing look in Beau, Huck and Granger's. The divide between those who have their women and those who have no idea what this feels like is expanding, but no matter what, I know they're all here for me.

By the time I crawl into bed, my mind is spinning with everything I need to do to secure my future with my new family. No matter how much I wish it was, this isn't as simple as just telling Lulu she's mine and fucking her till she agrees. I still intend to fuck all of that sass and snark out of her, until she's unequivocally claimed in every way; but after talking it out with my family I know that she'll need to know this is more than just a sexual connection before she allows me to change both her and her daughter's life.

When I'm naked beneath my sheets, I still wish she were here and I pull out my cell and text her. I wish I could call, but if she's in bed I don't want to risk waking Poppy up.

Me

> I wish you were here with me or I was there with you. My dick is aching to be inside of you, feel you gripping me tightly while I fuck you raw. One timeis all it'd take for you to know you were mine

I'm not really expecting her to text back. I can already tell she's stubborn, and I like that about her. As much as I love Alice, the way Granger and her are together wouldn't work for me. I want my woman to be independent, but willing to give herself over to me completely. I need that control, to be the one in charge. But I want to take that control from her, because she can't help herself, not have it offered it up on a silver platter.

That's one of the main problems I've found with the other women I've have pseudo relationships with. They wanted to play at being mine, to them it was all a game while they tried to top me from the bottom and that's just not my fucking kink. I'm no one's bitch and still the women I've fucked in the past have tried to play me like one.

Five seconds in Lulu's company told me all I need to know about her. Winning her will be the ultimate challenge with the sweetest prize, and I can't wait to win. My cell pings and I almost send it flying off the side of the bed in my haste to check it.

Lulu

eyeroll emoji If your dick's hard, you have two hands or I'm sure you could find a willing hole to stick it in.

My smile is wide as I quickly type out a reply.

Me

The only holes I'm interested in are your cunt, your ass and your mouth. If you're offering, then I can be in your bed in thirty minutes, but I'll have to gag you so you don't wake up Princess when you're screaming my name.

Lulu

Wow! Someone's full of themselves. I said WILLING hole, so that counts me out.

Me

Your cunt was more than willing earlier; I can still smell your sweetness on my skin.

Lulu

Every girl likes to get off and it's been a while **shrugging emoji**

Me

I'll make you come over and over; we both know the moment I touched you, you'd be more than willing.

Lulu

I'm impressed you could even get through the front door with how big your ego is.

Me

My ego's in direct relation to the size of my dick, so, massive.

Me

photo

Lulu

Dude, isn't it like illegal to send unsolicited dick pics these days? #notcool

Me

My dick belongs to you now, I figured you'd want to assess your assets. Your turn, send me a pic of your wet little kitty with three fingers stuffed inside it.

Lulu

I have no interest in owning any of you. You and your monster dick should just stay away from me and find a more willing victim to stalk.

Me

I couldn't stay away if I wanted to, which I don't. Sweet dreams, Kitten. Say the word in the morning, and I'll make your cunt all juicy and dripping for me as a breakfast treat.

Lulu

Night, stalker. Lose my number.

Smiling to myself, I grab my dick and squeeze. I think about jacking off, but decide I want to save all my cum for her. Women are super fertile after they have a baby and the thought of making Poppy a sibling is incredibly appealing. I fall asleep with my dick in my hand and dream of all the filthy ways I'm going to claim Lulu. I have the sweetest dreams I've ever had.

The next morning, I get to Chloe's house early in case Lulu decides to try and leave without me. Chloe answers the door when I knock it, she's still in her bathrobe, her hair a little disheveled, a cup of coffee gripped in her hands.

"Coffee's in the pot and Poppy's breakfast is cooling on the counter if you want to help. Lulu's running a little behind this morning."

"Sure," I smile, stepping into the house and immediately heading for my princess who is gurgling happily in a playpen set up at the edge of the living room. "Good morning, Princess, you hungry?" I ask, leaning over the pen and scooping her up into my arms.

The moment I straighten and look down at my little girl, she flashes me a wide smile. I thought I was a sucker for her mama, but Poppy melts my heart with just a grin and I know I'm going to be a complete pushover for her for the rest of our lives.

"She sits in her highchair to eat, make sure you strap her in, because she's a wriggler," Chloe calls.

Nodding, I carry Poppy into the kitchen, spotting the pink chair with a white plastic tray set up next to the dining table. I don't remember it being here last night, but honestly I wasn't paying too much attention to anyone but Lulu by the time we sat down.

Carefully lowering her wiggling legs into the seat, I fumble for a minute with the straps, eventually figuring out that her arms go through loops on either side and fasten to a clip that goes between her legs to stop her from scooting down and falling out the chair. It's a bit like a racing harness, I've fitted into cars before. There's a fabric thing on the plastic tray and when I lift it up, I see it's a bib that I fasten around her neck.

Grabbing the pink plastic bowl from the counter, I glance down at the sloppy oatmeal and grimace a little.

"Check it's not too warm," Chloe calls, she's behind me in the kitchen now although I didn't realize she'd moved, I was too involved with getting the princess settled.

"How do I do that?"

She chuckles. "Try some, if it's hot against your lips, it's too hot for Poppy."

Pulling out a chair opposite to Poppy's highchair,

I nod, gripping the long plastic spoon in my massive hand and dipping it into the beige goop. I'm not a fan of oatmeal, the texture has always freaked me out a little, and I fight a grimace as I bring the spoon to my lips and test the temperature. It's warm, but not hot, so I pull the gross stuff away from my mouth and hold it out to Poppy. Her look suggests that she's about as impressed with the oatmeal as I am, but with a little coaxing she parts her lips and lets me slide the spoon into her mouth. When I pull the spoon back about half the mush comes back out with it and I use the spoon to push it back in.

I've never fed a baby before and I've no idea if I'm doing it right, but after five minutes, about three quarters of the bowl is gone and Poppy is only wearing about half of that.

Lulu comes rushing downstairs just as I'm making airplane noises and dive bombing a spoon full of mush toward Poppy's mouth. She giggles and I take advantage and slide the spoon straight in.

"What? What's going on?" Lulu asks, her eyes wide as she looks between me, Poppy and Chloe who's leaning back against the counter, half watching me, half watching the morning show that's playing quietly on the tv.

"Morning Kitten, sleep well?" I flash her a smirk, raking my eyes over the fitted dress she's wearing that clings to her curves, accentuating her hourglass figure and fantastic boobs.

"Err, morning, what are you doing?"

"Feeding the princess her breakfast," I say, focusing my attention back on Poppy and pushing another spoonful of disgusting beige mush into her mouth.

"I see that. I meant why are you doing that?" she asks slowly.

"Because Chloe said you were running a little late this morning and I thought I could help out," I tell her simply.

"Oh, err, well, thank you. I can finish up if you want."

"Nope, me and Princess are bonding, you get some breakfast, I'd love a cup of coffee though."

"How do you take it?"

"Black, one sugar please." I can feel her eyes on me, but I don't turn and look at her, no matter how much I want to get another eyeful of how sexy she looks. A moment later she slides a mug of coffee onto the table beside me. "Thanks."

We all fall into an oddly comfortable silence as I feed Poppy, while Lulu sits on the other side of her daughter eating toast and Chloe watches the tv on the couch. It's a strange kind of domesticity that I can't wait to get used to. Once Lulu and Poppy move in with me, we'll be surrounded by family who'll dote on my woman and Poppy as much as I will.

When the oatmeal bowl is empty and Poppy is wearing

almost as much as she's eaten, I stand from the table and search the sink for a cloth I can use to clean her up.

"I'll clean her up, you guys need to get going so you're not late for work," Chloe says, grabbing a pack of something and quickly wiping Poppy's face clean. Lulu coos to her daughter, covering her now clean face in kisses.

"Bye Princess," I say, leaning down and booping Poppy carefully on the nose with the tip of my finger. "You ready?" I ask Lulu, and she gives Poppy one last lingering look, before she kisses Chloe on the cheek and then marches toward the front door.

"You hate leaving her, don't you?" I ask once we're outside and walking toward my mustang that I've parked at the end of the driveway.

"I hate it so much," she whispers.

"Does her dad—"

"Poppy doesn't have a dad, she has me and she has Chloe. The person who provided the other half of her DNA doesn't even get a mention in the footnote of her existence," she says forcefully.

"Okay," I say with a smile. "Did you dream about me last night? Why don't you tell me what I was doing to you?"

"Jesus," she hisses.

"What's up, Kitten?"

"The things that come out of your mouth, you have zero filter."

"Why do I need a filter with you? I'm happy to tell you all about my dreams. You were underneath me, your legs spread as wide as you could get them, your cunt dripping wet, your clit all swollen from where I'd sucked on it and I was pounding into you, your tits bouncing as you held your legs open so we could both watch my dick fill you." My dick hardens at my own words and I glance across the car to her. I can see her chest moving up and down rapidly, her fingers white as she grips the seat tightly beneath her.

"Are you imagining what it'd feel like to be helpless beneath me, a slave to do whatever I say? Begging me for more and knowing that you won't get it unless I decide to give it to you."

A quiet groan falls from her lips and she squirms in her seat. When she goes to cross her legs, I stop her, pushing my hand between her knees and forcing her legs wide.

"Is your pussy all sticky and wet for me, Kitten? Part your legs and let me see."

When she moves, it's instinctual. Her thighs part, and I push my hand up her skirt and cup her cunt, feeling the heat pouring from her and the wet patch across the front of her panties.

"Kick off your shoes and put your feet on the seat," I order.

"No," she groans.

"Now Kitten, don't make me ask again. Do as I say and I'll make you come. If you don't, I'll edge you till we get to work, but I won't let you come and I'll leave you wet and needy until later."

"I can make myself come," she rasps.

"Maybe, but it'll pale in comparison and you'll only feel more needy because it's only my touch, my fingers that'll sate that need. Then later I'll punish you for touching yourself, because this cunt is mine," I growl.

She fidgets for a minute, then slowly lifts her feet off the floor, balancing the edges of her heels onto the seat.

"Good girl," I croon, pushing her panties to the side and running my fingers through her wetness, before I thrust two fingers inside of her and find her clit with my thumb.

Her gasp seems to echo around my car as I try to watch where I'm going while I finger fuck her. When my attention leaves the road for the second time, I swerve to the side and stop, putting my car in park and turning all my attention to Lulu's pussy.

Leaning over her, I capture her lips with mine as I use my now free hand to rub her clit until she's panting and lifting her ass off the seat and grinding into my fingers. "That's it, Kitten, come on my fingers again, come for me."

A whimpering gasp is followed by a full body shudder as her orgasm crashes through her. Eyes tightly shut, her lips part and she moans throatily as her cunt clamps down on my fingers, pulsing as she explodes from the outside in. In this moment she is utterly enthralling, so beautiful when she's consumed by passion that I wish I could take a picture so I could capture this image forever.

I keep moving my fingers slowly, fucking her though her orgasm, until her body unfurls and her feet slide to the floor.

"Fuck," she pants.

"Watch your mouth, Kitten, I don't like hearing you curse."

"Well you're probably going to be shit out of luck, fuck is one of my favorite words," she smiles, her eyes still closed.

"Don't worry, I'm keeping a count, I'll decide on your punishment later."

"Punishment?" Her eyes crash open and she tips her head in my direction.

"You like that idea? I bet no man's ever tried to take you in hand have they? No one's ever taught you to mind your behavior, but don't worry, I will."

As I watch, she swallows thickly, her pussy drooling as a fresh surge of sweetness coats my fingers that are still buried inside of her.

Clearing her throat, she tries to push my hand away, but I ignore her, thrusting my fingers in a little deeper in a silent warning. Putting the car into gear I pull out onto the road, my fingers still deep inside of her. Her hands try to push mine away, she tries to cross her legs, but I refuse to move, forcing her to stay impaled on my hand the entire way to her office.

"Penn," she snaps.

"What's the matter, Kitten?"

"Your fingers."

"Are buried deep inside your cunt," I smirk.

"It hurts."

"No it doesn't, your pussy hasn't stopped gushing since I slid inside of you. It's practically begging me to replace my fingers with something bigger, but I'm not going to claim you for the first time in my car like some horny fucking teenager."

"Your cock isn't going anywhere near my pussy; I shouldn't have let you touch me at all."

"Adding lies and bullshit to the things I punish your mouth for saying too. I hope you like the taste of jizz, because it looks like I'm going to have to spend a lot of time washing your tongue with it."

Shock flashes across her expression as she stares silently at me.

"You wouldn't—"

"I wouldn't what?" I interrupt. "I wouldn't dare to force you to your knees and fuck all the sass right out of your mouth with my dick in your throat? I sure as fuck would. You're mine, Kitten, and you'll learn to mind me, just like I'll learn to make you scream with pleasure. I love your fire, but I won't tolerate you lying to me."

The moment she realizes her mouth has fallen open she snaps it shut, glaring at me as she doubles her efforts to remove my hand from between her legs. "I need to go to work."

"Kiss me first," I demand.

"No."

"Kiss me, or I'll keep you here in this car and fuck you with my fingers over and over till someone calls the cops because of how loud you're screaming."

"I hate you," she hisses.

"That's another."

"Another what?"

"Time you've lied to me."

"I'm not lying," she says through gritted teeth as I force my thumb through her gripped thighs and rub at her clit.

My laugh is low and soft. "Yes you are. Now kiss me, Kitten."

Her eyes hood and she glares at me, venom shooting from her eyes. Maybe she does hate me right this minute, that shouldn't amuse me as much as it does. I'm still smiling when she leans forward and pecks her lips against mine.

"Nope, that's not a kiss."

"It's all you're getting," she snarls.

The walls of her cunt are swollen and puffy from her orgasm, but I still manage to push a third finger into her sex, how wet she is easily allowing her to stretch.

"Oh fuck," she pants as I slowly start to move my fingers. "Stop."

"Is that what you really want? Or do you want me to fuck your cunt until you come again so hard, your cum with be dripping off my hand and soaking into the seat. My car will smell like your pussy for the rest of the day, it'll torture me every time I open the door.

My fingers keep up a steady pace, fucking her slow and deep as I work her clit with my thumb.

"Oh. Oh god," she moans, as her legs part again, allowing me access, her dress bunched at her waist.

"Ask me to make you come," I order.

Her teeth find her bottom lips and she bites down, sucking in a breath as she shakes her head.

"Kitten, ask nicely."

"Please, oh fuck, please make me come."

"Kiss me," I demand.

Her lips find mine and she kisses me properly, moaning

into my mouth as I fuck her to release again. I swallow all her sounds, unwilling to share them as she shakes against me. "Good girl," I praise, stroking her jaw with my thumb as I collar her throat with my free hand. "See how good I make you feel when you mind me," I praise, waiting until her internal muscles stop fluttering before I slide my fingers from inside of her, and pull her panties back in place, covering her pussy and the sopping mess I've made of it.

"What are you doing to me?" she questions, her eyes glazed with confusion.

"Owning you," I tell her simply, stealing a kiss from her lips before I open my door and climb out. Circling the car, I open her door and offer her my hand, trying not to smile at how disheveled she looks.

She doesn't fight me for once, taking my hand and letting me pull her out. I take a moment to smooth her dress, as her legs steady. "Have fun at work, I'll come get you and we can have lunch together at one-thirty. Call me if you need me, I'm only around the corner."

Her nod is a little dazed and I smile again. "See you later, Kitten." Swatting her on the butt, I watch until she pushes into the building, then I climb back in my car and suck her taste from my fingers before I start the engine and pull back onto the street.

EIGHT

LULU

What the actual hell was that? When I woke up this morning I was determined to set him straight, to tell him I couldn't deal with whatever this thing between us is anymore. Then I came downstairs and he was feeding Poppy. This huge beast of a man was leaning over my tiny baby girl, feeding her oatmeal from a pink bowl like she was the most precious thing in the world to him.

I swear my ovaries burst and I ovulated right then and there from the sight. The way he touched me last night, and the things he texted me meant my dreams were plagued with thoughts of him. I woke up hot and needy to the sounds of Poppy awake and ready for her day to start.

Perhaps if I'd had time to take care of myself I wouldn't be so susceptible to him, but somehow I doubt that's true. The moment his hands are on me, or he uses that voice that makes goosebumps come to life across my skin, he's impossible to resist.

Heat fills my cheeks as I wave a quick hello to Annette then rush to my office. I just let him finger fuck me in his car on the way to work. My panties are damp and half up my butt from where he pushed them to the side so he could fill me with his fingers. I'm a mess and my brain is only functioning at half capacity because the orgasm he gave me has addled my mind.

I want him. If he'd have whipped his dick out on the side of the road I've have jumped right on and ridden him to orgasm town without an ounce of reservation because he makes me irrational. It isn't until I'm out of his orbit that I get all of my faculties back and I realize I've let him affect me again.

Pushing my purse below my desk, I bring my computer to life and sign in, opening my email. Groaning quietly, I eye the impossibly long list of tasks Janet has already sent me, starting at 5.30am this morning. I wonder how long she's going to spend testing me before she accepts I'm really good at my job and starts to actually utilize my skills. I get the feeling it's going to take a while.

Exhaling, I stand and head for the bathroom. I pee, remove my wet underwear—there's nothing fun about sitting in wet panties all day—and then wash my hands and head back to my office. Stashing my panties in the bottom of my purse, I set the coffee pot I never used yesterday to brew and get to work.

My cell buzzes a while later and I fish it out, checking the time and realizing it's after 1.00pm and I haven't moved anywhere except to the coffee pot and back all morning. I offered Janet coffee earlier, but she just nodded her head in the direction of her own coffee pot and went back to working without saying a word.

She's not exactly communicative and I wonder how well she deals with clients. It seems unusual that she's not left the office at all so far in the last two days to meet with anyone, but perhaps she has certain days for meetings and has the rest of her time set aside for the paperwork side of the law.

Looking back down at my cell, I have five texts. One from Chloe and four from Penn. I open the one from Chloe first and find a selfie of her and Poppy at the park. My baby girl's bright eyes are smiling widely and her lips are parted in a toothless grin. She's so beautiful it actually makes my heart hurt just knowing that I made her. She's my greatest achievement.

I reply quickly.

Me

Love this pic, hope you're having fun.

Chloe texts back with another picture, this time it's of Poppy, fast asleep on the couch, her pacifier in her mouth, her long eyelashes resting against her lids.

Chloe

I wore her out at the park, she crashed after lunch.

Me

Heart Emoji

A pang of jealousy hits me so quickly my eyes fill with tears. I love Chloe and how she so graciously opened her home for me and Poppy, happily agreeing to look after my daughter so she wouldn't have to go to day care with strangers. But now I'm working, I hate that I'm missing out on these moments with her. I want to take her to the park, to spend my days with her making memories, I don't want to miss anything, but I needed to support myself and as a single parent that means working a full-time job.

Eventually I want to get my own place, somewhere that's ours, just mine and Poppy's and to be able to do that, I need to work. At least it's Chloe looking after her and taking a thousand pictures so I can be there in spirit if not in reality.

Sighing wistfully, I click out of Chloe's texts and into

the ones from Penn.

Penn

My dick is so fucking hard for you. I can still smell your pussy on me.

Penn

How's work?

Penn

I'm really hoping you're busy and not just ignoring me.

Penn

On my way to pick you up for lunch.

The last message was from only a few minutes ago and I exhale slowly as I try to build some walls to protect myself from his addictive presence. He disarms me so easily that I probably need a safe room to save myself from him, but I have to try no matter what.

Standing, I take a moment to stretch, my muscles tight from being bent over my laptop all morning. Making my way to Janet's office, I knock on the door then wait.

"Come."

Pushing open the door, I peer around it. "I'm going for lunch; did you want me to grab you anything?"

"No thank you," she replies curtly, not bothering to look at me again.

"Okay, see you in an hour." I close her office door

before she can ignore me again and grab my purse. I pop into Dave and Taylor's office and ask them if they need anything, but again Dave tells me they both brought lunch from home.

Stepping into reception I part my lips to ask Annette, but Penn appears from nowhere and presses his lips to mine before I can make a sound. He kisses me like we're reuniting after a decade of missing each other, like I'm his one and only, like he won't survive without it.

When he pulls back, his fingers still tangled in my hair, we're both panting and I'm sure my lips are kiss swollen and puffy. "I missed you," he whispers.

"It's been five hours."

"Exactly. Bay had to threaten to tie my ass to a chair to stop me from coming to get you all morning."

"Bay?"

"My brother."

"Oh," I nod.

"Come on, I'm starving, let's go to Grannie Annie's."

Dazed, I allow him to take my hand and tow me toward the door before I remember Annette, whose cheeks are tinged pink, a coy smile etched across her lips. "Annette, did you want me to grab anything for you?"

"No thank you, sweetie, enjoy your lunch. Bye Penn."

"See you later, Annette," he calls over his shoulder, not even pausing in his single-minded intent to get me out of the building.

"Hey, slow down," I protest as he pulls me so fast I almost stumble out of the door.

"Sorry, Kitten," he purrs, releasing my hand and dropping an arm over my shoulder instead.

"How far is this place?"

"Just around the corner," he smiles, bending down and stealing a quick kiss before straightening again, a smug smile stretching his mouth "We're having a proper lunch today, no eating at your desk."

"What if I'm too busy to eat out?" I ask, being deliberately combative. I hate eating at my desk and I need a break from all the mindlessly pointless tasks Janet has me doing, but his kiss has destroyed all the walls I've rebuilt this morning and right now being a bitch to him is the only defense I have.

"Tough," he chirps, guiding me across the street and toward a mom-and-pop style diner complete with the red and white gingham drapes at the windows.

The diner is packed, but Penn waves at an elderly woman behind the counter who points to an empty booth at the back. He guides me to the table, then slides in next to me, instead of opposite, his thigh touching mine.

"You'd have more room over there," I point at the empty bench set across from us.

"My brother and his wife are joining us."

"Oh, err, okay," I stumble over my words, surprised that he's introducing me to more members of his family.

"Don't worry, you'll like them," he says, his hand landing on my thigh, slowly pushing the fabric upwards.

"Stop," I chide, slapping my hand over his in an attempt to stop his movement.

"No one can see. I bet your pussy is missing me, I bet she wants to be petted." Ignoring my attempts to stop him, he continues his movement toward my core, stilling the moment he finds bare flesh and not cotton. "Where the fuck are your panties?" he growls.

"In my purse."

"Why?" he demands, swiveling around in his seat, heat blazing in his angry eyes.

"Because they were wet," I say barely above a whisper, my eyes moving from side to side to make sure no one is listening to our conversation.

"I don't give a fuck. There's men in your office, you need to be wearing fucking underwear." His hand forces my thighs apart and he spears me with two fingers, shoving them roughly inside of me. "This is mine. I don't fucking share. I don't give a fuck if your panties are dripping with cum, you'll wear them and keep my fucking pussy covered. You get me?"

He's angry. Really fucking angry, his eyes not leaving mine, even as two people arrive at our table and slide into the booth opposite us. Turning his head for a second he acknowledges their presence only long enough to snarl. "We'll be right back." Then he pulls his fingers out of me, grabs my hand and drags me out of the booth and toward the back of the diner.

Opening the door to a large bathroom, he pulls me inside, closing and locking the door behind us. "Lift up your dress."

"No," I cry, yanking my hand free from his hold.

He's holding my purse, I hadn't even noticed he'd grabbed it. He takes his eyes off mine and starts to root through my bag, dropping it to the floor with a thud when he finds my balled-up panties, gripping them in his hand.

"Pull up your fucking dress or I'll bend you over and fuck you for the first time right here in this fucking bathroom."

When I don't move, he closes the distance between us in a single stride. Grabbing the sides of my dress I lift it up, revealing my bare pussy to his furious gaze. The hand with my panties in wraps around my throat, while the other forces it's way between my thighs.

Two fingers shove inside of me and I grunt from the pain, which quickly morphs into pleasure as he ruthlessly fingers my pussy.

"Take out my cock," he orders and I do as he says, fumbling with his zipper.

His dick pops free and I swallow thickly at the sight of it. He wasn't lying about the size or girth of it. He's blessed in the cock department, it's long and thick and intimidating as hell. Even after having a baby, I'm not entirely sure that thing's not going to rip me apart if he tries to get it inside of me.

"Jack me."

His words are an order and I instantly comply, wrapping my hand around him, noting that my fingers don't touch as he fucks me with his hand. His movements are rough, angry and possessed as he forces an orgasm on me, my body barely having chance to recognize it's coming before it barrels through me, making my knees weak and a startled cry fall from my lips.

He rips his fingers from inside me and wraps his hand over mine on his dick, increasing the speed of my glides up and down, forcing me to hold him tighter. His grip on my throat tightens and he tenses as he comes, spilling his seed over my pussy, coating my bare skin in his release as he aims his cum to cover as much of me as he can.

When his dick stops twitching, he slowly releases his grip on my hand and loosens his hold on my throat as his eyes focus on the mess he's made on me.

"Can you pass me the tissue?" I ask quietly.

"No," he snarls. Releasing my neck, he bends down and holds out my panties for me.

"I need to clean up first."

"No," he snaps again, gripping my calf and forcing my foot off the floor. "You'll wear your fucking panties, you won't wipe me off you."

"Penn," I gasp, outraged.

"Put them on. Now. Or I swear to fucking god, I'll redden your ass with my hand, then force them onto you."

Shocked to silence I don't protest as he manhandles me into my underwear, pulling them up and pressing the fabric down over my pussy, forcing his cum to absorb into the cotton. The instant feeling of wetness pressed against my skin is disquieting. "I can't sit in cum soaked panties all day," I protest.

"You can and you fucking will. I'm not having *my* woman sat at her desk with *my* pussy out on display. You're either in wet panties, or impaled on my dick for the rest of the day, your choice."

"You're an asshole."

"No, Kitten, I'm a fucking Barnett. You belong to me and you'll behave like it."

"And if I don't?" I don't know why I'm provoking him. It's clear he's really fucking unhinged.

"Then you won't be going back to work until you do."

"You can't control my job," I shout, outraged.

"Watch me. I've known Taylor my whole fucking life. Nothing and no one will get in the way of me and you, including you learning to do as you're told."

"I hate you."

"No, you just wish you did."

Reaching out, he smooths down my skirt, unlocks the door and picks up my purse before grabbing my hand in a grip so tight I'm sure my fingers are going white and drags me back to the table, herding me back into my seat as he takes the one beside me, blocking me from leaving.

"Sorry about that, just had to sort a couple of things out," Penn says to his brother, smiling like it's an average, normal day.

"That's okay," the guy says. It's obvious that he and Penn are related, they share similarities, like the dark hair and strong bone structure, but where Penn is half mountain, this guy is slimmer, less muscular. Even his demeanor is less threatening than Penn's.

"Granger, Alice, this is Lulu," Penn says. "Lulu, this is my brother and his lovely wife."

"It's a pleasure to meet you, Lulu," Granger says, holding his hand out to shake.

"Nice to meet you too," I say as cordially as I can muster, considering how angry I am with the asshole sitting beside me.

"Hi Lulu, welcome to the family. We need to exchange phone numbers, because from the way you look like you're ready to stab Penn with your butter knife, I can see that you're going to need to talk to Bonnie, Cora and me. Trust me, if anyone is going to get exactly how you feel right now, it's going to be us." She's so softly spoken that I'm shocked by her words and the warm knowing smile that's gracing her lips.

"Any tips on how to get rid of him?" I ask.

Her giggle is melodic. "Not any that work, the others might though." She winks conspiratorially and I can't help but smile back.

The waitress appears at the side of the table and I notice the menus and full water glasses in front of us. I quickly scan the selection while the others are ordering, then ask for a grilled cheese and tomato soup, with a coke.

Nodding, she collects the menus from us and leaves. Penn tries his best to get my attention, sliding his hand beneath my dress and fondling me over my very wet panties, but I pointedly ignore him, not even glancing in his direction while we wait for our food.

Granger looks between me and Penn, smiling knowingly as he fills the silence. "So you've just moved to town?"

"Yeah, I got here a week ago, it's a bit of a change from Chicago."

"You're a big city girl then?"

"Yep, born and raised, but child care in the city

116

is expensive and I didn't want my daughter to be with strangers all day. Here, she can stay with family and it's free," I smile.

"How old's your daughter?" Alice asks.

"Almost six months." I grab my cell from my bag and quickly pull up a picture, turning it toward them like the cliché proud mama that I am.

"Oh she's beautiful," Alice smiles.

"You guys don't have any kids?"

Alice shakes her head, a faint blush filling her cheeks. "Not yet."

"We're working on it," Granger says, pressing a kiss to Alice's temple as he pulls her closer to him.

"So what do you guys do?"

"We own a bespoke furniture company," Granger says proudly.

Alice rolls her eyes. "Granger owns a bespoke furniture company, I just do the paperwork, because he's too messy to know where anything is."

"It's *our* company, we work together, I make the furniture, she keeps me organized, runs the showroom and does all the book work," Granger says, arching an eyebrow at his wife and conveying a silent message that has her squirming in her seat. Maybe he is as threatening as Penn, just in a different way.

I'm grateful when the food arrives, noting the time on

my cell and realizing I only have twenty minutes left of my lunch break. There's some small talk as we eat, but I don't really engage, just wanting to eat my food and get away from the domineering asshole beside me, no matter how nice his brother and sister-in-law are.

By the time I've finished, I have ten minutes left to pay and get back to my desk. "I'm so sorry to eat and run, but I only get an hour for lunch and I have to be back at my desk and working in ten minutes."

I push up to standing, dropping some money to cover my lunch on the table, but Penn doesn't move. "Excuse me," I say stiffly, still refusing to meet his eye.

"Put your money back in your purse."

Not wanting to argue over less than twenty dollars, I pick up the cash. "I need to go," I say stiffly.

"I'll walk you."

"I'd rather you didn't."

"I wasn't offering you a choice," he snarls, slowly pushing up from the table and edging his way out of the booth.

"Here's my number," Alice says quietly, her brow furrowed as she slides a business card with a cell number hand written across the back. "Call me later."

"Okay," I nod, not really meaning it.

A small, soft hand lands on my wrist. "Please call me."

Turning, I look at her, a knowing look is staring back

at me and I wonder if maybe the spouses of the rest of the Barnett brothers are perhaps the only ones who can help me get rid of this infuriatingly, sexy man. "I will, I promise."

She nods, lifting her hand and leaning back into her husband.

"It was lovely to meet you. I promise my baby brother isn't always as much of an asshole as I'm sure he's proved to be today," Granger says winking at me, a smirk twitching at the corners of his lips.

"Nice to meet you both," I say politely.

Shuffling out of the booth, I try to push past Penn, but he grabs my arm, stopping me as he puts some cash on the table and then says goodbye to his family.

"Let me go, I'm going to be late," I hiss from behind gritted teeth.

He doesn't release me, but he does start moving, guiding me forward with his unrelenting hold on my wrist. I go with him, hoping to escape him the moment we're out of the busy diner, only instead of letting me go, his grip just tightens once we're out on the sidewalk.

"I'm not going to apologize." His voice is low and steely.

"Whatever, I'd rather you just didn't speak at all."

I'm grateful that Rockhead Point is so small when we get to my office building moments later, yanking at my arm to free myself. "My lunch break is over."

"Come kiss me and you can go," he drawls, the confidence in his tone instantly pissing me off.

"I don't want to kiss you."

"I don't give a fuck, get your ass over here and kiss me, you won't be going in until you do."

"Fuck you."

His scoff is low and lethal. "That's another."

"Fuck," I drag the word out until it sounds like it's twenty syllables. "You."

Yanking my arm so hard I worry it might come out of the socket, he pulls me toward him so violently, I bounce against his rock-hard chest as he holds me to him with a death like grip on the back on my neck. "Kiss me," he demands.

"No." I'm not sure why I'm arguing, he's showing me that he can use his size to overpower me, but if he wants a kiss he'll have to take it, I won't offer it to him.

"Kiss me or I'll finger fuck you to an orgasm right here on the street."

"You wouldn't," I gasp.

"Test me," he taunts, grabbing my ass and pulling my dress up as he gropes me.

Seething, I breath in and out through my nose, so angry I can see the black haze closing in from the sides of my vision. "I hate you," I hiss, before I press my lips to his.

He doesn't let me get away with a dry peck, he forces his tongue past my lips, devouring me like a caveman. The only rebellion I can offer is to not kiss him back. I don't fight him, but I don't offer him anything in return staying a passive, unwilling participant.

Growling, he releases me. "Go to work. Keep those fucking panties on, don't test me on this, Lulu." Then he turns and strides away, his palpable fury following him like a cloud.

NINE

PENN

Fucking pain in the ass, stubborn fucking woman.

Rage and anger and annoyance are my companions as I stomp across town to where our garage is situated. Bay is bent over, his head inside the engine of a Honda, not bothering to look up at me as I kick an empty oil pan out of the way. Picking up the tools from the bench beside the car I was working on earlier, I throw them back into my rolling tool case, seething with anger.

"Nice lunch?" my asshole brother asks. At some point during my tantrum, he's moved across the workshop and is now beside me, a smirk twitching at his lips.

"I swear, that fucking woman. Why was I so excited to

find her? She's a pain in the ass."

"Would she be the right one for you if she just instantly submitted to whatever you wanted?"

His words make me freeze and I slowly turn my head and look at him.

"You don't want an easy lay. This town is full of them. Full of women prepared to jump in your bed and spread their legs for you. Be honest. When you think about your future, do you see some little mouse always saying yes, or do you imagine Lulu, fighting and snarling?"

Fuck, he's right. Even pissed at her, I love her fire and the way the flames only dull to a smolder, never going out completely even when she gives in to me. When her body melts at my touch she's gifting me her submission and that makes it a million times more valuable. I hate it when my brothers are right, the smug assholes.

"My work here is done," Bay says with a smirk, throwing his arms wide as he turns and saunters back to the car he's repairing.

I sit and stew in my anger and annoyance for another hour. I know everything he's said is right. Lulu is perfect for me in every fucking way. I doubt my dick would even twitch for anyone else now it knows she exists, but I'm still pissed that she took her fucking panties off at work. I'm furious that she refused to even acknowledge my presence at lunch and I hate that she wouldn't kiss me back when I dropped her off at her office.

She's mine and she needs to start fucking acting like it.

It's thirty minutes later before I pull my cell out and send her a text.

Me

Send me a picture of your panties.

The tick flashes up beside the message and I know she's seen it, but she doesn't reply.

Me

It's either send me a picture or I come down there and check they're still where they're supposed to be.

The tick appears again, but no reply. I don't know why I'm smiling, but I am, a low laugh bursting from my lips when she still doesn't reply.

Me

Be there in five.

The tick and then the three dots appear, letting me know that she's typing.

Lulu

Picture

The picture she's sent is a view up her skirt, showing her panties and her hand with her middle finger saluting me. I laugh again, my smile widening.

Me

Good girl. I'll be there to pick you up at 5.30

Lulu

I'd rather get a cab.

Me

There you go thinking I was offering you a choice again. I'll be there to pick you up at 5.30, you WILL be there waiting for me.

A few minutes later, a new message pings through and I'm surprised to find it's from Lulu. It's a link to a you tube video. Clicking it, I burst out laughing when a music video starts playing. It's called "Fuck you" by Lilly Allen. I watch the entire video, listening as the singer boldly sings "fuck you" pronouncing her hatred for whoever she wrote the song for. My kitten has claws and there's no point in pretending I don't like it.

Over the rest of the afternoon, Lulu sends me several more links to music videos with fuck in the title or as the theme of the song. I'm kind of impressed, because honestly I had no idea there were so many angry songs out there. Each song makes me laugh a little louder and by the time 5.15pm rolls around, I'm not even that pissed at her anymore. I still want to bend her over and spank her ass until she promises to do what she's told forever more; but honestly, I've wanted to do that since the moment I set eyes on her.

I'm almost jovial as I wave goodbye to my brother and climb into my car, driving the short distance around to her office and parking my car in the lot at the back of the building. Pushing through the door, I wave to Annette, who is on the phone, and then drop my ass into the couch in the waiting area.

It's 5.45pm before Lulu and Dave appear in the corridor, he's talking to her, making her smile and I'm glad I know he's happily married to a man, else I'd have a serious fucking problem with the way he has his hands on my woman. Despite knowing he's gay, I still hate the way she's smiling at him. I hate it more that her smile dims when she sees me, it's like being kicked in the balls. I don't like that she's pissed at me, I want her to light up when she sees me, not wilt like a fucking depressed flower. I thought she'd gotten over her anger with all the fuck you song links, but apparently not.

Standing, I move toward her, smiling widely at Dave as I push my way between them, separating them and dropping my arm around her shoulders, pulling her tight into my side.

"Hi Penn, you and your brothers all still straight?" he asks.

"Last time I checked. You still married?"

"I am, but Brian and I already agree that if any of you

boys decided to dip your toes in the gay pool, you're all both of our hall passes," he laughs flirtily.

"Well, I'm firmly in camp pussy, but if any of the others ever change their minds, I'll let them know about your and Brian's deal."

"You do that," Dave purrs, turning and winking at Lulu before he heads for the door.

"You ready, Kitten?" I ask, letting my palm slide down her back to rest just above her ass.

"Ready to get a cab? Yes. Ready to go anywhere with you? Not particularly."

"There you go thinking you had a choice again," I smile, adding a little pressure to her back and encouraging her to move forward.

"Asshole."

"Night Annette," I call, ignoring Lulu's insult as I hold open the door and urge her outside.

"Night Penn, night Lulu," Annette calls, her amusement clear in her tone and a soft chuckle follows us outside.

"I really don't like you. You know that don't you?" Lulu hisses, walking faster in an obvious attempt to get away from me.

"You liked me well enough this morning when you were coming on my fingers." I smile.

"Sex has nothing to do with like. I don't have to like

my vibrator to let it give me an orgasm."

"That's true, but no plastic cock can make you come the way I do." I sound smug, but I can be because I know it's the truth. I'm good at sex, I know how to make a woman come and I can almost guarantee that Lulu has come harder on my fingers than she ever has on another man's dick or any fucking plastic cock. "Kitten, you can ride a dildo like a cowgirl and it still won't make you feel the way I can with two fingers."

"So full of yourself," she mutters under her breath as I open her car door and help her inside.

Quickly moving to the driver's side, I climb in and turn to look at her. "Not as full as you're going to be when I fill you up with my cock. I can't wait to hear you beg for it… and you will beg. Mindless and cum drunk, you'll beg and plead, you'll worship my dick because you'll know you're ruined for anything else but me."

"Your cock isn't going anywhere near me," she snarls, her lips pressed into an angry line. Turning away from me, she shakes her head as she stares out of the window, ignoring me.

"Want to make a bet?"

"No."

"You chicken? I bet I can make you beg for my cock in less than ten minutes and if you're a good kitten, I might even give it to you."

"I might have enjoyed the orgasms you've given me, but I'll never beg for your dick," she sneers.

"Then you'll win."

Stilling, she slowly turns to look at me. "What do I get if I win?"

"I'll leave you alone." For at least an hour or two, I say silently.

"What?" her brow furrows and I can see the skepticism on her face.

"If you win, I'll leave you alone."

"Let me get this right. You get ten minutes to try to get me to beg for your dick and if I don't—which I won't—you'll leave me alone."

"Yep," I nod, smiling widely.

"Okay, fine, pull over, I'll set a ten-minute timer on my cell."

"Not in the car. I want you on a bed."

"Poppy."

"I know, we'll go to Chloe's, get Poppy bathed and into bed, then I'll take you to my place and you can set all the timers you want there."

"Your place?"

"Yes, my place. I'm not going to be able to make you scream when Princess is ten feet away from us. Plus I want you to see my home, meet the rest of my family, tell me what Poppy will need for her room so we can get it all set-up for her."

"Poppy's room?" her confusion is fucking adorable.

"Princess is going to need her own room and I want it to be perfect for her, so you'll check it out and let me know what I need to get."

"Why the fuck would my daughter need a room at your house?" she snarls.

"For when you move in, Kitten," I reply cockily.

"I'm not moving in with you."

"Sure you are, I could even take the weekend off and we could decorate and get it ready for you to move in next week," I shrug, traversing the roads to Chloe's house with ease and pulling into the driveway while Lulu is still staring at me incredulously.

"I don't..." she stops talking, shakes her head and then sighs. "I don't even know how to respond to that. I'm really starting to think you are actually completely insane. I mean, who suggests moving in together after they've known each other for two days?"

"People who know without a shadow of a doubt that the person they're asking is theirs and will always be theirs."

"And psychos."

"And possibly psychos." I shrug, smiling widely.

Before she has a chance to say anything else I open my door and climb out, rounding the car and opening her door while she just sits looking stupefied.

"Come on, Kitten, Princess is waiting." At my reminder that Poppy is inside waiting for her mama, Lulu sobers, ignoring my hand and climbs out of the car. I can't help but smile as she barges past me and storms straight up to the front door. Following behind her, I let myself into the house and find Lulu cuddling Poppy tightly, talking to her in a cooing tone on the couch, while Chloe pulls a bottle of wine from the refrigerator.

Deciding to give Lulu a moment, I saunter into the kitchen area and smile at Chloe. "How was your day with Princess?"

Chloe's eyes soften and she smiles. "Every day with her is a pleasure, she's the happiest baby I've ever known. I'm so glad they're both here."

Turning, I rest my butt next to hers against the counter and sigh as I watch my woman with her daughter. I want some claim on them both, but right now Lulu is fighting me as much as she's letting me take control. I need her to understand I don't just want her; I need her like I need air to breathe.

"What are you doing with her?"

Chloe's voice pulls me from my daydream and I turn my head to look at her. "They're mine."

"Both of them? Because they're a package deal. What Lulu's been through for that little girl—"

"Both of them," I interrupt. "Lulu's my woman, knew it the moment I laid eyes on her. Poppy's mine too, that little girl had me twisted around her little finger the second I saw her in Lulu's arms. I want to be her daddy and Lulu's man. I've just got to make Lulu understand what it means to be mine. She's pissed at me, but I think I have a way of fixing things. Do you have plans tonight? I want to take her back to my place for a while, we'll get Princess all sorted and into bed before we go."

"If you hurt either of them, I'll castrate you myself, Penn Barnett," Chloe warns.

"If I hurt them, I'll deserve it," I agree, making sure to look her in the eye so she can see how serious I am.

Chloe nods, then smiles again. "I like you, Penn, always have. I'll watch Poppy tonight, I wasn't planning on going anywhere anyway. Are you going to steal my girls from me?"

"As soon as I can convince them to move in, yeah, but that's okay, you'll just have to start coming to dinner a few times a week like Hal does."

"Deal. And I'll even give you a pointer. Actions speak louder than words with Lulu. She's been let down a lot the last year or so, lots of people have tried to sell her with pretty promises and zero follow through. She's not just going to roll over and accept you at your word, you're going to need to show her."

Nodding solemnly, I bite my tongue so I don't ask who's hurt my girls. I don't want to hear the story from Chloe, I need Lulu to tell me and to get her to do that, I need her to trust me. As much as I wish I could just kidnap her and Poppy and stop them from leaving, that won't work. Lulu needs to see that what I'm saying is true, and I have no problem backing that up with my actions.

Picking up the glass of wine from the counter, I press a kiss to Chloe's cheek and make my way over to the couch. Lulu is on the floor, helping Poppy to build a tower out of pink bricks. The moment the fourth brick goes on the top, Poppy knocks them all down and giggles, clapping her pudgy hands together in glee.

Instead of sitting on the couch, I get down onto the floor, handing Lulu her wine.

"Hey princess, have you had a good day?" I ask Poppy, smiling at the beautiful little girl when she turns her huge blue eyes at me.

She makes an adorable cooing noise, then slaps at the bricks that are on the floor between her legs.

"What are we building? Are Mama's towers no good?"

Poppy slaps at the bricks again.

"What about a castle for the pretty princess?" I ask her, then start to build the bricks up into a sort of castle shape while Poppy watches me. Working quickly, I place the last brick on the top and watch as Poppy giggles, then slaps the bricks, sending them skittering across the floor. "Oh no," I gasp, slapping my hands to my cheeks in mock shock. "A giant knocked the princess's castle over."

Poppy giggles, slapping at the bricks as a line of drool falls from the corner of her parted lips.

"I should go get her bath started," Lulu says quietly from beside me.

"Say, no Mama, I want to make more castles," I coo, booping Poppy on the nose and using the triangle fabric thing around her neck that's already wet with drool to wipe the spittle away.

Poppy claps and even though I can't see it, I can feel the soft smile on Lulu's lips. It's the same one I've seen her give her daughter whenever she looks at her. "One more castle to smash and then it's bath time."

"Yay," I cheer, lifting Poppy's chubby arms into the air and waving them around.

We play for another thirty minutes, then I push up from the floor. "I'll go run her bath, you keep playing and I'll shout you when it's ready. Any particular jammies for tonight?"

"I can do it," Lulu argues, moving to stand up.

"I've got it, Kitten," I assure her, squeezing her shoulder lightly. "You stay and play with princess."

Warm, grateful eyes lift to mine and my dick twitches with the way she's looking at me. It's not at all sexual, but the gratitude and thanks in her expression mean more than she could understand. Lulu is fighting my need to look after my girls and I fucking love it, but I'll do whatever it takes for her to understand that her and Poppy are the most important things in my world. Running our princess a bath so her mama can spend ten more minutes playing with her is just one tiny way I'll show her how happily I take care of what's mine.

I head upstairs and set the tub to fill, then go into Lulu and Poppy's room to find jammies, a diaper and everything else I remember her pulling out last night. Taking a moment to look around, I hate that this room doesn't feel like theirs. Their stuff is here, but it's obviously a spare room that they're using rather than home. Boxes are stacked up against one wall and furniture has been moved out of the way to make room for Poppy's crib and changing table.

This feels temporary, which maybe it is. That thought unsettles me even more. I still don't know why Lulu is here and what happened to make her move from Chicago. She mentioned that child care in the city was expensive and that she didn't want Poppy to be around strangers all day, but surely she has parents, maybe even siblings? Where are they? Why has she moved clear across the country?

The unknown answers to all of those questions consume me as I turn off the taps and lean over to check the temperature of the water. It's a little hot so I add some cold water, securing Poppy's bath chair in place and adding some bubble bath to the water, swishing it around until the surface is covered with a layer of fluffy bubbles.

Setting out a cloth, shampoo and baby soap, I head back downstairs and find Poppy in Lulu's lap on the floor while she sings quietly to her. Poppy's eyelids are heavy and she's sucking on her finger, her head resting against Lulu's breasts.

Crouching down, I brush my finger across the apple of Poppy's cheek. "You ready for your bath, little one?"

Tired eyes look up at me and I melt, I fucking melt. Carefully lifting her from her mama's lap, she nestles into my shoulder as I hold out a hand for Lulu. I'm expecting her to reject my offer of help, but instead she gently places her hand in mine and lets me help her up from the floor, her expression soft as she watches me hold her daughter.

We bathe Poppy and I blow bubbles at both mama and baby while Lulu does the actual bathing part. Then I tidy up the bathroom and make Poppy's bottle with a little assistance from Chloe while Lulu gets her dried and ready for bed. This time when she settles onto the bed to feed her, I lie down behind her, wrapping my arm around both Lulu and Poppy as Lulu whispers a story about a princess living in a castle, and a giant and a knight in shining armor.

The sense of contentment I feel just lying here with my girls shocks me, but makes complete sense at the same time; and I'm almost reluctant to release them when Lulu pulls the bottle from Poppy's mouth and starts to move.

"Stay, don't put her down yet."

Lulu stills for a minute, then sighs and relaxes back into me, her finger tips stroking the soft swell of Poppy's lips.

"She's so perfect," Lulu whispers.

"Just like her mama."

Scoffing lightly, she tenses when I press a kiss to her shoulder. "Perfect," I whisper.

Reluctantly, I let her get up and lay Poppy down in her crib, then I take her hand in mine and lead her downstairs.

"I can cook dinner here, or we can grab something at mine."

She opens her mouth to argue, but I silence her with a kiss. "I already spoke to Chloe, she doesn't have any plans tonight and doesn't mind watching the baby monitor while we go to mine for a while."

"It's not fair for me to expect Chloe to watch her all day, then again at night," Lulu protests.

"I agree and normally I wouldn't have asked, but it's only for a couple of hours and it's a one off. Once Poppy's room is set up at my place, we'll just take her with us."

She starts to argue again and I press my lips to hers, enjoying this way of keeping her compliant. When she kisses me back I slide an arm around her hip and hold her to me, grinding my hard dick against her stomach as I slowly dominate her mouth.

"Get a room," Chloe calls from the living room, then cackles loudly.

"We've got two but one's got a baby in it, the other's thirty minutes from here," I call back, smiling against Lulu lips as I turn her, walking her toward the couch with my arm wrapped around her waist. "Go sit, I'll see what I can rustle up for dinner."

The refrigerator is full, so I pull out the stuff for a stir fry, eager to eat and get her to my place as quickly as possible now we're on a time limit. As much as I want her in my bed all night, Lulu's right, it's not fair to expect Chloe to do extra babysitting or for Lulu to spend even more time away from her kid just because I want her all to myself in a room with a bed and no baby.

The ladies watch tv, while I pull out a pan, chicken, veggies and make a quick sauce and throw them together, cooking the fresh ingredients hot and fast. I'm a good cook, my mama made sure all of us boys knew how to take care of ourselves and our women when we found them. But it's more than just a life skill, I enjoy cooking, I find it weirdly calming. I even enjoy the days when it's my turn to cook for the family, and cooking for Lulu feels even better.

I want to provide everything for her, including food, a home and money. My woman and kid will have everything they've ever desired and I'll do whatever it takes to make that happen. Ten minutes later, I divide the food onto three plates and lay the table, grabbing the wine bottle from the refrigerator and a bottle of water for me. "Dinner's ready, ladies," I call.

Lulu gets to the table first and I hold out her chair for her, like the gentleman my mama tried to make me, pressing a kiss to her cheek as I place the plate of food in front of her.

"You cook?" she says breathily.

"I do."

"I don't," she laughs.

"That's okay, I'll look after you." I wink, sliding into my chair beside her as Chloe disappears into the hallway, returning a moment later with a frown on her face.

"You okay?" Lulu asks.

"Yeah, just my god damn daughter being a pain in the ass again," she sighs.

"Oh," Lulu says, not asking anything further as she grabs her fork and stabs some chicken and noodles from the plate.

"Apparently I'm a terrible mother because I won't

give her five thousand dollars to bail her waste of space boyfriend out of jail," Chloe hisses. Opening the bottle of wine, she fills her glass all the way to the top, lifts it to her lips and takes a healthy drink, before slamming it back down to the table hard enough to make some of the liquid spill out the side. "I mean five thousand dollars that I'll never see again to get that idiot out of jail, when the best place he could be is locked up and away from my daughter."

"Who's she seeing?" I ask cautiously.

"Dirk. I mean, really, who the hell calls their child Dirk? She met him at a bar in the city, I've not even met him, all I know is that she's saying they're engaged and I need to give her money for a fancy city wedding and a ten thousand dollar dress and a honeymoon to the fucking Seychelles." Chloe is full on ranting now, and when I glance at Lulu, her face is pale, her expression grim as she stoically eats.

"I'm sorry, Chloe, you know this is because I'm here."

"It's not your fault, Lulu. She's a selfish brat. You're family, but she's always been jealous of you and she's acting out like a child. She hasn't lived here for years and it's not like you and Poppy are even in her bedroom, you're in James' and he couldn't be happier knowing you're here." Chloe shakes her head and angrily stabs her fork into a baby corn, snapping the end off with her teeth and ruthlessly crunching down on it. "Oh Penn, I'm sorry, this is delicious. Thank you for cooking."

"It's no problem. Is there anything we can do to help with Roxanne?" I'm really hoping she says no. It took me months and several really nasty and uncomfortable conversations with Roxy for her to understand that my dick had zero interest in her anymore. Even after I'd spelled my disinterest out to her a dozen times, she still told me she'd be waiting for me to apologize and beg her to come back to me the last time I saw her. I'm not sure how a woman hears that she was just a wet, willing hole and spins that to her being the great love of my life. But the more I pushed Roxy away, the more she thought I was interested.

"God no, the best thing you and Lulu can do is stay as far away from Roxanne as possible. There is no point her screaming at everyone. I'm her mother, it must be at least partially my fault she is the way she is, so I'll take the brunt of her drama," Chloe laughs weakly.

The rest of dinner passes in a tense haze. I know I need to tell Lulu about the fuck buddy situation I had with Roxanne, but I need to get things solid with her before I throw any unnecessary drama into the mix.

When we've all finished eating, I wash the dishes, while Lulu disappears upstairs to shower and change. I'd rather we go and she can shower at my place, but I bite my tongue and instead make myself useful cleaning up while she's gone.

"Okay, I'm ready," she announces from the doorway.

Turning to look at her, I almost swallow my tongue when I spy her standing in the doorway, in a pair of skin-tight jeans and a knit sweater that hangs off one shoulder, revealing a tantalizing glimpse of skin that I want to lick and suck. I can't see a bra strap and I'm really, really hoping she's not wearing one, even though her tits are probably too big for her to go without.

Dropping the cloth I'm holding, I wipe my hands and close the distance between us, wrapping my arms around her and pulling her until she's close enough for me to kiss. "Fuck, Kitten, I'm not sure how I'm even going to last the ride home without touching you."

"See you in a couple of hours," Chloe calls, reminding us that she's sitting on the couch and can probably hear everything I just said.

"Are you sure you don't mind?" Lulu asks, unease lacing her beautiful face.

"No, it's fine, go, go. Poppy rarely wakes up in the night," Chloe waves away her concern before turning back to the show she's watching on the tv.

"Come on, Kitten, we won't be too long, and I've got a bet to win." Winking at her, I take her hand in mine and pull her out through the door.

TEN

LULU

My heart is hammering against my chest as Penn drives us out of town and up the narrow winding roads that traverse the mountain. "You don't live in town?" I'm not sure why this is the first time I've asked this, he's mentioned that it's a drive to his place, but I just assumed he lived in the next town over, not that he lived in the middle of nowhere on a mountain.

"Nope, my place is about halfway up the mountain, it's a pain in the ass if you need to get a cab home, but the views are amazing," he laughs.

"And you live with your family?"

"Sort of," he chuckles. "Until recently, my brothers

and I still lived in our family home. I know it's weird, but we're close, none of us enjoy living alone and the house is huge. When Beau and Bonnie got together and we had to listen to them fucking, we all agreed that unless we wanted to move out we needed to change the layout. We did a huge reno last year and now we basically all have our own two bed apartments and then a communal space that we can use, or not."

"I'm an only child, I can't imagine wanting to live with my family. I moved out for college and never went back again," I sigh, inwardly cringing at just the thought of living with my parents.

"We know it's unusual us all living together in our family home, but when you see it, you'll understand why none of us ever wanted to leave."

Falling into a comfortable silence I watch the sun set, the colors in the sky setting the Montana mountain range alight with reds and oranges and pinks. I never knew the sky could look like that until I'd gotten here, nor that so many stars filled the sky once the light show had faded. We slow, then turn down an unassuming gravel drive, and I focus all of my attention ahead of me as the huge log house comes into view. The house itself is single story, squat, with a pitched roof and looking entirely too much like it's dropped off a cowboy movie. Light glows through the windows and somehow considering it's alone, halfway up a mountain, it feels... homely.

Several cars are parked outside the front and Penn slows to a stop behind a huge jacked up truck that I'd need a ladder to get into. "Come on then, Kitten," he says excitedly, jumping out of the car and rushing around to pull me out of my door. "So this is home. What do you think?"

He's excited, more so than I've ever seen him, almost childlike in his enthusiasm to show me this house, this home that he loves so much. "It's gorgeous," I say truthfully, because it is, even if for some reason it wasn't what I was expecting.

"My daddy built it himself, every log in it he cut himself and shaped into a fucking house."

Taking my hand he tows me to the front door, opening it and pulling me inside where the scent of vanilla and cookies hits me, along with several sets of eyes. The room is huge, open plan and full of people. I recognize Bonnie, Alice and the brother from the diner today, Granger, but everyone else is a stranger to me. Strangers who are all staring at me with a sense of familiarity, like they all know who I am.

"Kitten, come meet everyone," Penn says happily, closing the front door behind us and pulling me further into the room.

"Everyone, this is Lulu," Penn announces to the room

at large. Pulling me forward, he sits down on a huge sectional couch and drags me down next to him. "Lulu, this is my oldest brother Beau and you met his wife Bonnie the other day." He gestures to the biggest guy I've ever seen. Seriously, I thought Penn was built, but this guy makes him look small in comparison. "Then this is Cody, Bay and Teddy." He points to three guys in turn. "This is Huck and the mama to be is his fiancé, Cora."

The red headed woman smiles at me, her face a little flushed, her hand rubbing absentmindedly at her swollen pregnant belly. "You've had a kid, right? Be honest, do you feel better once you squeeze them out, or am I going to feel like shit for the next six months?" There's no preamble or pleasantries, she just blurts the words out.

"Peaches," the guy sitting beside her chides.

"Huck Barnett, you did this to me, you should be lucky I'm letting you sit this close to me right now. I am so mad at you for this," she shouts, lifting her hand from her belly and punching Huck right between the legs.

All of the guys hiss in synchronized unity as Huck crumples, slithering into a heap on the floor.

"I'm serious, I need to know," Cora asks, completely ignoring the man moaning in pain at her feet.

I glance around for the others' responses, but the guys are all wincing in sympathy and Bonnie and Alice are smirking, both of their shoulders shaking with restrained laughter.

"Well?" Cora prompts.

"Err, how long do you have left?"

"My due date was ten days ago, if this baby doesn't come in the next forty-eight hours they're taking me in."

"Wow, okay. Err yeah, you'll feel better, then the sleepless nights come and you'll be exhausted but it'll still be better than you feel now."

Cora nods as if processing my words, then she glances down to her fiancé. "Huck."

"Yeah, Peaches?"

"I want pie."

"Okay baby," he nods, cupping his balls as he slowly gets up from the floor and heads for the kitchen, pressing a soft kiss to her lips as he passes.

I have no idea what the hell just happened and as I glance at Penn, he's smiling fondly at his sister-in-law, like she didn't just punch his brother in the dick and she's just the cutest thing he's ever seen.

"Come on, Kitten, I'll give you the tour," Penn says with a grin, standing up and tugging me up with him.

"Nice to meet you, Lulu, things aren't normally this weird," the big guy Beau says, his smile lighting up his face.

"Err sure. Nice to meet you too."

Penn pulls me away from his family, pointing out

things to me as we walk, but I'm not really paying any notice, until we stop beside a door.

"And this one is mine," he announces, pushing it open and gesturing for me to walk inside.

Even though he told me he basically had a self-contained apartment off the main house, I wasn't expecting an actual self-contained apartment, but that's what this is. A small, open living, dining, kitchen space, then two bedrooms and two bathrooms. It's bigger than the apartment I had back in Chicago and it's beautifully decorated. The living space has one whole wall of windows that I'm sure have beautiful views in the daylight, as well as skylights that give you a glimpse at the inky blackness above us. The walls are a warm grey, the couch a deep red with a mix of black and grey throw pillows. The kitchen has white granite counters and white cupboards with brushed chrome appliances. It's comfortable and modern and I feel instantly at home.

"This would be Poppy's room," he says, smiling as he opens a door and shows me a large bedroom. At the moment it's empty apart from a desk and chair. "We could paint it pink, then get some of those decal stickers that go on the walls with a castle and a princess and all that shit."

"Penn," I sigh.

"Kitten, it's happening so you might as well get on board. I'm not going anywhere and I'm not going to let you go anywhere, so you and Poppy moving in is an inevitability."

"Penn, we've known each other for two days. I'm not moving in with you and I'm certainly not moving my daughter in with you and a whole host of other people I don't know. In normal circumstances if it was just me, I'd want to be seriously dating someone for a year or so before I'd co-habit, now I have Poppy to consider so I'd need even longer. I can't introduce someone into her life until I know if they're going to become a permanent fixture. You seem like a nice guy, and maybe we can date and see where things go, but at least for a while I need you not to try to be around Poppy, it won't be fair on her in the long run." I feel better after I finish speaking, like I've taken back control of this runaway train of a situation. This is right, setting some boundaries, making sure he understands my priorities.

"That's not happening, Kitten."

"What?" My head snaps up and I gawp at Penn, who is shaking his head and looking down at me indulgently.

"I'm not staying away, I'm not backing off from being a part of Poppy's life, I'm not prepared to *date* and see where it goes. I don't need to do any of that bullshit stuff because I already know this is permanent. I'm happy to go down to the courthouse in the morning and make this official, then we can sort out adoption papers for Poppy so you're both legally mine. I'm not walking away, I'm not giving you a chance to build walls, so here's how it's going to go. I'm going to give you a month to get used to being with me, for that month we'll stay at Chloe's during the week; on the weekend you and Poppy will stay here and you can redecorate, change the furniture, whatever the fuck you need to do to make this home. I get that you're used to being on your own and you have a shit ton of walls up to protect you and the princess. I don't know what happened with Poppy's dad, I'm hoping soon you'll trust me enough to tell me, but know this, I'm not like any other guy you've known, dated, or fucked. You are mine. I'm not going to change my mind; I'm not going to get bored or lose interest. You're it for me. I'm going to marry you, give you my name, then as many babies as I can convince you to have. You can work or stay at home, you can cook or let me look after you. But the one thing you won't ever get to do is leave me. I'd chase you to the ends of the earth and drag you back over my shoulder, because you are my fucking life now."

His eyes are wide and wild and so full of honesty I step back to shelter myself from the intensity of it. Who the hell says all that and means it? I've heard guys tell me they love me, I've heard them declare they want a future and a life with me, right up until the moment they change their minds. But none of them, not one has ever looked at me the way Penn is looking at me right now. I didn't know honesty was a visceral thing until now, because I know with every fundamental part of me that he's telling me the truth, and that scares the fucking hell out of me.

Shaking my head, I try to deny his words, to hide from them, from him even when he's standing right in front of me.

"Yes, Kitten, yes. No bullshit, no lies, just god's fucking honest truth. Run and I'll chase, hide and I'll find you, I won't let you deny this when you feel it just like I do."

"I need to go home, this is too much, I need to…" I trail off, not sure what the hell I need.

"Not yet, I've got a bet to win."

"Bet?" I'm so bewildered I don't even realize how close he is to me until his arm curls around my back and I'm pressed into his hard, warm chest.

"Ten minutes to make you beg, Kitten. Are you still doubting that I can do it, or do you understand now the affect your man has on you?"

His voice has gone from brutally honest to lust drenched sin, and I swear my pussy actually moans as arousal gushes from me.

A laugh burbles from his chest and I close my eyes trying to defend myself against him. "The way you look, Kitten, I'll barely have to touch you."

His fingers find mine and he tangles our hands

together, turning me and slowly reeling me to him, guiding me out of the room. My eyes open without my consent the moment my feet start to move and I follow him, like a moth drawn to a flame even knowing it'll burn.

He's made me come more than once, but somehow I know that if he gets me on a bed, in private and without the risk of interruption, I'll lose myself completely to the pleasure he evokes and then I'll be powerless to fight him. The last eighteen months have been long and hard and scary. So much change, so many shocks, my life's been like a merry-go-round that dips up and down but never stops.

If I didn't want him, this would be so much easier, but until his hands slid up my dress the other day, I'd forgotten what pleasure felt like.

I let him lead me into his bedroom and close the door behind us. I feel almost blinded by the need to let him win this stupid bet. If he loses he said he'd leave me alone, but considering what he just told me he either knows he can win, or his offer to stay away is him just bullshitting me, because I don't think either of us could walk away now if we tried.

Swallowing thickly I take in the room; the walls are white, the bedding black, it's stark and monochrome and kind of perfect for Penn. His bed is huge like I expected, the dresser and bedside tables look like charred wood and are chunky and definitely not from pottery barn. It's clean, almost empty and I scoff as I imagine all my mess and chaos taking over his space.

"Come here, Kitten," he coos, drawing my attention back to him.

"Penn—"

"No Lulu. No thinking, rationalizing or arguing. The next ten minutes are mine and all I'm going to allow you to do is feel," he rasps, his fingers squeezing mine, the only point of contact between our bodies.

Suddenly his hands are on my waist, peeling my shirt up and over my head. My jeans go next and then I'm standing in the middle of his bedroom in just my bra and panties. My stomach is covered in red, angry stretchmarks that haven't faded yet despite it being six months since I was pregnant. I'm fighting the urge to cover them with my hands when he drops to his knees at my feet and he runs his fingers over my stripes, caressing the lines reverently. "I can't wait to see your body swelling with more babies. You're a fucking warrior, Kitten, and these are your battle scars. I love them."

His tongue licks a hot wet path on one mark that goes from my bellybutton all the way to the waist of my panties and I find myself standing a little straighter, my fingers finding his hair instead of insecurely clenching at my sides.

"Go lie on the bed on your back," he orders, his voice

becoming husky as he demands my compliance.

Slowly, I do as he asks, aware of his eyes on me as I climb onto the comforter and wait for him to come to me.

Smirking, he exaggeratedly pulls his cell from his pocket, sets a timer for ten minutes, turning the screen to show it to me before he places it on one of the bedside tables and hits start. I expect him to pounce on me, but instead he slowly walks to the bottom of the bed and takes a moment to look at me.

His eyes rake over every inch, settling on the fabric between my thighs that I know is damp and clinging to my folds. "Part your legs."

Shuffling my knees to the side, I spread my legs for him. I could fight him, drag things out and try to prolong this, but we both know he's going to win and fuck it; I want him to. I want to be lust drunk and begging, and I want him to be the one that makes me that way.

Unfastening my bra, I pull it down my arms and throw it to the side, his eyes land on my nipples and I feel them harden beneath his gaze. My body heats and I move my hands to the waist of my panties and push them down, revealing myself to him. Kicking my legs free of the damp fabric, I spread them wide for him again, putting my wet pussy on display, taunting him silently to do his worst and make me beg.

"Naughty, naughty, Kitten. Your cunt is so fucking wet

I could blow on you and make you scream, couldn't I?"

I nod, and his smirk becomes cocky and knowing.

"You don't want to play anymore?" he questions.

I shake my head.

"Good girl, now beg."

I shake my head again.

"Beg, and instead of taunting you until you're writhing and desperate, I'll just slam my fat cock into you right now and we can make the most of the time we have by me fucking you raw."

A groan slips out and I feel my arousal seeping from me and coating my thighs.

"Beg," he demands, his voice going stern and unyielding.

"Please," I whimper.

"Please what?"

"Fuck me. Oh god, please fuck me."

His lips spread into a wide smile and he blinks at me, smug and knowing and infuriatingly sexy as he stands there fully dressed while, I'm naked and squirming and literally begging him to touch me and fuck me without him even having to lay a finger on me.

Oh so slowly, he pulls his t-shirt over his head, dropping it to the floor. Kicking off his boots, he pushes down his jeans and boxers together, pulling them and his socks off his feet until he's gloriously naked.

"Fuck," I whisper as I take him in. His chest seems even bigger without clothes, broad and defined and covered in tattoos. In fact, most of his torso and arms are covered in bright bold Japanese images, pink flowers, orange fish, a green dragon. He's a living work of art and if this were any other moment, I'd want to look at each thing in turn; but he's naked and so am I… and I need his dick.

Holy fuck.

I let my eyes drop to his dick and all of the air in my lungs puffs out of me in a single, shocked exhale. Most guys boast that they have a big dick. They think it's a badge of honor to be well hung, but truthfully, ninety percent of the time they're nothing but average sized with an over inflated ego. Penn is nothing like those guys. His dick is obscenely large. I had my hand wrapped around it at lunchtime, but I swear it didn't seem this big. It's like a fucking bat hanging between his thighs, long and as wide as my wrist, there is no way that thing is fitting inside of me, absolutely no fucking way.

I shake my head, shutting my legs together with a slap as my skin meets and locks my pussy down.

"Spread your legs, Kitten, it'll fit."

"No, it won't."

"I promise it will. I'll get you so wet and ready you'll be panting to ride it even as I stretch you."

"I don't—"

"Now," he orders, his patience finally gone as he climbs one knee onto the bed and forcibly spreads my legs so he can settle between them.

His lips find mine and he kisses me, his tongue forcing its way into my mouth as his hand finds my breast and cups it. I feel the slight pinch of pain as his fingers squeeze down on my nipple, rolling it as he owns my mouth.

I gasp and he swallows the sound, his fingers pinching down a little harder on my nipple as the hint of pain makes my back arch. I've always enjoyed a little pain with my pleasure, but the majority of the men I've known have been more into their own appetites than interested enough to bother understanding mine. Penn isn't like that. He always seems to know exactly what I want, like he's reading my thoughts. So it doesn't surprise me when his free hand tangles with my hair, yanking roughly, turning me exactly where he wants me to go, while I try to rub my pussy against him, desperate for friction.

"Fingers on your nipples, I want you to pinch and tug on them while I get your cunt ready for me. Don't go easy, make it hurt, just the way you like it. You stop, and I'll stop playing with your pussy, you get me?"

I nod manically, lifting my hands to my breasts and rolling the peaks of my nipples between my thumbs and forefingers while he shuffles down the bed until his face is level with my sex.

"Such a pretty, wet cunt. Who does it belong to?"

"Right now, whoever makes it fucking come," I pant, unable to stop sassing him, even when I'm desperate for his touch.

"Wrong answer," he chuckles, lifting his hand and spanking my sex.

The pain is instant, raw and burning and I yelp. "Hey."

"If this cunt belonged to anyone but me it wouldn't be dripping right now, so tell me, Kitten, who would you rather have between your spread thighs?"

"No one. You."

"So, who does this wet slit belong to?"

"You."

"Good, Kitten. Spread those thighs nice and wide, I'm going to stretch you out so you can take all my cock like a good little kitty cat, but first you need to ask me nicely."

"Penn," I warn, the pain from my nipples almost overtaking my desire.

"Ask. Me. Nicely," he demands, speaking slowly and enunciating each word.

"Penn, please."

"Ask me."

"Please stretch my pussy out so I can take your obscene cock."

A single finger slams into me and I yelp. Fucking me with his hand, his tongue finds my clit and I swear to god

I black out as an orgasm crashes through me. When I become aware of what's happening to me, my pussy is stretched wide and it feels like he has his entire, huge hand inside of me.

"Too full, oh god," I cry, writhing as a second orgasm barrels toward me, threatening to hurtle me over the edge again.

"That's only two fingers, Kitten, I need to get three, maybe four into you before I can take you with my cock."

"No, I can't." Thrashing my head from side to side I try to close my knees, but his broad shoulders between my thighs stops me.

"You can, and you fucking will," he says as he nips at my clit, and I explode into a second orgasm. This time I stay conscious as his fingers keep moving inside of me and when he crams a third, thick digit into me it feels like I'm stretched beyond anything I've ever felt before. I'm so full it hurts, but it feels amazing at the same time and as tingling starts in my toes, I know that if I orgasm again I'll scream so loud the entire house will hear.

"Walls are soundproofed," Penn laughs, sensing what I'm thinking without me even having to say anything. "Come again, and then I'm going to bury my dick inside of you and claim you."

I don't know what he does, but it hurts in the very best way and my entire pussy clenches as I feel arousal gush from me as I come again, my whole body tensing and then releasing with a burst of euphoria that I've never experienced before in my life.

Somehow, I'm still working my nipples and he pushes me away as he crawls up my chest and takes one into his mouth. "Delicious," he smirks, then kisses me. I taste myself on his lips, but he doesn't give me a chance to protest as the broad head of his dick pushes against my entrance.

Even after three orgasms and him filling me to capacity with his fingers, the head still feels impossibly large. "Oh fuck," I gasp.

"Relax and let me in, my entire cock is going in you, Kitten, so you need to spread your legs as wide as they'll go and let me take control. I swear I'll make it feel so fucking good."

I nod, clinging to his shoulders as his lips find my neck, nipping and kissing as he slowly works his behemoth cock into me. Pushing and retreating, I whimper as he fills me slowly, the pain gradually morphing into a tingling pressure that makes me pant and moan until he's finally all the way inside of me.

"Good girl, that it's, Kitten, take me. I can't fuck you with all of it, but I wanted you to feel what it was like to be stuffed full of my cock."

"Oh god," I breathily gasp.

"I'm going to take your mouth and your ass too, there won't be a part of you that I haven't touched and filled and fucked."

"You're not putting that thing in my ass," I moan, as he pulls out and then slowly slides back into me, not all the way, but far enough that the head hits my g-spot and I see stars.

"Yes I am, I'm going to fill your ass with my dick and then when I come I'm going to spank your ass while my cum drips out of your gaping hole."

His dirty words, combined with the way his thick cock is filling me, makes me unable to speak. Burying my face into his neck, I hold on to him tightly as he uses my body for his pleasure, mini orgasms sparking to life with every thrust. I'm going to hurt tomorrow, honestly, I'm not sure I'll be able to walk, but I've never been fucked like this before. This is a whole body experience, every single one of my nerve endings from the top of my head to the tips of my toes are alight and buzzing with euphoria.

His pace increases until he's fucking me with abandon, only using about three quarters of his dick, making sure not to actually hurt me until I detonate around him, clamping down on his cock so hard that it hurts, even as I scream and pant with pleasure. He comes too, and I feel the heat of his release burst inside of me, filling me up as he jerks above me, his moans of pleasure stifled against my head.

I'm not sure how long it takes us both to come back to reality, but I don't loosen my hold on him, needing to be close to him and make this moment of ecstasy last as long as possible. If I let him go, reality will creep in and I don't want that, because we just had sex, very, very unprotected sex and I'm not on the pill.

ELEVEN

PENN

Holy fuck. I love sex. I mean, show me a man who doesn't, but what Lulu and I just did was so much more than just sex. My brothers have hinted that fucking their women has been different, but I had no idea what they really meant until now. Lulu is everything I've ever fantasized about in a sexual partner. She's submissive, without being meek, she's wild and abandoned and fuck me, her pussy is perfection.

It's selfish to confess that although I've always made sure my previous sexual conquests have had a good time, I've never been hugely concerned with making sure I was ticking all of their boxes. Fuck buddies are fun, but as long as they got off and so did I, I never found myself giving a crap about what they needed, or at least not more than just a good fuck.

Everything about Lulu is different. It's been years since I wanted to try and get my entire dick inside a woman. I know I'm blessed with a hefty load and once I figured that out, I also worked out how much I could use and which bits of my dick were unlikely to feel the inside of a warm, wet hole. There was no way I could be content with that with her. No way could I fuck her with the full length without hurting her, but this first time and hell; probably every time, I needed to be all the way inside of her, to claim her with every inch of me and she took it.

Her pussy is so tight I've been chanting "Don't come, don't come, don't come," inside my head since the moment the head of my dick slid into her platinum fucking cunt. I have never felt so much, enjoyed anything so vividly, or come so hard in my entire fucking life, and even though my balls are empty I'm ready for round two. This is the first time I've ever fucked a woman bareback. I had no clue how good it would feel and now I know, there's no way I'll ever put anything between my dick and her cunt again.

This is *my* woman and I feel that right down to my bones, to the very core of me.

"Fuck, Kitten, that was unbelievable," I rasp against

her cheek, dragging my lips to hers and kissing her.

"I..." she trails off, like she can't quite muster the strength to speak. She's still clinging to me, her arms around my neck, her legs wrapped around my hips, a mixture of my cum and hers dripping from around my dick and coating us both in our release. Slowly, I withdraw my dick from her heat and her arms slide from around my neck as I pull back until I can look down and watch the head of my cock slip out of her. Her pussy is pink and puffy, her lips and entrance slick and glistening with wetness. "Jesus, I wish you could see what I can. Your cunt is gaping and dripping with my cum, I wish we had time for round two, I'm already getting hard just from the sight of your slit.

"Penn." The sound of my name on her lips has me looking up, but instead of the bliss I expect to find on her face, her expression is... Worried? Unsure?

"What's the matter? Did I hurt you? Are you okay?" Fear overwhelms me and as much as I needed to claim her, I worry that I've damaged her, that maybe she didn't enjoy it like I thought she had.

"I..." she pauses, swallowing visibly, then pushing herself up onto her elbows. "Err, we weren't careful, I didn't even think. I should have."

"What the fuck's going on, Lulu? I'm clean, I should have said something, but there's no way I'd have touched you if there was any chance."

"I'm not on any contraceptive," she blurts.

"Okay," I nod, waiting for whatever it is she's worried about telling me.

"We didn't use anything and I'm not protected."

"So?" I laugh. Is this her only problem, that we weren't careful?

"I haven't needed to be on the pill, or whatever, not since before Poppy."

Placing my palm on her stomach, I lean down and kiss her. "Kitten, I never had any intension of being careful with you."

"What the hell does that mean?" she snaps, glaring down at my hand on her stomach like it's offending her.

"It means I want to breed you as soon as fucking possible, I want your body swimming in my cum until my baby is in your belly. I want to make a house full of brothers and sisters for Poppy."

"Breed me?" she hisses angrily. "Breed me? What the fuck do you think I am, a horse?"

"Kitten, you need to watch your mouth and your tone, right now."

"I," she shrieks, "I need to watch *my* mouth and *my* tone, do you hear yourself? You need to fuck off, just oh my god, what the fuck?"

I don't think, just act. Flipping her to her stomach, I

part her legs and fill her with my dick before she even has a chance to argue. My palm connects with her ass cheek a moment later and I keep spanking until her skin is pink and she's screaming and moaning while I punish her. Sliding my thumb into my mouth, I lave it with my tongue, getting it plenty wet before I part her cheeks and circle her ass, making her instantly freeze beneath me.

"Penn, don't you dare," she demands.

"Dare what?" I taunt, pushing against her tight ring of muscle, refusing to back down until the muscle relents and the tip of my thumb slips inside of her.

"Penn," she cries.

"I told you to mind your tone, I've been warning you to mind me since we met, and I told you there would be consequences for your mouth. Now your ass is a fucking perfect shade of pink and my thumb is inside your tight ring where my dick will be shortly if you don't stop giving me attitude."

"Get off me," she growls, trying to buck me off.

With my dick impaled in her cunt and my thumb up her ass, she isn't going anywhere. "Oh you're looking to get ass fucked aren't you, Kitten? Do you want me to fill your naughty girl hole with my big dick?"

"Your dick is not going anywhere near my ass," she cries.

"Oh it is, Kitten. I hadn't planned on that happening

tonight, but if that's what you need to stop being a brat then I'm happy to comply."

"I'm not being a brat. We had unprotected sex and you're acting like it's completely fine. It's not. I could be pregnant and you're talking about breeding me like I'm a freaking brood mare."

I don't know if she realizes it, but she just got through her entire rant without cursing at me and I can't help smiling. "Kitten, I've told you what I want from you and I want all that now. I want a ring on your finger, you in our bed every night, our daughter in her room down the hall and a baby in your belly. I haven't lied or bullshit you about how you're mine. My dick's been inside of you, my cum is coating your pussy walls and hopefully taking seed in your womb. I don't think you're a brood mare, I think you're my fucking woman."

My dick's hard inside of her, but I'm not fucking her, I'm just keeping her still and reinforcing my claim on her literally from the inside and out.

"This is all happening too quickly, it's too much," she whimpers, her voice breaking.

Sliding my thumb from her ass and my dick from her pussy, I lift her from the bed and cradle her in my arms. "I know this might feel like a lot, baby, it's fast, but don't you feel how right it is too? If you didn't feel it, you'd be fighting me harder, but you're not. You throw a tantrum when you feel like you need to rebel against how much this makes sense, but when it comes down to it you settle down the moment my hands are on you. Because you're mine, and even if your mind is rebelling against that fact a little, your body and soul know exactly who owns them."

"You don't own me, you can't own a person, that's barbaric."

Pressing my hand against her heart I take hers and press it over mine. "My heart is only beating for you. I'll never want another woman, never need anyone else but you and as much as you might want to deny it, I know you feel the same way. Your heart beats for me and nothing and no one will ever change that now."

"I don't want that," she says brokenly.

"Liar," I whisper back.

Her head moves from side to side. "No, it's the truth, I don't want to be with you, I don't want this..." she pauses, her soulful eyes staring intently at me. "I don't want you."

Anger and blind fury barrels through me and the next thing I know I'm above her, my hand around her throat, my dick slamming home into her wet cunt. "Tell me to stop, Lulu, tell me you don't want me, tell me you don't want this," I shout, punctuating each demand with a hard thrust. "Tell me," I roar.

Her eyes are squeezed tightly shut, but she's not speaking, not telling me no. I stop moving, dragging my dick all the way out of her, the head pressed against her entrance, but not inside. "Tell me to stop, or beg me to keep going," I demand.

"Penn," she groans, her eyes falling open as she blinks up at me.

"This is your one chance to stop this, Lulu, if you don't I'm going to come inside of you and I'm going to keep fucking you until all you can taste and smell and see is my fucking seed. I'll keep fucking you until you're pregnant with my kid and nothing you say will stop me. I'll claim you over and over until you can't function without me, until you crave my dick, until you need it like you need air to breath and food to survive. I'll make you so reliant on me you won't know how to move without me." Pausing I give her a chance to speak, to do something, anything to protest against my furious words, but she doesn't say anything, just keeps looking up at me through eyes wet with tears.

"Tell me to stop, or beg me to take you. Choose."

I watch as she swallows, then her lips part and she says the sweetest words I've ever heard. "Please Penn, take me."

Slamming my dick back into her, I fuck her hard and fast and brutally, not taking care not to hurt her as I fill her with my dick over and over. I don't pause even when she comes, fucking her through one release and straight into a second, until my balls tighten and I feel my own release explode from my dick with a force I've never experienced in my life. I come and come, my seed flowing from me as I do exactly what I promised her I'd do, fill her cunt with my cum.

It takes a while for my body to calm and I stay inside of her, lifting her hips and tilting her pelvis up, keeping my cum in her while I keep her pussy plugged with my dick. If I could, I'd stay like this, pushing my seed inside of her all night, but even without looking at the time, I know we need to get back for Poppy.

I thought my anger would have abated with the way I just used her body, but if anything, sating myself in her cunt has barely taken the edge off. I'm pissed at her and I have no idea how to resolve the fury I'm experiencing.

Reluctantly I slide my dick from inside of her, noticing her wince when I drag my cock free from her heat. "Did I hurt you?"

"No," she shakes her head.

"Don't lie to me, Lulu."

"Fine, you didn't hurt me in a bad way. I'm just a little sore and tender."

Nodding, I don't speak again as I slowly climb off her and start to collect our clothes from the floor. Handing hers to her, I sit down on the edge of the bed, not looking at her as I get dressed.

"I need to clean up."

"No."

"Penn."

"Unless you want me to make your ass mine tonight too, I suggest you get dressed," I spit angrily.

We both fall into a weighted silence for agonizingly long moments until she speaks. "Are you okay?" she asks, her fingers brushing along my arm.

"I'm fine," I spit curtly. "We need to get back for Poppy." Standing, I pull away from her touch and move to the door, glancing back over my shoulder and watching as Lulu fidgets with her shirt, then slides her feet into her shoes.

Silently she walks past me as I hold open the door for her, her expressive doll eyes begging me to say or do something. But I have no fucking clue what to do, so instead I open the door that will lead into the main house and twine my fingers with hers as I drag her outside and into the car, ignoring all of the questioning looks from my family as we go.

Neither of us speaks as I drive us back down the mountain to Chloe's place. I have an overnight bag in the trunk, but honestly right now, I don't know if staying with her will help calm me, or just make me angrier. She wants me, that much is obvious, but she doesn't want a relationship with me, to start a life with me, or to allow me to be a part of her and Poppy's future. I know my brothers' women have all fought their relationships, but I don't think any of them ever said they didn't want them the way Lulu did.

"I'm sorry."

Her voice is tiny and I can't help but look over at her sitting in the seat beside me.

"What for?"

"For saying all that stuff, it's not true."

"I know you want me," I scoff, a little more harshly than I intended. "You can lie, but your body can't."

We fall into an uneasy silence again, I know she wants me to say something, but I'm too fucking angry at both her and myself. She shouldn't have said all that bullshit, but I shouldn't have reacted the way I did either. I touched her with anger, I didn't hurt her, I never would, but I fucked her hard and fast to punish her. It doesn't matter that she came more times than I can remember, I still should have taken more care with her.

"You scare me."

"I'd never hurt you," I say quickly, slamming my brakes on and skidding to a stop in the middle of the road.

"I know. Physically I know you'd never hurt me, but I don't mean you scare me like that. I mean you scare me because you seem so sure."

"I am sure," I tell her confidently.

"I know and that…" she pauses. "That terrifies me."

Twisting in my seat, I take her in. She's tiny, petite but with a woman's body, all curves, tits and ass. "Why does it terrify you?"

"Because I don't think I've ever been as certain about what breakfast cereal I want as you are about wanting to be with me, wanting a future and a family with me. It's a lot, Penn, it'd be a lot after a couple of years, it's just too much after a few days. I need some time to come to terms with everything but you won't give me a second."

"I can't. You have this look in your eyes and I know I can't give you space because you'll try and talk yourself out of how right this is. Can't you just trust me, just put your faith in me and let me be sure enough for both of us?"

"I don't know if I can," she shakes her head. "That's asking a lot of me. We don't even know each other."

"See that's where you're wrong, Kitten. We know the important things. You trust me with your body, you trust me with your daughter, you trust me with your heart. It's the inconsequential things you're fighting, but you have to see, if I own the very core of you, what else is there for you to put at risk?"

She freezes as she takes in my words and really hears them. Putting my car into gear I pull off again, making my way back down the mountain and giving her at least a little of the time she asked for.

Pulling into Chloe's driveway I turn off the engine and get out, circling the car and opening Lulu's door a moment later. Taking my hand, she lets me help her out and doesn't fight to free herself from my grip when I keep her fingers entwined with mine and lead her up to the front door.

The house is quiet when we enter, Chloe is fast asleep on the couch, the baby monitor next to her, the tv playing on low in the background. Closing the door behind me, I release my hold on her hand and watch as she crosses the room to Chloe and gently wakes her.

"Hey, we're back, why don't you go on up to bed. Thank you for keeping an eye on Poppy for me."

Chloe blinks sleepily and waves Lulu's words away. "She slept; all I did was sit next to the baby monitor. Night."

"Night," I say as Chloe passes me, heading up the stairs and away from us.

Neither of us speaks until we hear Chloe's bedroom door shut, then it's just the two of us again, the tangible atmosphere thickening between us. I can't fuck her again; I was too rough with her earlier and she'll be even more sore in the morning after the pounding I gave her cunt. But I don't want to leave. Being away from her feels wrong, but so does constantly forcing my will on her.

"I want to stay," I blurt, when I can't decide a delicate way to word it.

"I'm sore, I—"

"Not to fuck you," I interrupt. "I want that, but I know I was rough. I just want to be with you, leaving you here and going home without you. I fucking hate it."

"I don't…"

"Stop thinking so fucking hard," I growl. "Do you want to wake next to me? Sleep in my arms all night?"

Her teeth appear and she bites down on her plump bottom lip, dragging it along as her brow furrows. Then she nods, a barely perceptible nod. "Yes."

"Thank you," I praise, curling an arm around her back as I dip my head and kiss her. "Let's go to bed."

Turning off the tv and lights, I lock the front door and check the windows before I lead Lulu upstairs to her bedroom. She immediately moves to Poppy's crib, peering down on the tiny sleeping princess, before she kisses her fingers, then softly rests them on Poppy's forehead. Watching her, I will my dick to calm down, but seeing her care for her daughter is so sexy and my cock hasn't got the memo that we're not getting laid again tonight.

Lulu stares down at Poppy for a few minutes, then she smiles and turns to her dresser. She pulls out some pajamas, but I lay my hand on her arm and stop her.

"Naked."

"I can't sleep naked, what happens if I need to get up with Poppy?"

"You got a robe?"

"Yes, of course."

"Then if you need to leave the room, you put on the robe, but when we're in bed together I want to feel you against me."

She bites down on her lip again, but I tug it free with my finger.

"Bed."

I help her undress, then pull off my own clothes and crawl beneath her comforter. She's on the other side of the bed, so I drag her to me, cupping her still wet pussy with one hand and banding the other around her waist.

"I thought we agreed no sex," she says, a wary whispered laugh filling the silence.

"No sex, that doesn't mean I'm not going to touch you."

"Oh," she whispers as I part her folds and start to fondle her, circling her clit.

She sighs, her body relaxing into me when I find her clit with my thumb.

"You need me to make you come? I'll be gentle."

I feel her nod, and I smile. Slowly I slide one finger into her, gently pumping it in and out as I rub at her clit. I go slow, dragging her pleasure out until her cunt clamps down on my finger and she cries out. Her orgasm isn't an explosion, it's a slow burn of pleasure, meant to relax not be a preamble for more and after a moment, she relaxes into me.

***

A shrieking high-pitched wail wakes me and I bolt upright, scanning the room before my eyes land on Poppy who's sitting up in her crib, fat tears rolling down her cheeks.

"Morning Princess," I croak, my voice rough with sleep. Pulling on my jeans I cross the room to her and lift her from her crib. "Shall we wake Mama up? I don't know your morning routine yet, so we're going to need Mama to tell us both what to do," I tell her, glad that her tears and cries have stopped as I cross back to the bed and sit down on the edge, keeping Poppy cradled to my chest as I stroke Lulu's cheek, gently waking her up. "Kitten, Princess is awake and I'm not sure how mornings run yet."

Lulu reaches out sleepily and Poppy lurches toward her. Placing the little girl carefully in her mama's arms, I stay where I am and watch as Lulu holds her baby girl in the tightest of hugs. This right here is why I'll never be able to walk away, no matter what Lulu says. These two are mine, my family and I don't want my world to exist without them in it.

"What do you need me to do?" I ask, running my

fingers across Lulu's bare shoulder.

"What time is it?" she asks sleepily.

"Six thirty."

"Coffee." The word is more like a plea and I chuckle, scooping Poppy from her arms and holding her to my chest.

"I'll take the princess with me and start the coffee while you get a shower."

She doesn't speak, just shuffles her head back and forth across the pillow in a sleepy nod.

"Come on, Princess, let's go make Mama some wake up juice." Poppy smiles her gummy smile, patting my cheek with her hand. When we get into the kitchen, I pull out the highchair and strap Poppy into it, it takes me a few attempts to get the straps connected right, but eventually, she's secure and safe. Grabbing her a couple of toys from the playpen in the living room I place them on the tray in front of her, then busy myself with the coffee machine.

For the first time, I wish I had more experience around kids. If I did, I'd know how to help, how to make breakfast for Poppy so I could do more than just stand around and wait for Lulu or Chloe. Remembering that yesterday morning she had oatmeal I set about searching the cabinets, eventually hitting gold when I find the one that's full of baby food. Grabbing the box of banana flavored oatmeal I read the instructions, seeing that at her age Poppy should have it made with formula milk. I find that in the same cabinet, and make the princess breakfast.

It's a little warm once it's ready, so I turn on the stove and cook the eggs and bacon I find in the refrigerator. By the time Chloe and Lulu make their way downstairs, there's three plates of food waiting on the table and I'm half feeding myself, half feeding Poppy our breakfasts.

"You made breakfast?" Lulu asks, shock clear in her voice. "For Poppy too?"

"She had oatmeal yesterday, I wasn't sure if she had it every morning, but I figured two days in a row wouldn't hurt her. I haven't made her any formula because I wasn't sure if she had juice or something else. I made bacon and eggs for us and the coffee pot is full too."

"Your mama sure raised all you boys right," Chloe says, slapping me on the shoulder before she leans down and presses a soft kiss to my cheek.

"Thank you," Lulu smiles softly, leaning over to kiss Poppy on the head before she turns her attention to me. "Where the hell did you come from, Penn Barnett? Men don't do this, they don't cook and care for other people's kids days after they meet them."

"Barnett men do, like Chloe said, our mama raised us right and our daddy taught us to appreciate a good woman when we find her. I'll take care of you and our princess for the rest of our lives if you'll let me." Pulling her into me I kiss her hard and fast, then I let her go and carry on feeding our girl.

TWELVE

LULU

Our Princess.

Oh my god, my ovaries just popped out another egg and the air in my lungs isn't working. He called my daughter *our Princess*. What is he doing to me?

If this were any other guy, in any other town I'd think all this is bullshit, but I've questioned Chloe more than once about him since he decided I'm his and she always tells me the same thing. That Penn Barnett is exactly who he says he is. Chloe's known the whole family for years and apparently they really are as wonderful as they seem to be. According to her, the brothers are ladies' men right up to the point where they find *their* woman, at which point they settle down quick and of the three that are coupled up, two are married and one is engaged with a baby due any day.

If what she says is true, and I really can't seem to believe it isn't, then Penn is just a really nice guy. A really nice, really hot guy. A really nice, really hot, dirty talking, dominant guy who somehow brings every one of my dirty fantasies to life.

Fuck, what the hell am I going to do? I could keep on fighting but I don't think I want to and, hell, after last night I could be pregnant. The idea of having another baby so soon after having Poppy scares the hell out of me, but it'd be different with Penn. The circumstances around Poppy's conception weren't exactly normal.

I need to tell him. He needs to know the truth before I let things go too far. I can already see he adores my daughter and I doubt what I have to tell him will change that, but he needs to know the truth.

Everything about Penn is all consuming and that scares the hell out of me. He uses my body against me. He wants to control me and after being so out of control for the last year and a half, I don't know if I can give him what he needs. I don't know if I can allow mine and Poppy's futures to be in anyone else but my hands. He'd never hurt us, last night showed me that. But he's proved he's not above manipulating me with sex to get what he wants.

Truthfully, everything about him is just so much more intense than any guy I've ever met. You say commitment and future to most guys and they're out the door before you can finish speaking, but Penn's the total opposite. He wants it all and he wants it now, and the idea of waiting or taking some time is completely foreign to him.

I eat absentmindedly, most of my attention on him as he spoons mushy oatmeal into Poppy's mouth, occasionally stabbing some egg or bacon and eating himself. I can't take my eyes off him, or the domesticity of this moment, how can something so new feel so right?

The need to push him away is so strong, like an angel on my shoulder warning me that people are never what they seem, but the devil on my other side is telling me that maybe he's exactly what he and everyone else is telling me he is. If I didn't have Poppy I doubt I'd be questioning this, I'd have my legs spread and offering myself to him any which way till Sunday, but if this all goes to shit it won't just be me that's affected, it'll be Poppy too.

Standing, I go make Poppy some formula in the new sippy cup Chloe got for her and then hand it to her, ruffling her hair as she lifts it to her mouth. "Do you want me to finish up while you go take a shower?" He's still just in his jeans, the top button undone looking incredibly tempting.

"You haven't finished your breakfast."

"I can eat while I feed her," I assure him, holding in the wistful sigh that's eager to escape at how sweet he is for trying to take care of me.

"Okay, Kitten, shout if you need anything."

My eyes follow him out the room and I swear I hear Chloe actually swoon as his tight ass encased in jeans disappears up the stairs.

"Honey, if you don't marry that boy, I swear I'm going to take a run at him myself."

"Chloe," I admonish with a laugh.

"He is infatuated with you and Poppy, if I hadn't hit the menopause years ago I'd be pregnant right now just from watching him with your baby girl."

"He's impossible to dislike and god help me I've tried," I confess.

"He's a good man, he's exactly what I'd want for you in a husband. He'll take care of you both, he'll love you and be faithful."

"It's been three days," I whisper shout. "I can't think about marriage and any of that kind of stuff after three days. Maybe three years, but not days, it's crazy and I don't do crazy things anymore. Look what happened the last time I did."

"Oh honey, look what happened," Chloe sighs, smiling as she squeezes my hand and looks across the room at my beautiful little girl. "Don't push him away just because you think it's happening too quickly. Sometimes things happen on their own timescale and they turn out perfectly."

Poppy giggles, pulling both of our attentions to her and the conversation is forgotten, until Penn appears ten minutes later in fresh clothes, his delicious torso covered in a tight black t-shirt. His hair is damp and he looks sexier than ever as he saunters into the room like he's lived here forever. His confidence is sexy and I can't take my eyes off him as he rounds the table, lifts me out of my seat and sits down, pulling me into his lap.

"We need to go soon, else you're going to be late for work."

Sighing, I smile down at Poppy. "I hate leaving her," I confess.

"I earn plenty of money, Kitten, I can look after all of us. You can stay home if you want, or go part time, whatever makes you happiest."

His palm slides over my stomach and I tense at his unspoken words, that I might be pregnant, that he wants me to be. Shaking away the thought, I bury it at the back of my mind along with all the other things I don't want to think about right now and push his hand away, standing and grabbing a wet cloth to clean Poppy's face.

"You've got more breakfast around your mouth than

you got in it," I chirp in a sing-song voice. "Mama's got to go to work, but you and Auntie Chloe are going to have the best day." Unclipping the straps, I lift Poppy from her chair and cuddle her to my chest, loving how she nuzzles into me, her familiar baby smell surrounding me.

Strong arms wrap around my back and I tense for a second, before relaxing into his warm embrace. He's so big and somehow his arms fit around both me and Poppy and he's holding us both. It's so freaking perfect I think my heart misses a beat just so it can start up again in time with his.

Sighing, he reluctantly releases me and steps back. I turn and pass Poppy into Chloe's waiting arms, leaning down to kiss her chubby baby cheek. "Bye babycakes, see you tonight."

When I step back and grab my purse, Penn leans down and kisses first Poppy's head, then Chloe's cheek, speaking to her quietly before he steps away and places his palm on the base of my spine, guiding me toward the front door.

"Come on, Kitten, let's go."

We're both quiet on the drive to work, me because I'm trying to decide how I pursue something with Penn without losing myself to him completely and him because... Well, I don't really know why he's quiet.

"I want to take you and Poppy shopping tonight; we

can go get her straight after work and then have dinner at my place."

"I don't—"

"She needs stuff for at my place so you can both spend time there. I can pick it out, but I'd prefer we do it together."

"Penn—"

"Nope," he interrupts. "I'm not going to have this conversation again, Lulu. You think this is moving too fast, I disagree. I'm happy to prove how wrong you are, and that starts with you picking out stuff for you and Poppy to keep at my place. If you're right, then that's on me, and I'll have bought stuff I won't need, I'm okay with that. But I want you both at my home and right now that can't happen, so I'm going to do what I need to change that."

"Penn."

His hand reaches across and cups my pussy through my pants. "How sore's your pussy today?"

"What?" I say, startled by his sudden change of subject.

"I need to check how sore you are, because I've got a feeling you're going to earn yourself another punishment fucking if you carry on trying to push me away, and I want to make sure I'm not going to hurt you."

Outraged, I try to slap his hand away, but he just grips me tighter, grinding the heel of his palm against my sex.

"You can't threaten me with sex."

"Sure I can," he smirks. "You like my dick, I plan to keep you full of my cum, if a good fucking helps you learn to mind me and makes you see some sense at the same time, it sounds like it's working to me."

I can feel my mouth is hanging open and I stare at him, while his hand is still cupping between my legs. No man has ever treated me this way, this mix of caveman dominance, sexy control and out and out assholeness - I have no idea why it turns me on but it does.

"You need me to walk you in?"

My focus snaps back to the moment and I realize we're parked at the curb outside my office. "I think I can make it to the door on my own," I snarl, reaching over to unclip my seatbelt.

His hand between my thighs tightens while his free hand collars my throat. "Kitty, kitty, kitty, sheath those claws before I take you home, strip you naked and fuck your ass until you're begging to do as I tell you."

"Your dick isn't going anywhere near my ass."

"I'll only allow you to be so rude and disrespectful, Lulu, before I'll have to come up with a creative way to hogtie that temper of yours. If me filling your ass with my fat cock is the only thing that works, I promise you I won't hesitate, and I'll make you scream and beg and orgasm while I do it. You're mine, Kitten, and I'm a jealous, possessive, unreasonable, controlling asshole. I will worship the ground you walk on, do anything in the fucking world to make you happy, but that doesn't mean I'm a metro-fucking-sexual beta who will let you walk all over him. If you start behaving like a bitch I'll put you in your place, just like I'll expect you to put me in my place if I'm being a douche. Now go on into work and I'll pick you up at one thirty for lunch."

I'm so shocked by his words that I do as he says without thought, opening my door and sliding from the car in a haze of outraged lust. It shouldn't turn me on that he threatened me with sexual punishments, but god, it really does. He's turning me into a sex crazed freak and I'm not sure my snarky words and half-hearted attempts to disobey him are even me trying to really fight it anymore.

Pushing into the office, I say an absentminded hello to Annette before I stagger to my chair and slump down into it, staring blankly at my computer. I'm an idiot for him and it's only been three days. I have no idea if I can get off this bucking bronco of a life or if I even want to.

If I'm really honest with myself, I like him. I like the way he railroads me, I like the way he won't let me push him away and the truth is, I want someone to take care of me, even if I'm capable of looking after myself. Penn cares for me, he cares for Poppy and he's by far the hottest, sexiest, growliest man I've ever had the chance to have sex with... and I want to do it again.

My morning passes in a blur. Janet emails me another list of ridiculous jobs that I do and email back to her, even though she's never going to use any of the information she has me providing. But even though I'm functioning, my mind is on Penn. My body is tingling and the memory of all the ways he touched me and owned me keeps replaying through my mind. By the time 1.30 rolls around, I'm a bag of lusty nerves and I have no idea how I'm going to get through an hour with him without jumping him.

Grabbing my purse, I inhale a low, deep breath and try to get myself under control. It doesn't work, so with a dry, humorless laugh I push through my door and head out toward my man.

Penn's waiting in reception, chatting with Annette and looking sexier than any man really should. My nipples pebble at the sight of him and my sex clenches with awareness. I'm still a little sore from last night, but the pain does nothing to quell the shameless moan that tries to fight its way past my tightly clenched lips.

"You ready, Kitten?" he asks, his low, rough voice making my pussy drool in anticipation.

"Uh huh," I nod, moving toward him, sighing when he wraps his arm around my shoulders and pulls me into his side.

"You want us to bring you anything?" Penn asks

Annette.

"No thanks, enjoy your lunch," she says with a playful wink.

Swallowing thickly, I try not to rub up against his dick as he holds the door open for me, closing my eyes as he runs his hand across my ass. The moment I'm outside I pull in a deep breath, hoping the air will blast away the pheromones that are oozing from my pores.

"What do you want for lunch?"

"I don't mind," I say, keeping my eyes forward and trying my best not to look at him. I'm more horny than I've ever been in my life and right now I know if I look at him, and he has even an ounce of lust in his eyes, I'll jump him right here in the street.

"Hey." His fingers wrap around my wrist and he spins me to face him. "You still—"

His eyes rake over me and I feel myself melt at the heat reflecting back at me.

"Kitten, do you need me?"

Forcing my muscles to move, I shake my head.

"What did I say about lying to me?"

Swallowing I try to speak, but no words come out as he reels me in, holding me to him with one hand at the base of my spine and the other around my throat. Leaning down, he presses his lips to my ear, the warmth of his breath making me shudder.

"Do you need me? Do you need me to force your legs open and fuck you until you're panting and screaming?"

I don't want to admit it, I'm not sure I actually can admit my need out loud, but he knows; he can see it in me, probably smell it on me.

"Oh Kitten, you should have told me how desperate you were," he croons, pressing his lips to mine in a hard kiss before he pulls away and leads me down the street.

I can't find any words, but I don't fight as he moves me along the sidewalk, guiding my steps until we reach a huge, grey building with a Barnett Brothers Repairs sign hanging above the roller shutter doors. I recognize one of Penn's brothers inside, but before I have a chance to speak, Penn's dragging me up a set of stairs at the side of the building and into a small apartment.

The moment the door closes behind us, he releases his hold on me and folds his arms across his huge muscular chest, making his biceps strain against the fabric of his t-shirt. "Strip."

I freeze, lost to my eagerness and desperation.

"Now."

The single stern word forces me back to the present and I start to undress, unfastening the first two buttons on my shirt before pulling it up and over my head. Dropping it to the floor, I unzip my pants, pushing them down and letting them pool to my feet.

"And the rest."

His voice is gravelly, rough like he's having to force the words out. He wants me almost as badly as I want him, the heat in his eyes is unmistakable, as is the massive bulge in his pants.

Releasing my bra, I let it slide free from my arms, then push my panties down, kicking off my pumps as I step free, leaving my discarded clothes in a heap.

"How sore are you?"

"I'm fine."

"Go bend your sweet ass over the back of the couch, then spread your legs nice and wide so I can see your cunt dripping for me."

Panting wildly, I clench my hands into fists at my sides. God, his demanding nature calls to me, begging me to defy him almost as much as I want to do what he says. I'm not afraid of his punishments, a part of me craves them almost, taunting him to do his worst because even though I know he might spank me, or fuck me, he'll always make it good, make me beg and scream.

I move, padding on bare feet over to the black leather couch that fills most of the small living space and climb onto it, leaning my chest over the back and spreading my knees as wide as they'll go, pushing my ass toward him.

The rustling of his clothes makes my nipples pebble further in anticipation, my tips so hard the pressure of the couch beneath me is almost painful. My core is throbbing, the twinges of soreness only adding to my anticipation of the moment he'll touch me.

I expect the couch to dip beneath his weight, so I jump, startled when he grabs my hair and yanks me upright, pulling my head back as his warm lips find my racing pulse point and bite down on it.

"Does my kitten need to be fucked?"

I try to nod, but his hold on my hair stops me.

"Words."

"Yes," I gasp, my voice raspy.

"Beg."

"Please, please."

"Do you want my fingers, my tongue or my cock?"

"Your cock," I whine, moving my legs together, needing to clench my thighs to stem the tide of lust barreling through me.

"Open your legs," he barks.

I immediately comply, his puppet in this moment, lost to his demands.

"You want me to fuck this cunt?" he asks, sliding his fingers between my soaked folds, before he pulls back and spanks my pussy, making me squeal in shock. Before I have a chance to breath, he slides two fingers into me, fucking me roughly as he whispers against my ear.

"I want you wet, Kitten, I won't fill you with my dick

until your juices have soaked this couch. You don't just get to be ready; I want you dripping, your cunt begging for my dick."

He does something, adding a third finger and pushing them further into me as he moves, grinding his hand and making whimpering mewls fall from my parted, gasping lips. "Oh god," I whine, embracing the pain and barely stifling the urge to beg him to spank me, or choke me or just fuck me, because I need more.

"Your little kitty is so tight. You're clamping down on my fingers even as you drip with lust. I think you enjoy the pain, that's why you needed me even though your cunt is still swollen from the fucking I gave you last night. You're perfect for me, Kitten, fucking perfect. I can't wait to see you cry while you choke on my cock or hear you beg me not to stop while I slide into your tight ass. I'm going to own you inside and out, claim every hole, every act, every dirty fantasy."

I come with a strangled cry, my whole body shaking with the force of the orgasm that's ricocheting through me. I've only ever squirted once before and it was on my own with a dildo and a lot of hot porn, but that pales to the way he's playing my body right now. Liquid gushes from me, soaking my thighs as he rips his fingers from inside of me and rubs them over my clit, watching me soak the leather beneath us.

"Jesus, fuck," he growls as he pushes the head of his huge dick into me.

THIRTEEN

PENN

She's soaking wet, her pussy still squirting as I slide the head of my cock inside of her, not stopping my insistent thrust until most of my dick is filling her. Releasing my grip on her hair I force her forward, pinning her upper body to the back of the couch as I lose my fucking mind and fuck her like I'll never get a chance to touch her again.

The moment I turned her to look at me on the sidewalk outside her office, worried that she was pissed and saw the raw, feral lust in her eyes I knew it'd come to this. That I'd end up balls deep in her, fucking her like I'm a caveman and she's my prize.

She's my ultimate fantasy and my weakness all rolled

into the perfect package. Her sweet body calls to me and I'm helpless to resist her lush curves. Not that I want to. I want to indulge in her, sate myself over and over in her body until there's not a person alive in the world who doesn't know she's mine.

Last night was good, but this right here, this savagery is fucking everything. I want her sweet and soft too, but right now hard and animalistic is all I can offer her and what she needed. My dick's so hard it hurts, but she takes everything I give her, pushing back into every thrust as I brand her cunt with my dick.

Her cream drips from her every time I pull back and then slam into her again and when she screams out her release, her cunt somehow becomes even tighter, clamping down and strangling my dick until I explode. I slump over her back, my cock twitching inside of her as she milks every drop of release until I'm drained and spent.

"I…" she starts, then falls silent again.

A low chuckle falls from my lips as I lean down and kiss her bare shoulder. "We should clean up."

"Can't move," she whines softly.

"I'll carry you," I whisper, pressing another reverent kiss against her skin. Sliding my dick from her, I feel the wince she tries to hide from me. "I was too rough?"

"You were perfect, it was so hot, so. God."

"I felt you wince, baby."

"You have a big dick," she laughs and I feel a mixture of my cum and her arousal drip onto my dick that's still touching her entrance.

"Yeah I do," I smile, sliding my hand down her front and running my fingers through the soaked folds of her cunt. "Jesus, Kitten, I'm not going to lie, it's sexy as fuck feeling your cunt all sloppy and wet dripping with cum."

Lifting my fingers to her lips I push one into her mouth. "How do we taste?" Forcing a second finger past her lips, I don't give her a chance to speak as I drive them further into her mouth and she sucks eagerly.

"My dick's still hard, but we don't have time for round two. I need to get you cleaned up even though I'd rather send you back to work smelling like sex and my cum."

Pulling my fingers from between her lips, I grab her hair again and turn her head, kissing her hard as I slide my tongue into her mouth, owning it like I just owned her pussy.

"Come on, Kitten," I say, reluctantly stepping back before lifting her and standing her in front of me. My eyes dart back to the couch, and a smirk spreads across my lips when I see the shiny pool of liquid glistening against the black of the leather.

Turning her, I curve an arm around her waist, sliding my hand between her thighs to cup her mound. "Look what you did, Kitten, I told you I wanted you to soak the couch and you did. That's the hottest thing I've ever fucking seen." My fingers part her dripping folds and I slide two fingers back into her cunt. "I wonder if I can make you squirt again."

When she moans, its guttural and desperate, her legs parting without me even having to tell her to do it. I start to move my fingers inside of her, pulling out, then thrusting them back in again through her swollen muscles.

The blasting music of my cell phone ringing shatters the moment. Ignoring it, I try to keep us both in this haze of lust but as soon as the music ends, it immediately starts again. "Fuck," I hiss.

"Penn," she cries when I pull my fingers from her and cross to where I left my jeans, grabbing my cell from the pocket.

"What?" I answer, bringing it to my ear.

"Sorry bro, but it's been nearly an hour and Lulu needs to get back to work," Bay tells me, his voice apologetic, but laced with amusement.

"I fucking hate you."

He's still laughing as I end the call. "Sorry baby, we need to clean up real quick unless you want to call in sick this afternoon."

"I can't," she sighs sadly. "Do you have a shower up here? Who's apartment is this anyway?"

"Come on, I'll help," I smile. "And it's my apartment, there's another on the other side of the garage that's Bay's. We all have a place of our own like this to get away from the family if we need some downtime."

"So this is your fuck pad," she giggles as I guide her into the tiny bathroom, leaning past her to turn the shower on to warm.

"No, this *used* to be my fuck pad, now it's *our* fuck pad for when your greedy cunt can't wait until we get home."

Her cheeks turn the most delicious shade of pink, making me chuckle as I lift her into the small shower cubicle and follow in behind her. As much as I wish I could take my time cleaning her from head to toe, she needs to get back to work, so I coat my hands in soap as she does the same and then work it into her skin while she explores my chest with her hands.

Five minutes later my dick is still hard, her pussy still wet but we're dressed again. Her hair is damp on the ends and I watch her twist it into a bun on the top of her head as we make our way back down the stairs and onto the sidewalk outside the garage.

"You still need to eat," I tell her when I reach her side, draping my arm over her shoulders.

"Not sure I can tell Janet that I need an extra hour because I was too busying having sex," she giggles.

The sound is like fucking music to my ears and I hold her closer as we make the short walk back to the lawyer's office. "I'll go grab you something from Wake Up and Go Go. What do you fancy?"

"Oh, do they do iced coffee? I would love a Frappuccino and a muffin."

"I'll go find out," I smile when we reach her building. "Back soon." Grabbing her by the neck, I kiss her deeply, then release her and watch her enter the building before I leave to go and get us lunch.

Despite our shower, I smell her on me for the rest of the day. It keeps me rock hard and cursing my dick every time I catch it against the hood of a car as I lean into its engine. By the time 5.30 rolls round, I'm more than ready to go get her and have her mouth wrapped around me.

Pushing into the lawyer's office, I smile at Annette and instead of taking my usual spot on the couch I wait by the door, carefully adjusting my dick and really hoping I don't have a fucking obvious bulge in my pants.

"Your girl might need a little TLC tonight, Janet's had clients in this afternoon and that's never a fun time," Annette warns.

"What happened?"

"I'm not sure, I didn't hear any shouting, but Janet hates dealing with clients and she makes sure everyone, including the clients know it. Meeting day is when the last five paralegals she employed have left. Lulu's a trouper for sticking it out this long," Annette tells me with a sympathetic wince.

My dick instantly deflates. I hate that my woman is working for that bitch Janet. I'm all for women being strong, independent and rocking a kickass job in a male dominated world. But Janet is just a fucking harpy. She's childish, petulant and entitled. That bitch is just plain angry and instead of getting on with things, she tries to make those around her as miserable as she is.

In a small town like Rockhead Point, everyone knows when someone new moves here, especially when it's the relative of one of the town staples like Taylor. From the moment she pulled up in her flashy Mercedes in her expensive pant suits, she's been sour faced and pissy. I'd say she just needed a good fuck, but honestly I wouldn't recommend any man put his dick anywhere near her. I'm about ninety percent sure she's part praying mantis and would probably try and eat the poor bastard afterwards.

When Lulu appears with Dave, I expect her to be world weary and stressed, but instead she's smiling and laughing, the post sex glow still emanating from her.

"Hey Kitten."

"Hey," she smiles sweetly.

"Good afternoon?"

"Hellish, but it's over now and I'm ready to go see my

baby girl."

"Well then let's go get the princess." I smile, pulling her into my side and pressing a soft kiss against her upturned, waiting lips.

I don't speak again until we're both strapped into the car and pulling away from the lot and onto the road toward Chloe's. "Annette said she thought you might need a little TLC tonight after dealing with Janet this afternoon."

"My boss is a bitch, but she's not the baddest bitch I've ever met and if she thinks she's going to scare me off, she's got another thing coming. I went to law school, I've met plenty of women like her before," Lulu shrugs, resting her head back against the seat and stretching her legs out in front of her.

"You went to law school?"

"Yep, I was prepping to take the bar when I got pregnant with Poppy."

"That something you still want to do?" I ask.

"Yeah, eventually. I'll be a great lawyer, only maybe not a fancy litigator with a corner office like I imagined."

"Still plenty of people who need a lawyer, even in a small town," I say with a wink.

"And those poor people have to deal with Janet." She hisses her bosses name and grimaces. "To be honest, I thought it was odd that she'd gone all week without meeting with anyone. Apparently she keeps all of her client interaction down to one afternoon a week. We had clients in and out all afternoon and she was rude to every single one, barely acknowledging them, even though these people are paying her for her time. Taylor's so nice, I'm surprised he allows her to treat people that way."

"She definitely doesn't strike me as a people person," I joke as we pull into Chloe's driveway. "Right, how we going do this? You want to go have a quick shower and I'll have Chloe help me get Poppy ready to go."

"Where are we going?"

"Shopping, Kitten, then dinner at my place."

"Oh," she says quietly. "Poppy's going to be tired…"

She trails off and I know she's going to try to make an excuse to get out of going, but after last night and this morning, I need this. I need to have stuff at my place to encourage them to see a life with me.

"Poppy will be fine. It's one night, and you said yourself it's not fair to keep asking Chloe to babysit on an evening when she's had her all day. There's a big box store not far from town where we can get most of what we need, and Beau is meeting us there with his truck to help us haul everything home."

I watch as she tries to come up with an excuse, eventually sighing when she can't immediately think of one. "Come on, Kitten, let's go say hi to the Princess and then you can take a shower." Slapping her ass hard enough to sting, I arch my eyebrows in challenge when she glares at me over her shoulder. "Hurry up or I'll make that ass a nice shade of pink before we go to bed tonight."

"Promises, promises," she says quietly, smirking at me before darting up the front steps and into the house.

Twenty minutes later, we're on our way back out. I'm going to need a different car for when we go out as a family, my vintage muscle car is sexy as hell, but it doesn't have all the safety features of a modern car and without them it's not safe enough to be carrying around precious cargo. If I'm lucky, then Lulu is already pregnant so a new car is now my top priority after getting her and Poppy all moved into my place.

Tipping my seat forward, I clip Poppy's baby carrier into the base and make sure it's secure before I climb into the front and close the door. I've already text Beau to tell him we'll meet him at the store in about twenty minutes and I'm excited.

"So what exactly do you want to get?" Lulu asks.

"Everything."

"Penn, be serious."

"I am being serious. I get that you think this is happening too fast, but I disagree. If you want to pack up all of her stuff from Chloe's and move it to mine, I'm all for that, if not then we need everything we have at yours at mine too."

She's looking at me like I'm crazy, which I probably am, but I don't give a fuck. I'm crazy about her and I have enough money to buy whatever the fuck I want, to get my woman and my kid set up. Instead of arguing, I just flash her a huge smile and turn my attention back to the road.

It turns out shopping with a Lulu is a fucking nightmare. Poppy is wide awake and not at all impressed about being in her stroller. I end up having to carry her and push the cart, while Lulu pushes the empty stroller, arguing with me over every single thing I try to get her to buy.

"Kitten," I growl angrily. "You're being a pain in the ass. We're not leaving here until you pick everything we need and you being difficult is just making Poppy more tired and both of us more hungry than we need to be. Now just pick all the things she needs or I'll call Chloe and have her send me pictures of all the stuff you have back at her place and just buy exactly the same."

Scowling, she starts to shuffle down the baby aisle, reluctantly selecting things from the shelves and putting them in the cart. By the time we're done and back out in the parking lot, Poppy is asleep and Lulu has been scowling at me for the last thirty minutes.

"Go get Poppy back in the car, I'll help Beau load all this stuff into his truck," I tell her.

Nodding, she takes the keys from me and pushes

Poppy's stroller away.

"Jesus, bro, you leave anything in the store?" Beau laughs.

"Babies need a lot of crap. Give me a hand with this stuff, they're bringing the crib and mattress out."

Once Beau's truck is full, I climb into the car with Lulu and tense, feeling her anger. "You still pissed?"

"You just spent thousands of dollars, Penn."

"So?"

"So it's ridiculous, we've only been dating a couple of days."

"Lulu, this is old news, I've heard this argument and I don't want to hear it again. If this thing between us all goes to shit—which is won't... But if it does, then that's my problem and I'll be the one with a house full of baby stuff."

She parts her lips to argue again and I lose it, snapping my hand out and wrapping it around her throat, collaring her with my fingers. "Enough, Lulu, your doubt in us is starting to piss me off. You're mine and I'm yours, what the fuck have I done to make you question my sincerity?"

Her eyes fill with tears and in this moment she looks so fucking young. "Nothing," she whispers. "It's just people think they want something and then when it becomes a reality, they change their minds and it's me that's left picking up the pieces."

Her words sound casual, but I can tell there's more to it than that, something deeper and personal.

"Tonight, you're going to explain what you mean by that, but for now all I can do is tell you again that even though it might seem like I'm rushing blindly into this thing between us, nothing could be further from the truth. You and Poppy are my fucking world now. I'd love nothing more than to prove it to you than by taking you to city hall in the morning and marrying you, then adopting Poppy, but I know you're not there yet, so I'll wait. But you've got to stop questioning when I'm going to be an asshole and get bored, because the answer to that is never. I'll only ever want more of you, I'll never get enough."

Leaning over, I wipe the tear from her cheek and press my lips to hers. She doesn't need me to dominate her right now, she needs me to show her the truth in my words. So that's what I do, kissing her like she's my last breath, like she's my everything.

We make the drive back to my place in relatively comfortable silence. I keep her hand in mine, resting it on my thigh, staying connected to her like I know she needs, and she stays relaxed, as if my words have settled some of her doubts; at least for the moment.

Beau's already here, his truck parked in its usual spot, the bed empty of all of the stuff we bought when I pull up behind it. "Looks like they already unloaded."

Climbing out, I open Lulu's door, before circling back around and reaching Poppy's carrier out from the car as Lulu gets her bag full of diapers and other baby stuff from the truck. With Poppy in one hand, I reach for Lulu with the other and lead her to the front door. This feels momentous and I want to pull out my cell and take a picture of the first time I bring my woman and my daughter home.

Fuck it. Grabbing my cell from my pocket, I pull Lulu into my side, then lift the cell up high and snap a picture of the three of us. I don't care if it makes me look like a pussy, I want a record of this moment.

Lulu sighs then smiles, leaning into me as I open the door and guide my family inside.

FOURTEEN

LULU

My heart melts as he takes out his cell and takes a picture of the three of us. It doesn't seem to matter that Poppy's asleep in her seat, or that we were fighting less than half an hour ago.

Why is he such a nice guy?

It would be so much easier to keep my distance if he wasn't so freaking perfect, but he is. He's actually perfect.

The living room is full of people again when we step inside, but all eyes turn to us and then to Poppy. I'm not used to my daughter being under scrutiny and my mama bear instincts all rise to the surface ready to defend my daughter against anyone, including Penn's family. But then they descend on us and instead of distain there's nothing but warmth and acceptance.

"Oh my god, she's so precious."

"She looks so much like you."

"Dude, you're going to have to carry a shotgun with you all the time when she's older to keep the asshole boys away from her."

"I want one."

As his family coos over my daughter I can't help but lean into Penn's side, wondering how it is that this room full of strangers has shown me more affection and acceptance than my actual family ever has.

"Oh. Oh fuck."

Cora's loud exclamation has me immediately checking on Poppy, but she's still fast asleep.

"What's the matter, honey?" Huck says frantically.

"My waters just broke," Cora giggles.

"What?" Huck cries, his eyes going down to the puddle of clear liquid that's now around Cora's feet.

"Oh fuck, should I call an ambulance? Oh fuck is he coming? Oh fuck." Huck's frantic, grabbing Cora, then releasing her to move in one direction, then stopping and rushing back to her again.

"Huck, calm down," Cora demands. "I need to go get cleaned up and into dry clothes. You need to grab my baby bag and go get the car started. It's an hour's drive from here to the hospital so you need to give them a call and tell them we're coming in." Her voice is calm and relaxed.

"Okay. Fuck, okay."

"I'll call the hospital, Beau will grab the bag, you help Cora," Bonnie says, hiding a smirk.

Huck nods, then carefully helps Cora back to their door and into their apartment.

"Should we follow them to the hospital?" Granger says.

"Most hospitals only let the dad into the labor suite and it could be hours. I was in labor for twenty-eight hours with this one. Unless you want to be sitting in a waiting room all night, it's probably best you wait here," I tell him.

"Twenty-eight hours?" Penn looks horrified. "Who was with you?"

"Chloe."

"Not your mom?"

"God no," I laugh, while Bonnie makes a call and Beau reappears carrying a black carry-on bag.

"I'll go put this in Huck's car," he says to no one in particular.

Cora reappears a few moments later looking annoyed as Huck fusses behind her.

"What do you mean you've been having contractions for the last few hours? Why the fuck wouldn't you tell me that?" Huck snaps.

"Because I've been having Braxton hicks for weeks and I wasn't sure this was the real thing. Women don't have babies in minutes, it takes hours and there's no way I'm having the hospital turn us away if we get there and I'm not even dilated." She suddenly stops talking and grimaces. She breaths slowly while we all watch, then straightens and starts to walk again. "I'm pretty sure this is the real thing," she shrugs.

One by one, everyone takes it in turn to either kiss or hug Cora, then Huck. The brothers all do that man hug, shoulder slap thing, speaking quietly to Huck until finally they give us a wave and leave to have their baby.

"Keep in touch, let us know what's happening. If you need us, just let us know and we'll come on down to the hospital," Beau says with a firm nod of his head. If I didn't already know he was the oldest I'd have figured it out right now, he's a good big brother.

We all watch the door close behind them, a layer of tension for Cora and Huck still filling the air. That's the moment that Poppy decides to wake up with a screech and all focus turns back to us. Carrying her seat over to the couch, Penn sits down and unclips the straps holding her in, lifting her out of the seat and pressing a kiss to her head, before he turns and hands her to me.

She quiets the moment she's in my arms, her wet

cheeks pressed into my neck as Penn coos at her from beside me. "You want me to warm up her bottle and get you her jammies?" he asks.

"Please, this is well past her bed time, but she hates sleeping in her carrier."

"That's okay, you feed her and I'll get the pop up crib and the baby monitor set up in our room, that way she can sleep in there while we have dinner."

Biting my lip, I want to argue, but honestly what can I say? He's right, she'd be more comfortable in the crib than anywhere else. So I nod, and he stands from the couch and pulls the bottle I made up for her before we left from the bag, and disappears into the kitchen.

Suddenly feeling self-conscious, I focus all my attention on Poppy rather than deal with all the Barnett eyes that are on me. These brothers definitely have the intense thing going down and I don't really know what to do with it.

Grabbing the folding change pad from the bag, I lay it down on the couch and then lay Poppy on it, stripping off her cute leggings and shirt and unfastening her diaper. When the couch at my side dips down I glance up and find one of the brothers beside me, his smile soft as he looks down at my daughter.

"Hey, I'm Teddy, I doubt you remember. I know Penn sort of just threw names at you last night."

"Hi Teddy." He's younger than Penn, still attractive in the same way all the Barnetts are, but he's slimmer and I'd guess at shorter too.

"Can I do anything to help?"

"Could you hand me a diaper and the wipes?"

"Sure thing." Pulling the bag onto his lap he grabs out what I asked for and hands it to me, stroking Poppy's cheek with his finger and earning a tired smile from her cute baby face.

"There's a pink onesie in there too, if you wouldn't mind."

I clean her up and change her diaper as he roots through the bag again, pulling out every single pink thing in there until he finds her onesie, handing it to me triumphantly.

"Thanks," I chuckle, dressing Poppy in it, just as Penn appears with her bottle.

"Here you go, Kitten, I'll go set the crib up."

Unsure what else to say, I take the bottle from him and nod. He leaves with Beau in tow and I wish I could go with him, but it feels really rude to just get up and leave, especially when the couch is full of members of his family.

When the lights dim, I glance up and find Alice at the wall switch. "This is a strange place and we're all strangers, I thought it might make her relax a little if it was a more calming light."

"Thanks, that's great," I say, realizing that the dimmed lights have actually made me a little more comfortable as well. Shuffling back into the couch, I cradle Poppy against my chest and check the temperature of the formula before I bring the bottle to her lips. It takes her a little longer than usual, but she starts to drink as I stroke her cheek, and before long the bottle is empty and she's asleep in my arms.

"She's so perfect, how do you get anything done, I'd just spend all day staring at her," Bonnie says with a wistful sigh.

"I think I spent the first three months pretty much in awe that I made her," I say quietly. "I hate leaving her every day."

"Penn makes good money, you could give up work and stay home all the time with her," one of the brothers says.

"Penn and I have known each other less than a week," I scoff.

"So. You're his, so is she, the timescale isn't important."

Rolling my eyes, I look to Bonnie for some support but she's staring down at Poppy with a strange look on her face.

"Bonnie, Alice back me up here," I say, feeling like I need some support against all the obviously stubborn and unreasonable Barnett men.

"With any other guy I'd agree, but things work differently for the men in this family," Bonnie says.

Shaking my head, I sigh. "So you're telling me after a few days you'd have been ready to give up your job and just let a man take care of you."

"I moved Alice in here the day we met," Granger says, pulling Alice into his lap. "We got married five days after that."

"Holy shit," I say beneath my breath. "Bonnie?"

"Things were a little different for me and Beau, my family's ranch is right next door so I'd sort of known the whole family my entire life, but I'm so much younger than them. Beau kind of… I want to say stalked, but that sounds much worse than it actually was."

"He stalked you?" I ask, my voice shrill.

"You know I work at the coffee shop, right?"

"Yeah," I nod.

"Well I open up most mornings at like five thirty and then stay till close at eight thirty. Beau turned up as I opened and again at close for a year because he thought it was dangerous me being there by myself."

"A year together before getting serious I can totally understand, that's normal."

"Oh no," Bonnie laughs. "For a year he came in every morning and every evening, but he barely spoke to me. Took a guy asking me out in front of Beau for him to pull his head out of his ass and see what apparently the rest of the brothers already knew."

"Which was?"

"That she was mine." Beau's gravelly voice comes from behind me and I twist around to see him. "Once I figured it out, I never let her go."

"And Huck met Cora through me, we went on a girls' night out and the guys followed us, he took one look at her and he was gone, she was moved in within the week and pregnant within a month. By the way, never let Penn anywhere near your birth control, they can't be trusted," Bonnie says with a serious nod.

My eyes go wide and I stare at the guys as both Beau and Granger nod and the others all smirk. I feel myself go pale as I remember Penn's blasé attitude toward me being pregnant. We haven't been careful, and in the last couple of days he's come inside of me three times. Fuck, I really could be pregnant already and by the sounds of his family, Penn really might be crazy enough to be happy about it.

"Kitten, the crib's all set up, you want to come check it before you get the princess settled?" Penn says, walking back into the main house from the door to his rooms.

"Yeah sure," I say, trying to swallow back the rising panic that's building inside of me.

"Let me take her." He carefully lifts Poppy from me

and cradles her to his huge chest, she looks tiny in his arms and yep, you guessed it, I'm pretty sure my ovaries pop out another egg. Between his insane need to fill me with cum and my traitorous body's ability to ovulate at will the moment he's sweet to my daughter I really am going to be pregnant before the end of the week. He starts to walk toward the door to his apartment and I vow to stop being an idiot and get myself on birth control.

I follow him through the apartment to his room and find the pop-up crib all set up to the side, there's the new pink sheets we bought on the mattress and even a mobile hanging over the side that I don't remember seeing him put in the cart. The baby sleeping bag like the ones I use at home is spread out in the bottom of the crib, and the monitor is all set up and resting on the bedside cabinet.

"Is everything okay? Did I forget anything?" he asks.

"No, it all looks perfect."

"I'll wash all the sheets and everything tomorrow, I know we should have done that before she slept on them, but I'm hoping it'll be okay for one night. If you want I can build the proper crib in here, or we can use this until her room is finished."

"Penn," I sigh.

"I want you both here with me, Kitten."

How can I fight him when he's so sincere? God, how do I fight him anyway? I want him and everything he has to offer, but he needs to know the truth first. "There's some stuff we should talk about. About Poppy."

"Okay," he nods. "Dinner first, then we can talk."

My stomach growls almost on cue and he smirks, pressing a kiss to Poppy's forehead before he brings her to me and I do the same. He carries her in his huge, protective arms over to the crib and painstakingly carefully lowers her into it, zipping her into her baby sleeping bag before slowly moving away from her.

I don't know if I go to him, or him to me, but I'm against his chest and being held by the same strong arms that were just cuddling my daughter a second later. If she feels even half as safe and protected by him, no wonder she never protested at him holding her and taking care of her.

My stomach growls again and he chuckles. "Come on, let's go feed you."

Grabbing the baby monitor I turn it on, then let him guide me away from Poppy and back into the main house, where two huge dishes of pasta are being placed down on the massive dining table in the kitchen.

All the furniture must be bespoke, because where else do you find a table big enough to seat fifteen people? Penn guides me to it, holding out a chair for me and sinking down into the one beside it.

"I hope you like pasta?" a brother whose name I can't

remember asks. "I'm Cody by the way."

Smiling gratefully I nod. "I love pasta, thanks."

Everyone takes their seat and plates are filled and handed out while wine and beer follows. It's loud and chaotic and sort of wonderful and for a second, I sit back and imagine me and Poppy being here and being a part of it all. Growing up I spent most of my childhood either in daycare or with a nanny. My parents weren't natural child rearers, and as an only child I never had any siblings to make our home anywhere near as boisterous as this place.

"So you all eat together every night?" I ask.

"Not all of us and not every night, but most of the time yeah. We all have lives and with us each having our own kitchens now, we can cook for ourselves if we don't feel like being sociable, but most of the time, dinner is when we catch up, when we stay connected to one another's lives. We know it's weird, but we're close and we enjoy each other's' company. Bonnie's dad joins us three or four times a week and Cora's parents and brother are here at least once a week."

"Jesus, this really is like a commune," I say, then slap my hand across my mouth. "I'm so sorry, that was so rude."

Instead of being offended, they all laugh.

"Oh my god, this place is like a commune," Bonnie

giggles. "Ya'll need to grow long hair and moustaches."

"We could get a few VW vans to go with my RV and maybe a tee-pee," Alice chuckles shyly. "I think my sister thought it was some kind of cult the first time she met everyone too."

"She's not from here?" I ask.

"No, she's in the army and based out of West Virginia. But we're from Ottawa originally," Alice tells me, snuggling into Granger's side even while she's eating.

"How did you end up in Montana then?"

"My RV broke down on the edge of town. Granger pulled over to see if I was okay and needed any help, and he did his whole caveman 'Mine' thing. He convinced me to stay here for the weekend and I've never left."

"Wow, so that knowing at first sight stuff really has happened before?"

"Yep," she nods.

"And you were okay with that?"

Alice blushes. "Not really."

"I think we all fought it at the start, I mean they're a lot. But if you haven't noticed already, Barnett boys are hard to resist. At least Cora and I lasted longer than Alice though," Bonnie laughs.

"Hey," Alice half-heartedly protests.

"What? You know it's true, you lasted like a day, must be Granger's massive dick."

I choke on my bite of pasta.

"We didn't get the sound proofing till well after I moved in, I've heard more than I ever need to know about Beau's dick," Alice barbs back, blushing bright red.

Bonnie doesn't even show an ounce of embarrassment, she just nods and smiles, lifting her glass into the air and raising it in a silent toast. Alice lifts hers too and then both women turn their faces to me expectantly. "To big dicks and great orgasms."

Fighting a smile, I lift my glass and tap it against theirs.

"Welcome to the family," Alice grins.

FIFTEEN

PENN

Dinner is loud and rowdy and Lulu fits in perfectly. I love having her here, I love having Poppy asleep in our room. I want this all the time and I'm hoping that this might be the first step toward making that happen.

Once the table is clear and the plates loaded into the dishwasher, I wave goodbye to my family, take Lulu's hand and pull her into our rooms. I don't really know what she wants to talk about, but whatever it is, I doubt it will make any difference to the way I feel about her and Poppy.

"You go check on Princess and I'll get drinks. You want wine or coffee?"

"Just a little wine, I've already had a couple of glasses."

I nod and head for the kitchen as she disappears into the bedroom to check on Poppy.

"She okay?" I ask when she comes back to sit on the couch beside me.

"Fast asleep."

"So what is it you wanted to talk about?" There's no point beating around the bush, I might as well get straight to the point.

Inhaling slowly, she tangles her fingers together in her lap and cautiously lifts her gaze to me.

Shuffling forward until my leg is rested against hers, I push my fingers between hers and take her hand, bracing myself for whatever she's about to tell me.

"Okay, so this is weirdly harder than I was expecting," she clears her throat. "When I was in college, I was really close to the RA in my freshman dorm. Her name was Hayley and she was a senior when I was a freshman. She was awesome, she played mother hen to all the new kids who had never lived away from home. She looked after us all, held our hair back if we were sick, offered us a shoulder to cry on when we got dumped. After she graduated, we kept in touch. We'd meet up for dinner a couple of times a month and then when I went to law school, she helped me find an apartment in the city and we ended up being neighbors."

"Okay," I nod, confused what this has to do with

Poppy.

"She met this great guy, Dane. They moved in together and were engaged and trying for a baby. When it wasn't happening, they went to the doctors and had all kinds of tests and they told her that her eggs weren't viable and that her womb was inhospitable and basically that she couldn't have kids."

She's not looking at me, her gaze is lowered to her hands that are still trying to fidget despite me holding them.

"Hayley and Dane looked into egg donors and surrogates, but the fees were unbelievable and so she asked me."

"She asked you what?" I say slowly.

"She asked me to donate my eggs and act as their surrogate."

I freeze, unable to process what she's saying.

"She was my best friend and they wanted a baby so much and I just didn't know how to say no, especially because I knew without my help they'd never get to be parents."

"So you agreed?"

"I did. They paid for all the medical costs and I went into a clinic and had my eggs harvested and then they used Dane's sperm to artificially inseminate them and then they were implanted back into me."

"But how? Why?" I stumble over my words, trying to understand how she ended up a single parent.

"The day we found out I was pregnant they were overjoyed; we knew we only had one shot at it working because of the cost and I was just so happy for them. I was giving them the greatest gift in the world."

There's a solemn, sad expression on her face that has me tensing, but I don't say anything and just wait for her to continue her story.

"I was about eight or nine weeks pregnant and we'd been for a scan at the doctor's office, just to check everything was okay. Dane's cell rung like three times during the appointment and Hayley was getting really angry with him. It rang again the moment we got back to the car and she snatched it out of his hands, shouting at him that nothing was more important than the appointment and why couldn't he just turn it off. I was sitting in the backseat of their car, feeling super uncomfortable because they were having an argument right in front of me. Hayley answered his cell and he was trying to grab it off her, and then he just stopped and slumped down into the driver's seat, like he'd just given up."

"What happened?" I ask.

"The person on the end of the call was the woman he was having an affair with. Turns out she'd just found out she was pregnant and was pushing him to finally leave

Hayley. Apparently they'd been sneaking around almost the whole time Dane and Hayley had been married."

Closing my eyes, I brace myself for the rest of the story, even though I've filled in the blanks myself and I know what she's about to say.

"They screamed at each other the entire drive home and then Hayley packed her stuff and left the same day. I didn't see either of them for a month. She came first and told me that they were getting a divorce and that she didn't want the baby. She said that while they were married she would have been content knowing that half the child's DNA was Dane's, but that now she was on her own, the baby had none of her in it and she knew she'd always resent it because of the situation with him cheating on her."

"That bitch," I hiss.

"I was shellshocked. She'd begged me to be their surrogate, she'd cried and told me I was her only hope of having a child of her own and then when it came down to it, she just walked away because it didn't have any of her DNA."

"And Dane?"

She scoffs lightly. "He never even contacted me himself. I received a letter from his lawyer advising that due to the breakdown in his marriage he no longer wanted to proceed with the pregnancy. They provided me with a list of medical facilities they would pay for me to use to have the pregnancy terminated."

Her voice breaks and I pull her into me, wrapping my arm around her shoulder and pressing a kiss to her forehead.

"I couldn't do it. There was a baby growing inside of me and I couldn't just end their life because the people who were supposed to love it were assholes. So I got a lawyer. Dane, Hayley and I never signed any contracts. It was my best friend and her husband, I never thought we needed to. My lawyer advised Dane that I wouldn't be terminating, that I intended to have the baby and would keep her. His lawyers returned paperwork for me to sign, agreeing that Dane would waive all parental rights in exchange for me never contacting him about the baby or asking for any kind of child support. By the time I was four months pregnant, I was doing this alone."

"Jesus, Kitten, I'm so sorry that happened to you."

"I'm not, it's how I ended up with Poppy and I don't regret keeping her. I don't regret her being here, I never have, not even for a moment. My parents think I should have terminated, they think I'm an idiot, that I ruined my life. Chloe was the only one who supported my decision, she came and stayed with me in Chicago the last month of my pregnancy, she was there when I gave birth and the first month of Poppy's life. When she had to come home she begged me to come with her, but I wanted to stay in the city, I thought I could do it alone. Only daycare was so expensive and everyone I went to look at I hated. The law firm I was working at as an intern were great, they let me work from home, but interns don't get paid that much and I knew I wasn't in a position to throw myself into taking the bar with a newborn. Rent and the cost of living was killing me and honestly, I felt like I was drowning. My parents refused to even see Poppy until I told them we were moving and even after meeting her they told me I'd destroyed my future, that I was a fool. Chloe offered me a home, and to take care of Poppy while I worked, she's been amazing."

"I'm sorry you had to go through all that alone, Lulu, but I'm not sad it happened. Poppy is amazing and you're an amazing mom, I love her already and I only met her for the first time this week. If your parents can't see how precious a gift she is, then they're the idiots and they don't deserve to be a part of either of your lives. As far as I can see, everything that happened lead you here, to me, and I'll be grateful every single day that I have you, both of you."

Tears fill her eyes and I hate them, I don't ever want her to be sad, to cry. Dragging her into my lap I hold her in my arms, wiping away the tears with my thumb a moment before I lean down and capture her lips with mine. I don't devour her; this isn't about that. In this moment she needs to see how much I want her, how much I need her. That I won't ever leave her and Poppy, that I won't discard them.

She kisses me back, her bottom lip trembling as hot, wet tears hit my cheeks. I swallow all of her emotion and channel all of mine through our lips. Telling her she's mine, that I won't ever let her down.

Laying her back on the couch we strip each other's clothes slowly, not frenzied or desperate. "You're mine now, both of you," I whisper as I press my dick to her soaked entrance. "I won't ever let you go. I need you too much."

It takes me a while to work my dick into her, even though she's still stretched from how roughly I took her this afternoon. Once I'm seated all the way inside of her, I pull back, our bodies connected, and lock my gaze with hers. "I'm all in, Lulu, sharing a home, a name, a daughter, a life. I want it all with you, only ever you."

She nods as fresh tears spill down her cheeks. When her arms cling to my neck, I kiss her, making love to her slowly, branding her soul with every movement. I already own her body, now her soul, but I won't stop until her heart is mine as well.

Her entire body trembles beneath me by the time her third orgasm finds its peak and I allow myself to come, pumping my seed into her and silently claiming her all over again. Minutes, or hours pass as she clings to me, my dick still inside of her, neither of us speaking and I love it. I want her here in our home, in our bed, and tonight has made me feel like I might be one step closer. She trusted me with the fucked up circumstances of Poppy's birth, but knowing that she should have belonged to someone else doesn't change things for me. In fact, it's made things easier. I want both of them, permanently and legally and knowing that her biological dad won't ever be a problem has only eased that concern. I'm going to be Poppy's dad in every way she needs, and she'll never need to think about the person who provided nothing more than a bit of DNA.

"Come on, Kitten, let's go to bed."

"I need to go home, I don't have any clothes here."

"You do, I had Chloe pack a bag for you and Poppy, she's not expecting you guys home tonight."

"Penn," she sighs.

"Poppy's happy and asleep, I don't want to disturb her and I want to sleep with you in our bed. I want to wake up with you." I know I probably sound pathetic, but it's the truth and apparently I'm not above begging if it gets me what I want.

"Okay," she says sleepily.

"Good girl," I praise, holding her to me as I stand up from the couch, not releasing her, my dick still half way inside of her.

"Penn, she giggles, gripping me tightly, her arms and legs wrapped around me.

I carry her to our room, glancing down at Poppy before pulling back the comforter and lowering her to the mattress. Running back into the living room I grab the monitor and turn off the lights, then I crawl into bed behind my woman and fall asleep naked with her in my arms.

***

Morning comes too quickly and a pint-sized princess wakes me before my alarm can. Just like the morning before, I throw on some sweats and pick Poppy up out of her crib, cuddling her close and kissing her head before I wake Lulu up and hand her off to her mama, who pulls her under the comforter and holds her tight.

The highchair I bought yesterday is still in the box in the main living room, so I open the door to my apartment and head out, intending to grab it and take it back to my space. Except it's already open and set up at the big table. My heart just fucking melts that my family so easily thought of and included Poppy. I know Lulu might be more comfortable eating in my apartment, but I want her and Poppy surrounded by all the other people who are important to me. Instead of moving it, I leave it where it is and instead go and grab the bag Chloe packed for the girls from the trunk of my car and bring it into the house. We're all early risers, even more so with Bonnie having to open the coffee shop four or five times a week, so even though it's barely six thirty, one by one, doors open and my brothers and sisters start to appear.

"Any news from Huck? I haven't had a chance to check my cell yet this morning," I ask Beau.

"He text about 5.00 am saying she'd had a tough night, but they'd finally taken her down to delivery and he'd call as soon as the baby was here."

Nodding, I head back to the door to my rooms and go straight into the bedroom, finding a giggling Poppy sitting in Lulu's lap in bed. "Morning. We normally all eat together if that's okay?"

"Oh, err, yeah sure, I need to shower and get dressed," Lulu says, her cheeks tinged pink, her shoulders tense.

"Let me change Poppy's diaper and get her dressed while you get ready, although no one will care if you go out there in my shirt and boxers. What does she normally have for breakfast? We got some of that banana oatmeal stuff last night, or I can make her eggs or something."

"She has oatmeal most days, but she likes eggs or mashed banana and yoghurt."

"Okay, I can do that. You go take a shower and I'll sort the princess."

"Are you sure? I can get her dressed then get myself

ready," Lulu starts to protest.

"No, baby, let me help, that's what I'm here for."

She doesn't look convinced, but I take Poppy from her lap, kissing Lulu quickly before I head into the living room to grab the bag with the diapers in. I've never changed one before, but how hard can it be?

Ten minutes later, I've realized that it's definitely harder than it looks. Poppy is finally in a fresh diaper and lying on our bed as I try to coax the squirming baby into clothes. How the fuck does Lulu make this look so effortless?

A soft chuckle has me looking up. Lulu is wrapped in a towel, her hair twisted into a bun on top of her head, laughing at me.

"How do you do this?" I smile.

"Fast," she shrugs. "I'll get dressed and take over."

"No, I can do this," I say, refocusing on Poppy, moving quicker and managing to get both arms through her onesie. "Yay," I coo at Poppy, leaning down and blowing a raspberry against her belly before I pull the onesie down and fasten it over her diaper between her legs. The rest of her clothes are a little easier to get on and by the time Lulu is smoothing her hair into a ponytail, Poppy is fully dressed and smiling widely.

"Let's go eat."

Keeping Poppy in my arms, I take Lulu's hand and tow her out of the privacy of our mini apartment and into the main house, that's filled with the hustle and bustle that comes with lots of people all awake and moving familiarly together.

Lulu tenses, like she's expecting everyone to stop what they're doing and stare, but no one takes any notice of us as we make our way to the dining table and I strap Poppy into her chair. "Coffee?"

"Yes please," she says quietly, taking the seat to the right of Poppy and immediately focusing on her daughter.

Heading for the kitchen where Bay is busy flipping pancakes, I pour two cups of coffee and then ask Bay to make some eggs for Poppy while I grab a banana and some yoghurt. I remembered to put the bowls, cups and spoons we got last night to sterilize, so I grab what I need and make my way back to Lulu and Poppy. Bonnie is sitting beside Lulu, chatting to her, and she smiles at me when I slide into the seat on the other side of Poppy's chair.

"I asked Bay to make Princess some eggs, but I got her a banana and some yoghurt too."

"Thanks," Lulu says, taking the banana from me and starting to peel it.

I hand her the bowl and spoon and she quickly makes a disgusting banana, yoghurt mash, passing it back to me like she expects me to feed our princess. I fucking love it.

"Oh, let me go grab her a bib, else she'll be wearing

more than she eats," Lulu says, jumping up and heading back to our rooms, returning a minute later.

I settle in to feed Poppy as Bay places down huge platters of eggs, bacon and pancakes in the center of the table.

"Do you want me to take over so you can eat?" she asks me quietly as everyone descends on the food like wild animals.

"No, but can you make me a plate?"

She smiles and nods and I fucking love how domestic and normal this feels. I hope she likes it too. I want this to be their home, and I think she'll only agree to that if I can make her feel accepted and comfortable.

Beau's cell rings and we all fall silent, aware that this could be Huck. It's a video call and Beau places it at the end of the table and clicks answer while we all crowd in to see the screen.

"I have a son," Huck chokes out, tears freely falling down his face as he spins the screen around to show an exhausted looking Cora, cradling a tiny thing wrapped in a blue blanket.

There's a chorus of congratulations, until Beau silences us all. "Have you guys decided on a name yet?" he asks.

"Maverick Beau Barnett," Cora says, lifting her eyes from her new son for a moment to stare at the camera.

Glancing at my big brother, I'm surprised to find

tears in his eyes. Most of my life he's been the strong one, setting an example for us all to live up to, so I'm not at all surprised Huck and Cora decided to use his name as a middle name for their son. He's going to be just as amazing an uncle as he has been a brother.

"He's perfect," Huck whispers reverently, moving closer and zooming in on the infant's scrunched up face, his eyes tightly shut.

"Congratulations. Mama and baby doing okay?" Beau asks.

"Tired, but happy. Cora wants to sleep in our bed tonight so if the doctor says everything is okay, we'll be home later. If not, then tomorrow."

"Okay, you need anything brought to the hospital?"

"Not right now, I'll let you know."

"Okay, you take care of them both, we all love you."

"We love you all too," Cora and Huck say in unison. "Talk to you later."

"Bye," we all call just as the video ends.

"We have a nephew," Beau says shakily.

"I want one," Bonnie says loudly.

"What?" Beau answers.

"I want to have a baby."

Beau doesn't speak, just stands, lifts Bonnie from her seat and stalks back to their room.

"Twenty bucks says she's pregnant by the end of the

month," Teddy laughs.

I glance over to Lulu, she's smiling but there's a sadness in her eyes that I don't really understand. My gut tells me she's reliving Poppy's birth and the fact that she didn't have any one to video call to tell them that her precious baby girl was here and safe. I hate that she went through that and I'm even more grateful for Chloe and how much she's been there to love to support my girl. I just wish I'd met her when she was still pregnant, I would have been the one announcing my daughter's arrival, and Lulu and Poppy would have known they were loved and supported by my entire family.

Unable to resist, I stand up, move to Lulu's chair and pick her up, dropping her back down in my lap, my arms banded tightly around her waist. I don't say anything, I just hold her and I know it was the right thing when she leans back into me.

When we've all finished eating, I leave Lulu to clean Poppy up and get her into her baby carrier while I go and take a quick shower and get ready for work. By the time I get back into the living room Teddy is entertaining Poppy, playing peek a boo with her while Lulu chats animatedly to Bay.

"You ready, Kitten?" I ask.

"Yeah, Bay was just telling me he went to school in Chicago."

"He regaling you with his tales of living it up in the big city?" I smile.

"Just talking about familiar haunts, turns out Lulu worked at a sports bar me and my buddies practically lived at for four years. Shame I hated city living, else I might have met her before you did," he winks.

Pressing a soft kiss to Lulu's lips I reach around her and punch Bay in the arm. "Mine, hands off," I snarl.

Bay's laugh is loud and amused. "Don't worry, I'm not gonna start hitting on my new sister."

"Sister," Lulu coughs.

"Yep, you and Poppy are family now. I'll add you to the group chat."

Her eyes go wide and she looks to me like she's expecting me to deny it.

"Mine," I mouth.

I turn away from her as the reality of what was just said sinks in. I'm not gonna lie to her just to shield her from the truth, so it's better that she starts to get used to the fact that I have nine siblings who all now class her as their sister and Poppy their niece. This is what us Barnetts do.

SIXTEEN

LULU

Is it possible for people to be too nice? If it is then that's the problems with the entire Barnett Clan. Before Hayley and Dane, I was a naturally trusting person, at least to the people I was close to and considered pseudo family. After my best friend walked away from me and the baby she'd begged me to carry for her, I'll be honest, my faith was rattled. The day I received a letter from a lawyer's office advising me they wanted me to terminate the life growing inside of me, it was completely destroyed.

Chloe, Poppy and now Penn are all helping me to heal, but I'm still dubious. I mean if a couple who were so desperate to have a baby could just walk away, how am I meant to have any trust that anyone's motives are honest?

Penn grabs Poppy's carrier in one hand, the bags over his shoulder, his free hand on the base of my spine as he guides me toward the front door.

"See you guys tonight, it's my turn to cook and I'm making my famous chili and cornbread," Teddy says, waving to Poppy before he presses a kiss to my cheek.

"I'm not sure—"

"We'll be here, Chloe will be with us too, so be sure to make plenty."

"Don't worry, Hal and Cora's mom and dad are coming too, so we'll have a full house," Teddy smiles, stepping aside so the rest of Penn's brothers can take it in turns to say goodbye to both me and Poppy.

Until this morning, I had sort of deliberately forgotten that Penn had such a huge family. Being an only child myself, the idea that he has six siblings and their spouses was daunting enough that I pushed it to the back of my mind and dropped six ton of concrete on the top to stop myself from thinking about it. But now that I've spent time with them, it's impossible to pretend they don't exist, especially when they're calling me sister.

I mean, what the fuck is that all about?

Penn guides me out to his car, opening my door for me, before he fastens Poppy's seat into the back. Somehow he's stepped into the role of dad, caring for her without me even having to ask. I think I like it. If there wasn't this fear whispering to me that this won't last, that guys don't take on other men's children just like that, especially not men like Penn, I could maybe believe this was all true. He seems almost obsessed with getting me pregnant, but if he does, will he stop caring for Poppy the way he is now? Will she just become mine if we make a baby that's ours?

That doubt is enough to keep me quiet on the drive back into town. We have to drop Poppy at Chloe's for the day, then we both have work and I'm grateful for the reprieve. I need some time to think and when I'm around Penn he doesn't allow me breathing room, let alone a chance to consider how him and his family could affect me and Poppy.

He's the first person I've told about how Poppy came to be, outside of my family and Chloe. I was worried that he'd call me a fool or worse, that he'd think I should have ended my pregnancy like my parents thought I should. But instead he'd been angry for me, angry that the people that should have stepped up to care about me and Poppy didn't.

He even said that he was glad it all happened because it led me to him, and I suppose he's right. I never would have moved here if it hadn't been for Poppy.

I'm so inside my head I don't even realize we've stopped, or that we're at Chloe's. Shaking the fog from my brain I open my door and climb out, rushing around to take Poppy's seat from him and run it into the house as he grabs her stroller from the trunk.

"Hey," Chloe calls as we step into the living room. "How was your sleepover?" she winks.

"It was fine. Maybe a heads up that you'd packed me and Poppy a bag might have been nice," I say with a pointed glare.

Instead of being even slightly chastised, Chloe laughs, unclipping Poppy from her seat and lifting her up. "Honey, if I was thirty years younger I'd be panting after that man myself. I assumed you'd be over the moon you got to spend the night."

"His entire family was there," I hiss.

"In the room?" she balks.

"What? No. I mean they all live in that house."

"I know, they always have. His brothers are all just as fine as he is."

"Chloe," I scold.

"What, I'm old, not blind."

Shaking my head, I purse my lips and stay silent as Penn carries the stroller in and puts it in the coat closet by the door.

"You 'bout ready, Kitten?"

"Yeah, I'll be right there."

He nods. "Chloe, do you want us to come and pick

you up for dinner, or would you rather meet us at my place?"

"I'll meet you up there."

"Wait, when did you organize Chloe coming for dinner?" I ask.

"Last night," Penn winks. "I'll come grab Poppy off you before I pick Lulu up from work, that way we can go straight home and you can come on up whenever you're ready."

"Okay then," Chloe says, but she's not really listening, she's too busy tickling Poppy.

"Err," I try to think of an argument but nothing comes to mind before he pushes me toward Poppy to say goodbye and herds me out the door.

"You got something to say?" he asks once we're both in the car and heading toward work.

"You want to pick Poppy up without me?"

"Makes sense. Then me and her can come get you and we can go straight home rather than driving backwards and forwards all over town."

"She doesn't really know you that well."

"It's ten minutes, Lulu, you don't trust me with her for ten minutes?"

A part of me wants to say no. To insist that she's mine and that he can't have her, that I won't share. But the truth is as strange as it sounds, I do trust him. I know he'd never do anything to hurt her, or me. "No, it's not that, it's just—"

"That she's your baby and we haven't been together for too long."

Feeling terrible, I nod.

Smiling, he nods back. "I get it. I'll pick you up first, then we can swing straight back round to get the princess."

"Thank you," I whisper, feeling like a grade-A bitch when Penn has never done anything to suggest he couldn't pick Poppy up and drive the three miles to my office without me.

"I've never been a parent; I can't pretend to understand when the level of trust required to trust me with her will come. But we'll get there and when you feel comfortable, you just let me know."

Slackening my seat belt, I lean over to him and press a kiss to the side of his mouth. "Thank you. I really care about you and I know you care about me and Poppy. It's just, she's my entire world."

"I get how that feels, because you and her are my entire world."

When he pulls up outside my office, I grab his face and pull him in for a kiss, needing to show him how much I like him. I've been fighting this so hard, but maybe it's time for me to give in and enjoy him. He's a good guy and he just keeps proving that to me over and over again. Instead of assuming the worst, I need to recognize how wonderful he is.

"I really like you, Penn."

His smirk is pure sin. "I really like you too, Kitten."

"I'm going to stop trying to fight this."

"Good, you were never going to win anyway. You're mine and I wasn't ever planning on letting you go."

"Arrogance isn't sexy," I playfully chide.

"Nothing arrogant about what I'm saying." His hand slides between my thighs to cup my pussy. "Your body is begging for me, your soul knows it belongs to me, there's only your heart I have left to convince."

Blushing, I don't bother trying to deny his words. He's right, my body craves him in a way I've never known before. I can feel my core leaking in preparation for him even though we had sex more than once yesterday, and a deep-seated soreness is still lingering between my thighs.

"Go to work, before I take you home and make you ride my dick until you pass out."

Swallowing past the lump of want and need in my throat, I let him collar my neck and kiss me deeply before I slide out of the car and walk in a daze toward my office.

The rest of the day is a blur, Penn grabs us takeout for lunch and we eat it while he drags me to a gorgeous baby boutique to pick out a present for Cora and Huck's new son. The store has an embroidery service, so we end up getting a blanket embroidered with Maverick's name and date of birth, a couple of cute outfits and a pack of milestone cards that Cora and Huck can use to take pictures of all the special moments over the first few months.

The store makes me a little broody. Even though Poppy is only six months old, she's so big in comparison with the tiny newborn I bought home from the hospital. The reminder that Penn and I aren't being careful, that I could already be pregnant fills my thoughts, and I wander aimlessly through the store... my head full of images of a perfect newborn that looks just like his daddy.

No.

I shake the picture free and blink, trying to force myself back to the real world. Where getting pregnant within a week of meeting someone is really fucking stupid. If only he didn't make me feel like I truly was the most important thing to him in the world.

"You ready, Kitten?"

Gentle fingers lace with mine and he turns me to face him. "Sure." I nod and let him lead me out the store and back toward my office. I need a distraction from him and if that's the mundane, time-wasting tasks that Janet is still assigning me, then so be it.

The afternoon drags and it takes me longer than it

should to send Janet all of the research she's asked for. It's been almost a week and she still hasn't left her office during the day at all. I'm assuming she must have a private bath back there, else she must have some serious bladder control.

I get why she's lost so many paralegals, if I didn't know this is the only law office in town, I'd probably have said fuck it and quit by now too. Sitting in a windowless office all day with no one to talk to and a boss who only communicates via email is boring as hell. But I need this job and it's only a stopgap until I take the bar and become a practicing lawyer.

Closing down my computer, I tidy my desk and am just grabbing my purse when Janet's office door opens and she emerges from inside, her eyes taking me in. "Lucile."

"I really do prefer Lulu," I say with a saccharin sweet smile. She might think using my full name will intimidate me, but I've known much scarier people than her.

"You intend to practice law with a name like Lulu?" she sneers. "Who would take you seriously?"

"Those who think I'm incapable of doing my job because of my name, are the kind of clients I'll be happy not to represent," I say, not letting my smile slip even an inch.

"Hmm," she grunts. "So, you and Penn Barnett are a *thing*?"

She says the word thing, wrinkling her nose in the same way you might if you were discussing dog shit.

"We're dating, yes," I nod, fighting the urge to tell her my personal life is none of her goddamn business.

"Those brothers," she spits, "they don't appreciate a strong, capable woman. They're all looking for submissive little mice to do as they say." Her gaze roves over me from head to toe. "You're not a mouse."

With that she turns and re-enters her office, closing the door behind her with a decisive click. What the hell was that? Was that a warning, or a compliment, or just another weird test that she's hoping I'll fail so she can fire me?

Bewildered, I grab my purse and leave my office, moving on autopilot through reception and outside to where Penn is waiting for me. Sliding into the car, I flash him a small smile and then reach for my seatbelt only to find his fingers on my chin, forcing me to turn and look at him.

"What's the matter?" he growls forcefully.

"Oh, nothing. I just had a weird conversation with Janet."

His grip loosens marginally but he doesn't release me, or let me turn away. "What did she say to you?"

"Nothing really, she asked about us. I said we were dating and she said that you and your brothers don't want strong women, that you only like submissive mice. Then she said I wasn't a mouse and left."

His brow furrows.

"I don't really know what her point was, or if she was insulting me, or you, or both of us."

"She's a bitch who doesn't know what she's talking about. Bonnie, Cora and Alice are hardly fucking mice and you're a badass single mom." Pulling me into him, he claims my mouth in a hard punishing kiss that leaves my panties damp and my chest heaving when he finally pulls away.

"Buckle up, let's go get the princess."

Breathless, I nod, reaching back and pulling my belt around me as he watches me with intense eyes. How is it possible that he can own me with just that look? Wetness has filled my panties and my nipples are straining against the confines of my bra.

"Just because we own our women, doesn't mean we don't want them to be strong, feisty and independent. I fucking love how capable you are, it makes you submitting to me and letting me take care of you that much sweeter, because you don't need me, but you're giving yourself to me anyway," he says quietly before he turns his attention back to the road.

When we get to Chloe's, she has Poppy all strapped into her carrier and a bag packed for each of us.

"I don't remember agreeing to stay the night again," I inform Penn with an arch of my brow.

"That's okay, Kitten, I don't remember asking. Doesn't mean it's not happening though."

Before I have a chance to argue, he smacks my ass, hard, then grabs the bags and disappears through the front door.

"Asshole," I hiss, rubbing at my sore butt.

"I'll see you later," Chloe laughs, lifting Poppy's carrier off the floor and handing it to me.

"Bye." Shaking my head at her amusement, I make my way outside. Penn takes Poppy from me the moment I get near the car, situating her seat into the base in the back seat and checking it's secure twice before he gets in. These are the moments when he's completely irresistible to me. I could cope with the good looks, massive dick and dominant personality that turns me on more than I'm willing to admit out loud. But the moments when he is sweet and caring and protective of both me and Poppy are the moments that really get to me, when he shows me how good of a partner and father he'll be. I didn't even know that would turn me on until he showed me how sexy hot daddy is on a guy.

The drive to Penn's house seems to pass quickly and before I know it, we're pulling to a stop behind the row of cars that are parked outside. Now that I've been here a couple of times, I don't feel the sense of trepidation I did on my first visit and jump out the car while Penn grabs Poppy.

"Here, Kitten, you get her while I get the bags," Penn says, handing off the carrier to me while he grabs the two bags that I notice are larger than I realized.

"Why are there two bags?"

"One for you, one for Princess."

"But it's one night, that could easily fit into a single bag."

"I asked Chloe to pack up some stuff for you guys to leave here too," Penn says with a shrug.

I part my lips to ask him why, but he grabs my throat and silences me with a kiss. When I've melted into him, my lips parted and eager, he pulls back and smirks down at me. "Come on, I have a surprise to show you."

Taking my hand he pulls me into the house, briefly acknowledging Teddy and Beau who are sitting in the living room as he leads me through the door and into his apartment. This is the fourth time I've been here, but it still shocks me that he has an entire apartment built off the original house.

Dropping the bags next to the couch, he takes Poppy's seat from me and quickly unstraps her, lifting her into his arms. "Come on," he says, reaching for my hand and rushing me through the room and toward the bedrooms.

When we reach his spare room, he pauses for a minute, smiles at me, then at Poppy, then he releases my hand, reaches out, turns the door handle and pushes the door open.

My mouth falls open as I take in the pink, princess paradise. The walls are a soft pale pink, the crib we picked out is built and set up with a pink patchwork bed spread covering the mattress. Several plushies are sitting in the crib and there's a beautiful mobile hanging over the end. A super soft looking pink rug covers the floor and an overstuffed white armchair sits in the corner with a changing table and a dresser pushed against the wall. It's so perfect I can barely take it all in. Princess Poppy is painted in swirling letters above her crib and tears fill my eyes at the most beautiful girly nursery I've ever seen.

"What do you think? We can change anything you don't like."

"When did you do this?" I choke out through the emotion that's filling my throat.

"Today. I dropped you off at work, then came back here and Beau and Teddy helped me. She won't be able to sleep in here for a couple of days because of the paint fumes..." He trails off and a faint blush coats his cheeks.

Stepping forward I slam my lips against his, showing him with my actions how much I love that he did this. Poppy's squeal grabs both of our attention and we pull away from each other, laughing as we turn to my daughter who's pudgy hand is batting against Penn's cheek, patting him and demanding his attention.

"Do you like the room Penn made for you?" I coo.

Poppy makes babbling noises and smiles her gummy grin that always makes my heart melt.

"You like it then?" he asks.

"I love it, Penn, it's beautiful."

We spend the next couple of hours feeding Poppy her dinner, bathing her and playing with her on the couch while we watch tv and generally just hang out. It's the first time we've done nothing together and it's kind of perfect. When Cody calls in to let us know that Chloe is here and dinner will only be about ten minutes, I glance at Poppy. "I should probably get her ready for bed."

"Keep her up while we eat, then I'll help."

"It's late."

"I know, but I swear if she gets up in the night, I'll get up with her. My family want to get to know her and I want to show you both off," Penn says, flashing that smile that I just don't seem to be able to say no to.

"Okay, fine. But this is a tonight thing, not an always thing."

"Of course," he says with a wink.

We show Chloe Penn's apartment and of course she already knows the entire Barnett clan, as well as Cora's parents and Bonnie's dad who are all also eating here tonight. Even with Huck and Cora missing, we're still fourteen for dinner and we all fit comfortably around the huge wooden table. Considering this is a blend of several families, everyone just gels like… well, like one big happy family, which I suppose it is.

Dinner is loud and messy and fun. As the only child here, everyone dotes on Poppy, taking turns to keep her on their lap when she gets fussy in her highchair. I like it more than I'm willing to admit I do. Because if I allow all the feelings of family and acceptance to settle in, I'll only be even more upset about the total lack of what I've received from my actual family.

By the time the plates are cleared and dessert has been demolished, Poppy is fast asleep, her head on Penn's shoulder. It's another one of those ovary popping moments that I keep having around this man, it'll be a miracle if I'm not pregnant at this rate.

"It suits you," Bonnie says to Penn, a soft smile on her face.

Penn glances down at Poppy, then at me, his eyes glittering with happiness and contentedness. "I know," he tells her. "I can't wait 'till this house is full of Barnett boys and girls. All our kids growing up together would be awesome."

Bonnie sighs wistfully, then turns to glance at Beau.

His eyes heat and he paces over to her, lifting her off her seat and kissing her like there isn't twelve other people, including her dad in the room.

When he speaks, I know he doesn't intend for it to be loud enough for anyone else to hear, but apparently his volume control got lost with his ability to tone down his desire for his wife in mixed company; and so I hear every word.

"Baby girl, the moment your dad leaves I'm going to strip you naked, tie you to the bed and keep you there until I put a baby in your belly. I'm telling that fucking coffee shop you quit because my dick's going to be in you twenty-four-seven until there's so much of my cum in you, you'll be pregnant for the next ten years. Once I watch you grow with my baby, I'm going to want to see it over and over and I can't wait to get started."

I feel my eyes widen at his words and watch as Bonnie gasps for breath, her mouth parting without any sounds coming out. Worried that I'll be caught listening to what should have been a private conversation, I look away, but as I do Beau catches my gaze and winks at me, before he turns to a still visibly horny Bonnie and drags her away.

"Holy fuck," I whisper.

Penn's soft chuckle comes from behind me. "Let's go say bye to Chloe."

Blinking through my revelry, I nod and let Penn guide

me over to the door, where all the parents and Chloe are saying their goodbyes. She steps toward us, separating herself from the group and presses a gentle kiss to first Poppy's cheek, then Penn's. When she reaches me, she encases me in a tight hug. "I want this for you more than you could ever know," she whispers against my ear.

"What?" I whisper back.

"A big family that loves you and Poppy, that will always be here for you. It's what your mom and dad have never been able to give you, even when you were doing everything they wanted you to. They weren't built to love the way you do, with your whole heart. I know it's a leap letting Penn in, but if it feels right, then promise me you'll try."

Tears fill my eyes at the way her voice breaks. If Chloe was my mom, my life would have been so different, but I'm so grateful for her anyway. "I'll try," I promise, looking to Penn and finding him frowning at me.

"You okay?" he mouths.

I nod, holding Chloe tighter for a minute before I pull back and surreptitiously wipe beneath my eyes.

"Goodnight, my loves," Chloe smiles, then she says goodnight to everyone else, promising to come for dinner again soon.

Penn takes my hand the moment the front door closes and leads me back to his apartment, not sparing his family any attention. The moment his door is firmly closed, he backs me up against the wood and kisses me, firm and deep. "I'll go change her diaper and put her down."

I nod, watching him go, my legs too jellified to follow after him. He comes back a few minutes later, the baby monitor in his hand and a feral look on his face.

"On your knees, Kitten, I want to feel your lips around my dick before I fuck you."

Shock at his sudden change of pace keeps me frozen to the spot, my body heating at his dirty words and forceful tone.

"Knees," he repeats, his eyes hooding as his tongue dips out and wets his lower lip. His fingers grip my chin tightly, before he releases me and puts pressure on my shoulder, encouraging me to move.

I'm not as graceful as I wish I was as I slowly drop to my knees at his feet, looking up at him from my position on the floor.

"Open your mouth."

His voice has a ragged quality that only intensifies this moment. He's as powerless against me as I am to him. The knowledge settles me and I feel my heartbeat start to slow, the bordering on painful buzz that has been zipping through my veins slowing to a hypersensitive awareness.

Parting my lips, I look up at him from beneath my lashes, basking in the power that emanates from him. His maleness is almost overwhelming, but it calls out to some primeval part of me that wants to submit to his power.

Rough fingers touch my cheek as I wait there for him on the floor at his feet. His thumb slides over my bottom lip, dipping into my mouth and rubbing over my tongue. "Suck."

I do as he says, closing my lips around him and sucking lightly. His eyes light up and he pushes his thumb further into my mouth until my lips are stretched around his hand as he moves his thumb back and forth, delving deeper with each movement.

"Good girl. Now open up."

I part my lips and he pulls his thumb free, smiling down at me predatorially.

"You'll take my dick, as much as you can. I'm going to fuck your mouth and you're going to take what I give you. When I come, I'm going to fill your throat and paint your tongue and you're going to swallow it all."

There's not a hint of playfulness left in him as he tells me in harsh, stern words exactly how he's going to use me. I should be appalled, or scared, or just down right insulted, but instead I'm hot and more turned on than I think I've ever been in my life.

Heat pools in my core with every vulgar word he says and I know my pussy is wet and dripping for him. I wouldn't consider myself particularly submissive, but the way he's towering over me, using his physical size and talking to me, I want to close my eyes and just give myself over to him. Right now he's a walking, talking wet dream bought to life, and a shudder of desire ricochets through me as he guides the broad head of his cock into my mouth.

Not taking a moment to let me get used to the sheer size of him, he shoves his dick to the back of my throat, gripping my hair and holding me in place as I gag around the invasion of his massive cock in my mouth.

"Breathe through your nose," he coaxes.

Slowly, he pulls back a little, letting me drag in air before he surges forward again, the head breaching my throat for a second then pulling back only to push forward again.

"Fuck," he rasps, his fingers gripping my hair even tighter as he starts to fuck my mouth. I wrap my lips around his girth and grip my fingers into the fabric of his jeans, holding on tight as he takes over, using me for his pleasure.

Tears fill my eyes as he steals the oxygen from my lungs with each thrust of his beer can wide dick into my mouth, but he doesn't pause, relentlessly thrusting into me. "I'm gonna come," he groans a moment before the salty liquid hits my throat.

Swallowing instinctively, I barely taste him until he pulls back and his dick twitches on my tongue, coating my mouth with his release.

His dick starts to slide from my mouth and I move to lean back, but his fingers release my hair and instead grab my chin, squeezing to hold me in place. "Stick out your tongue," he orders.

Looking up at him through watery eyes I slowly push my tongue out, knowing he can see the remnants of his release on me.

"Fuck, Kitten, I'm getting hard again just seeing my cum in your mouth. Your mouth belongs to me now, just like your wet cunt. When I need to remind you to mind me this is how I'll do it, using your mouth and coating your sharp tongue with me."

I blink up at him, shocked by the heat and possession in his words.

"Swallow, then come sit on my face, I want to see how turned on you are from being used."

SEVENTEEN

PENN

Her pupils dilate and her chest heaves as she slowly swallows, then takes the hand I'm holding out for her and carefully rises to her feet. Lulu is everything I've ever fucking wanted in a woman. Her naturally sexually submissive nature collides with her assertive kickass personality, blending to create this amazing mix of sweet and salty.

In day-to-day life I know she'll keep me on my toes, making me work for every concession to my caveman wants and needs. But the moment we're alone she becomes the perfect little doll, built for my pleasure, my hands, my desires. Sliding down onto the couch I undress her slowly, pulling her sticky wet panties down last, lifting my gaze and showing her how pleased I am with the mess she's made of her underwear.

"Wet, sticky and gushing with need. Your little kitty likes it when I fuck your face doesn't it?" Groaning, she nods, her teeth biting down on her lower lip. "Pull your lips apart, put yourself on display for me," I taunt.

She barely pauses before her hands dip between her thighs and she parts her folds, showing me her cunt and all the cream she's coated in.

"Perfect," I whisper, lying back and crooking a finger, beckoning her toward me. "Sit on my face. I want to eat you, before I bend you over and fuck you."

Smiling dazedly, she steps forward and climbs onto the couch, hovering above me, her legs spread on either side of my face. I wrap my palms around her thighs and force her down, licking at her pussy from her slit to her clit as a low moan fills the air. I eat her with gusto, feasting on her cunt as she grinds against my tongue, animalistic groans falling from her parted lips as I push two then three fingers into her, stretching her while I torture her clit with my tongue.

"Oh god, oh fuck, so good, so good," she chants, her full tits bouncing as she rides my face.

Finding her g-spot I curl my fingers, rubbing at the spot inside of her that I know will have her screaming out my name in just a matter of moments. Her cunt tightens, she's close, so I use my free hand to part her ass cheeks, pushing a finger against her tight ring of muscle and slipping into her ass as her orgasm splinters and she writhes above me.

I fuck her cunt and ass with my fingers as she rides out her orgasm, her eyes squeezed tightly shut, arousal dripping from her and coating my face. I fucking love it, love that her pussy is full, her ass stretched around my finger; that she's completely out of control in this moment.

My dick needs to be inside of her, right fucking now. Lifting her off my face, she slumps into the couch cushions but I don't ask her if she's okay, I just jump up, pick her up and position her over the arm of the couch. Kicking her legs apart, I grab her hips, tilt her body forward and slam my dick into her. Even though I've stretched her out with my fingers I struggle to get my cock inside until she pushes back onto me, helping me fill her.

"Harder, fuck, harder," she cries, her fingers tightening around the couch as she arches her back and I push another inch of my length into her.

"That's it, take it, your cunt is stretched so full I could watch my dick slide in and out of you all fucking day."

Lulu lets out a pained noise right before her pussy clamps down on me and she whines, shuddering beneath me as she comes around my dick.

"Fuck, Kitten, you're strangling my cock."

She cries out again, slapping her hand over her mouth to stifle the sounds that are falling from her lips as I slam into her, fucking her harder than I should, as I fill her over and over again.

"Oh god, I'm going to come again," she mewls, the words muffled from where she's buried her face against the couch.

"Yes, come on my dick," I urge, trying to hold back my own release until she's found hers. The moment her pussy clamps down on me I let go, slamming into her once more and filling her with my cum. My hips are still twitching when I slump over her back, pressing a kiss to her shoulder. "Fuck, Kitten, your cunt is perfect."

Her giggle is raspy and adorable. "I've had a baby, Penn, my pussy is most definitely not perfect, you just have a big dick."

"Nope," I smile, "your pussy is a fucking wonderland."

I don't want to, but I pull out of her heat, keeping her bent over with my palm on her back as I watch my cum drip from her slit. Biting my lip, I barely manage to hold in a growl of male pride. My woman's cunt, full of my cum. I don't know why it turns me on so much to know I've marked her in the most basic way, but it really does.

"Come on, let's go to bed," I say, running my hand down the length of her spine, parting her ass cheeks and taking a minute to enjoy the view before I step back and help her up. Her eyes are wide, her pupils blown, a soft satisfied smile gracing her full pouty lips.

"My legs are shaking," she giggles.

"Come here then," I say, scooping her off her feet and into my arms. Holding her like this, having her here feels so fucking right that I wonder what magic or voodoo or fate brought her to me. Whatever it was, I'm more grateful than I've ever been in my whole god damn life.

"I need to clean up, your cum is dripping down my legs."

"No Kitten, I want you to smell like me all night."

"That's kind of disgusting," she says, her lips curling.

Chuckling, I lower her onto the bed, following her down and claiming her lips with mine. "There's nothing disgusting about my cum being in you."

"Yeah, but it's not staying in me, it's dripping down my ass, that's the disgusting bit."

My dick wants to be inside her again, but I've already taken her hard once, if I try to go for round two right now, she'll be sore and off-limits tomorrow. Rolling to the side, I band my arm around her waist and pull her ass into me, her back pressed to my chest.

"I need to check on Poppy."

"Fine," I say dramatically, releasing her with a huff and rolling onto to my back, my hard dick slapping against my stomach.

Shaking her head, she climbs up off the bed and pads naked over to Poppy's crib, leaning over and touching the beautiful baby before she straightens. When she turns back toward me, I rake my eyes over her beautiful body. Her tits are full and heavy, her nipples a dark pink against her pale skin. Her hips are wide, her ass is full, she's stunning.

I wait for her to come back to me, but instead she pauses, glancing down and grimacing. "Eww, nope I can't sleep with this oozing out of me."

"Kitten," I warn.

Her eyes flash with amusement, then she darts toward the bathroom. Jumping from the bed, I catch her in two steps, grab her around the waist and spin her around, putting my back to the bathroom door. "Nope, not happening."

"Penn," she whines

"Not happening." Carrying her to the bed I throw her down and immediately follow after her, capturing her in my arms and holding her close while I rub my dick against her thigh. "Stay still or you're gonna be riding my dick again."

Stilling for a moment I wait for her to tell me she's sore, or that she's done for the day, instead her hands rub across my chest. "Wow, more sex." She laughs. "That sounds just awful."

Rolling her beneath me, I bury my face into her neck and lose myself to her, basking in how fucking perfect she is for me.

When I wake up the next morning I'm shocked to find that Poppy is still asleep, her tiny arms thrown above her head, her pacifier resting beside her, her mouth open. She's the most beautiful baby and despite her DNA, all I can see is Lulu when I look at her. My eyes move to the woman next to me, her hair is a rat's nest of tangles, spread out across the pillow. Just like her daughter, her mouth is open, her lips parted. The comforter has slipped down in the night and her naked body is on display for me. I fight the urge to part her legs and lose myself in her. My need for her is almost overwhelming, but the desire to just enjoy being here in the moment wins out and I settle back down, pulling her closer as an unexpected contentment settles over me.

Poppy's giggles pull me from sleep and a smile spreads across my face as Lulu wiggles out of my arms, climbs out of bed and lifts Poppy out of her crib.

"Come get back into bed," I call.

"We need to get up, my alarm went off ten minutes ago," she replies, glancing at me over her shoulder.

"Five minutes, then I'll go get the princess's breakfast while you get dressed," I say, picking up a pair of shorts from the floor and pulling them on.

With a soft sigh she turns and climbs back onto the bed, sitting Poppy against the pillow between us.

"Morning Princess," I coo.

Poppy wiggles excitedly, launching herself at me. I reach out and catch her, pulling her into me and blowing raspberries against her cheek as she giggles and squeaks excitedly. The mattress dips as Lulu climbs back into bed and my chest swells with happiness. This is it, this is the moment when I literally have everything I ever wanted. My woman, my princess and maybe another baby girl or boy growing inside of Lulu.

I want to breed her, I want to see my ring on her finger, I want to change both her and Poppy's surname to mine. I want to claim them as Barnetts and now that I've experienced this moment of perfection, I know there's no way I'll ever give them up.

Reluctantly climbing out of bed, I take Poppy through to the main house while Lulu showers.

"Cora, Huck and Maverick are coming back some time this morning. Apparently the nurses tried to get Huck to go home, but he refused. After he tried to sleep in the waiting room, they brought a cot into Cora's room and let him sleep in there," Cody says with a laugh, leaning down and kissing Poppy on the cheek.

"No way I'd have left either," I tell him, strapping

Poppy into her highchair.

"French toast, bacon and strawberries on the counter," Cody announces.

"Thanks, I'll grab something once I've fed Poppy."

"I can feed her, I already ate. Shall I make her the oatmeal you got for her? I picked up some yoghurt I found in the store that says it's good for babies too."

"You sure?"

"Of course, she's my niece and this place is going to be overrun with kids pretty soon, we all need to learn how to do this shit," he says with a laugh. "Teddy's taking bets on when Bonnie and Alice will be pregnant, I guess we need to add Lulu to it too."

"I'd put twenty on all three of them being pregnant in the next six months," I say with a smirk. In the kitchen I pour myself a cup of coffee, make Poppy's oatmeal and fill the sippy cup we bought her up with formula. Making up two plates, I cover Lulu's and put it in the oven to keep warm. I know she could have made her own, but the need to take care of her, to have her rely on me is so strong I can't resist. Taking my plate to the table I sit down next to Poppy and eat while my brother tries to figure out how to get food into a six-month-old. One by one the rest of my family emerges, all except for Bonnie and Beau who probably left for work hours ago. Finally Lulu appears, freshly showered and wearing a tight knee length skirt and a fitted pale pink blouse. All she needs is a pair of black glasses and she'd be the ultimate naughty secretary fantasy bought to life. Jealousy almost consumes me. There's nothing wrong with her outfit, it's not short or risqué, it's all her. She makes everything sexy and her skirt accentuates her ass in a way that makes me want to spank it, then fuck it, and I can't help but imagine everyone else that sees her today will feel the same.

"Kitten," I groan, jumping up from my seat and closing the distance between us.

"What?" she asks distractedly.

"You look fucking edible in this skirt."

"It's a plain black pencil skirt, Penn." Her brows are furrowed in a way that tells me she has no idea what she looks like and I love it. The thought of her dressing to be sexy for anyone other than me makes my inner caveman roar to life, swinging his club and beating his chest with the need to drag her back to my cave and keep her all to myself.

Palming her ass, I pull her against me, letting her feel how hard my dick is for her. "Kitten, my cock needs back inside your tight, wet—"

"Oh my goodness, you don't need to feed her, I can do that," Lulu exclaims, pushing me away as she rushes to the table.

"No, you eat, I'm fine, although I can't really blame

the little princess for not wanting to eat this, it tastes like lumpy nothing," Cody cringes, lifting the plastic spoon from the bowl and letting the beige mush fall from it.

"I..." she pauses, obviously unsure what to say or do. "Are you sure, I thought Penn was going to." Her eyes move to me and she narrows them. "He said he was going to feed Poppy, else I could have just kept her in her crib until I was out of the shower."

"I asked if I could do it," Cody says, waving away her concern as he makes choo choo noises, swooping the spoon down into Poppy's mouth. "This little one is my very first niece, she needs to get to know her favorite uncle," he says, smiling down at my princess like she hung the moon.

Lulu freezes, her arms stopping in mid-air, her eyes going wide, then a little watery. Grateful that Cody is oblivious, his attention on Poppy, I wrap my arms around Lulu and turn her to face me, lowering my lips to her ear.

"You're mine, she's mine. This is my family, and now they're your family too." I expect her to fight me, to deny my words, instead she sags against my chest and I pretend not to notice the tears that hit my skin.

EIGHTEEN

LULU

I can only describe the next few weeks as perfect. Janet is still sending me useless time wasting tasks, but I find I don't care, because my day revolves around Penn. He drops me off outside the office every morning, kissing me senseless before he leaves with a promise to see me at lunch. When one o'clock rolls around he's waiting for me in reception, a heat-filled smile etched across his lips the moment he sees me.

Some days we eat alone, others with one or more of his brothers, some days he drags me to the apartment over the garage and fucks me until my pussy is sore from his dick and my throat from screaming his name.

After work he collects me and drives me to Chloe's to collect Poppy. Despite what he said, we've spent every night at his place and even though I know I shouldn't, I've stopped arguing with him about it. Chloe's joined us for dinner three times in the last week, and each time I swear she looks happier and happier to see me and Poppy being embraced by Penn's crazy family.

Huck, Cora and baby Maverick ended up staying in the hospital for an extra night, but now they're home and the entire Barnett household is in a state of baby fever. With a shock of red hair just like his mama, Maverick is the mirror image of his dad in every other respect and is the most beautiful baby.

Despite my protest about it being a family thing, Penn insisted that Poppy and I be there to greet them when they came home, and instead of feeling like outsiders, it only reinforced how Penn's family have truly embraced Poppy and I as one of them. It was weird and wonderful all at the same time.

Maverick's Aunts and Uncles all fell in love the moment they set eyes on him and I wouldn't be at all surprised to find he'll be gaining some cousins in the next year. I swear I actually heard Beau growl, right before he lifted Bonnie clean off her feet and carried her back to their apartment.

Being with Penn is easy, so easy that I'm waiting for the other shoe to drop. After the last year and a half I deserve easy, but I can't help being suspicious and holding myself back. I like Penn a lot, probably more than I should after only a couple of weeks. Before I became jaded by men and life I always believed in love and happily ever after, only now it seems like I might be getting mine, I can't help but hold something back from fully committing.

"Kitten, can we move the rest of yours and Poppy's stuff in this weekend? I fucking hate you living out of a suitcase, you're not going anywhere so you might as well hang your shit up in the closet," Penn growls, putting the baby monitor onto the docking station on the bedside table and glaring at me from across the bed.

"Poppy and I don't live here."

"The fact that our princess is asleep in *her* crib in *her* room, kinda disproves that," he smirks.

Rolling my eyes, I turn my back on him, crossing the room to where the bag full of my clothes is perched on the armchair.

"I know you didn't just roll your eyes and turn your back on me," he growls, a moment before his arm bands around my waist, spinning me around as his hand grips my throat, tipping my head back and forcing me to look up at him.

"Penn—"

"No," he interrupts, spanning his palm over my stomach. "You're my woman and this is your home. That baby girl down the hall is mine too, I'm her daddy and the daddy to the baby that's growing in your belly right now. You're mine and I don't fucking appreciate you dismissing that like you just did."

"I'm not pregnant," I hiss, trying to force some conviction into my words, even though I'm lying to myself. We haven't been careful, not once since we started having sex and there's every chance I might be pregnant right now. The reality of my own stupidity hits me like a mac truck. I've been avoiding the fact that all the cum Penn's emptied into me might have taken root and I hate that he's bringing it up, when I've been studiously ignoring it up until now.

"Kitten, I've been fucking you raw every day since we met. I've pumped so much of my cum into your cunt that it'll be a fucking miracle if you're not pregnant with my kid right now." His voice is smug, his smile victorious.

"You want me to be pregnant?" I gasp.

"Hell yes I do. I want to watch your belly swell as it grows with our baby, I can't fucking wait."

"That's fucked up," I snarl.

Before I even realize what's happening, he spins me around, lifts me off the ground and dumps me unceremoniously over the edge of the bed, my toes barely scraping the floor. Pushing up with my arms, I try to move, but he presses his massive hand to the center of my back, holding me in place.

"There's nothing fucked up about me claiming what's mine," he drawls as his fingers work at the button of my jeans, peeling my pants over my ass until they're halfway down my thighs.

"Penn."

"Shut up, Lulu. The only words I want to hear you say right now, are you begging for my cock."

I feel the draft of cool air as he yanks my panties down, leaving me bare to him, my pussy dampening excitedly. Despite my protests, I'm more than aware of how he owns my body. My core clenches just at the thought of him touching me and I know my arousal will be dripping down my thighs by the time he touches between my legs.

"I own this cunt," he taunts, lifting his hand from my back, knowing I won't move now he's so close to touching me.

"Penn," I rasp, desperation edging into my voice.

"Quiet."

Biting my lip I wait, hanging over the bed, my ass and pussy naked and on display for him. I moan loudly when his fingers part my folds and he dips one inside of me. "Your cunt's dripping for me, it wants my cock, it wants to be filled with my cum. Do you know why, Kitten? It's because it belongs to me. No one else will ever touch it. No one else will ever push their fingers into your heat, run their tongue along your folds, or fill you with their hard cocks. No one but me ever again, and your cunt knows that, it's greedy for me, isn't it?"

Nodding, I turn my face to look at him, needing him to touch me, to stop torturing me. "Please."

"Please what?" he taunts.

Penn is normally a generous lover, he enjoys giving me pleasure, but he's also formidable and dominant in a way I've only ever fantasized about in the past. He pushes me past the point of ecstasy into a place where I'm only sensation, and it's glorious, but it's always on his terms and today won't be any different.

"Please touch me," I beg, knowing he won't give in to my defiance, only my submission.

"Here," he coos, running the tips of his fingers over the curve of my ass cheek.

"No." I shake my head.

Leaning over me he presses a kiss to my butt, glancing up at me with heat filled eyes a moment before he sinks his teeth into my skin and bites down on the globe of my ass.

Shrieking in shock and pain I try to move, but he stops me, spanking me hard right over the spot where he just bit, adding to the pain and making me cry out.

"Still."

I freeze, my body obeying him before my mind can

catch up.

His palm soothes the spot he just struck, his fingers dancing over the bite mark reverently. "I fucking love seeing my mark on you," he chuckles.

"You're an asshole."

"I like your asshole." Parting my cheeks, he runs his thumb over my tight ring of muscle and I instantly tense. "I can't wait to watch this stretch around my dick."

"Not happening," I growl, pulling my arm from beneath me to try to push him away.

Grabbing my wrist he pins it back to the mattress as he presses his body over my back, his lips finding my neck. "Oh it's happening, Kitten. I'm going to stretch you out, then my dick is going in your ass and you're going to love it. I can't wait to hear you begging me to fuck your ass harder, to fill it with my cum."

I shudder under the assault of his words. I shouldn't like it, I shouldn't react to his dirty promises, but I can't help it because my body isn't my own when he behaves like this.

"First my fingers are going to slide into your pussy, one, then two, then three and I'm going to make you ride them, to get yourself off on my hand. Then once you come and soak me with your cream, I'm going to flick your little clit with my tongue until you're screaming and begging me to let you orgasm. But I won't. Instead, I'll use all your cream to coat your ass. I'll fill you up until your tight hole is stretched. I might even get a plug so I can keep you open for me while I fill your cunt with my cock, plunging into you until your juices are coating us both. Then I'll come inside of you, painting you from the inside out with my cum. When you're dripping, your folds all puffy and swollen, I'll slide my dick that's still soaked with a mixture of my cum and yours into your tight ass. It'll hurt, but you'll take it all just like your cunt did, begging me to own you and I will. I'll take your ass slow, grinding you on and off my cock, watching your hole stretch around my girth until you're so blind with want you'll beg me to just take you, to use you. Only then will I slam into you and fill your ass with my release. After I'm done and you've come so many times you can barely breathe, I'll lay you out over my lap and watch as my seed drips from both your holes."

Panting, I squirm beneath him, aware of how turned on his dirty words are making me.

"I own you, Lulu, I have since the moment I laid my eyes on you and I will for the rest of both of our lives. I'll never let you go, never let you leave me, never let you run. We're end game, Kitten. Marriage, babies, happily ever after. Tomorrow, we go get the rest of yours and Poppy's stuff. In a week you're gonna pee on a stick and the moment the line turns blue we're getting married and I'm adopting Poppy. You can fight it all you want, but it's happening."

I open my mouth to argue, to tell him off for this bullshit, alpha male crap he keeps pulling with me, but then the head of his dick is pressing against my pussy and before I can utter a word, he's filling me, and every thought but harder and more and please flies from my head.

My body is deliciously sore the next morning when the sound of Poppy's cooing filters through the baby monitor. She started sleeping in the beautiful princess room Penn and his brothers made for her three nights ago, because no matter how much I argue that we don't live here, we're making this place our home despite my reservations.

"I'll get her," Penn says, sliding his hand from where he'd been cupping my mound and climbing out of bed, pulling on some shorts before he pads out the door. I hear him as he enters her room, his voice lowering and quietening as he speaks to her.

"Good morning, Princess, did you have a good sleep?"

There's cooing and laughing, then his voice fills the silence. "I told your mama I'm your daddy last night and I am, because you're my little girl in every way that matters." He pauses for a second then speaks again. "Poppy Barnett sounds almost as good as Lulu Barnett. My Barnett girls, I'm gonna love you and protect you both, I don't want either of you to know even a day of sadness, only happiness from here on out, you hear me, Princess? I know you can't speak yet, but if you could put in a good word with your mama, I'd appreciate it."

My heart thuds loudly in my chest as I listen to him talking to her. Men have made me promises in the past but Penn is the first one who truly means everything he says. I'm his, but so is my daughter and as he appears in the doorway, Poppy nestled against his chest, I realize that there's no point in fighting this anymore, because I really am his and he's mine too.

Watching him with soft eyes I kneel up on the bed, shuffling to the edge as he watches me warily. "You okay?"

"More than okay," I answer, wrapping my arms around his neck and kissing him.

Every meal in the Barnett household is a family affair and breakfast today is no exception. Penn insists that I don't need to get dressed, so I throw on a pair of shorts and a baggy t-shirt and follow him barefoot out into the main house. No matter how many times I see it, the hustle and bustle of the huge family always shocks me. When I lived with my parents, I was cared for by housekeepers or nannies, so weekend breakfasts were just like any other day with me eating alone.

In the Barnett home, weekends are packed with loud, raucous togetherness. Teddy scoops Poppy from my arms the moment he spots us, throwing her into the air and making her giggle loudly as he catches her, then brings her close to blow a raspberry on her cheek. "Good morning, little Miss Poppy, Uncle Teddy made you some eggs and some pancake fingers for you to try." His face lifts to me and he smiles. "I found a website about baby led weaning and there was a recipe for pancakes that said they were suitable for babies her age. Is that okay?"

Touched by his thoughtfulness I nod and he grins, turning and carrying Poppy to her high chair, talking away at her as he goes. When he moves to sit in front of her, he's unceremoniously shoved out of the way as Granger takes his seat and immediately coos at my daughter, chatting nonsense to her as he holds up a piece of pancake for her to try.

Penn kisses me quickly before steering me toward the seat next to Poppy. "Sit, Kitten, I'll get you some breakfast."

Doing as I'm told, I sink down next to Poppy and just take in the scene all around me. Bonnie is sitting in Beau's lap, their heads close together as they alternate between talking and kissing. Bay is beside them, his attention on his cell, a coffee in front of him as he absentmindedly forks food into his mouth. Alice is beside Granger on the other side of the table. I don't know her that well, but from the few times I've spoken to her, she seems shy and quiet but sweet. Right now she's watching her husband feed my daughter, a look of longing flashing in her eyes as she places a hand unconsciously on her stomach. If I had to guess I'd say she's either already pregnant or hoping she is.

Cora is a few seats down from me, Maverick held to her chest as she breastfeeds him, a smitten Huck standing behind her, watching them both with such intense love that I can feel it from here. I wonder if Penn would look at me like that if I was the one nursing a baby? Something tells me he would, that he'd stifle the air with his proprietary gaze. Cody is the only Barnett missing, and I wonder where he is. Perhaps he has a girlfriend somewhere, maybe he's the only one who doesn't buy into the whole instalove fantasy the other brothers all seem to believe in?

"Here you go, baby," Penn says, pushing a plate of food in front of me as he takes the seat at my side.

"Thanks. I really should go home today; I need to do laundry and spend some time with Chloe."

"This is your and Poppy's home, but we need to go to Chloe's anyway to get the rest of your stuff. You can visit with her while we load Beau's truck."

"Penn—" I start.

Without saying a word, he narrows his eyes and silently warns me not to argue with him. I narrow my eyes right back, but apparently I lack the menace and warning he has, because instead of minding me, he smirks, reaches out and grips my thigh tightly with his fingers. Leaning down, he presses his lips against my ear and whispers. "Behave, Kitten, or I'll bend you over this table and spank your ass right here in front of our family. I promise you they won't blink an eye at me taking you in hand."

I gasp, shocked, but all he does is chuckle lightly and slide his fingers a little further up my leg.

"Don't make me remind you who's in control, baby, because we already both know it's me. We talked about this last night and you're making it official and moving in with me. Today. It's happening, but if you need me to convince you again, I'm happy to drag you back off to our place to help you agree."

Heat starts at my toes and surges upwards through every nerve, cell and vein. His words are literally burning me up from the inside out and I can't help but love it. His voice, his tone, the single touch of his hand on my thigh, all of it flips that truly female switch inside of me that begs me to submit to my man. *My* man. Not just any guy who's trying to control me because we're having sex, but *my man*. Penn, who has owned me since the first moment we laid eyes on one another.

"Maybe I should be the one reminding you," I whisper back.

"What do I need to be reminded of?" he drawls silkily.

"That you're just as much mine as I'm yours."

His chuckle is low and gravelly. "I've never forgotten that, Kitten, you own my ass and I fucking love it." Nipping playfully at my earlobe, he presses his lips against my cheek and pulls back, lifting his hand from my thigh and draping it along the back of my chair. "Eat up, those boxes aren't gonna pack themselves."

Hours later, all of mine and Poppy's stuff has been loaded into the back of Beau's truck and taken back to the Barnett house, and both Penn and Chloe are looking at me with smug grins. I both hate and love how much they seem to think it's wonderful that I'm moving out. Penn because it means he's getting his way, and Chloe because she truly thinks that Penn is both mine and Poppy's happy ever after.

Sighing happily, I flop back into the couch cushions and glance around at the living room. It doesn't look that different, because all of the stuff I brought with me from Chicago is still here. Chloe will still be caring for Poppy while I'm at work, so it made sense to leave the playpen and all of the toys here. Also Penn insisted on buying so much stuff for her, that we'd just be doubling up if we took any of this back to his place. Despite our obvious presence in the room, there's a sense of emptiness. Mine and Poppy's clothes are no longer in the closet, all of my keepsakes and mementoes have been packed in boxes and all of a sudden, the finality of moving out hits me.

I came to Rockhead Point to find a home with people who love and care for me and my daughter, and Chloe opened her life up to us with wide, loving arms. She gave me the unconditional love you expect from your parents, when my biological family condemned me for the choices I made. I wish she was my real mother, and once again I'm envious that Roxanne and James have such an amazing woman as their role model.

"You happy?" she asks as she plops down onto the couch next to me and hands me a glass of wine.

I glance to where Penn is sitting playing with Poppy and exhale dreamily. "It's stupid, isn't it?"

"Being happy is never stupid."

"I'm rushing into this. If it were anyone but him, there's no way I'd let him around my daughter or be moving into his home, but…" I trail off, trying to find the words to explain the way being consumed by him feels.

"I didn't know Penn's daddy that well, he died when the boys were all still in school, but he had this magnetism to him. He was a looker, even though he was a lot older than me, but it was more than that, he had a forcefulness to him. Penn has that too, like it's just impossible to deny him anything that he wants. Its more than just charm, although he has plenty of that too," she smiles. "Hannigan Barnett was a good man, and so are his sons. But I'm going to be honest with you, if it was any other man who'd turned your head and you were talking about moving you and Poppy in with him, I'd be doing everything I could to stop it. But with Penn, he looks at you the exact same way his daddy looked at his mama, like you're the single ray of sunlight at the dead of midnight. That man loves you and he loves Poppy, so go, be happy, because you both deserve it."

Until right now I didn't realize how much I needed her approval, her blessing. Chloe might not be my biological mother, but she's my mom in every way that truly counts. Knowing she thinks I'm doing the right thing reaffirms what I know deep inside. That I'm in love with Penn. It's too fast and too much and it's scary as hell, but I do. I love him and I'm pretty sure he loves me too.

NINETEEN

PENN

Lulu knows she's doing the right thing moving in with me, but she's still battling with how fast things are moving between us. In her head, love and commitment should take a certain amount of time and it's tough for her to accept that what we have is different. We didn't meet in a bar and exchange cell numbers, we're not dating. The intense need and want and love that flared between us the moment we met is so much more than anything either of us has ever experienced before.

I love her.

But I haven't told her yet, or at least not in so many words. As much as I'm sure she's feeling it too, she's not ready for me to confess my feelings, or admit her own, and even though I'll happily push her on some things, getting her to tell me how she feels isn't something I want to fuck her into admitting.

But I do, I love her, I love Poppy too. My life irrevocably changed in an instant and I went from single and fucking unimportant women to scratch an itch; to knowing that Lulu and Poppy are my future, my everything. I'm ready for it. I'm ready to really start my life with my woman and my daughter.

Glancing at the two women on the couch, I watch as whatever Chloe says to Lulu makes a soft smile spread across her lips. It doesn't matter what they're talking about, if it makes Lulu smile then it's my favorite topic in the world. All I want for my girls is for them to be happy, to smile, to be okay, and if getting her godmother's approval does that for Lulu then I'm down for them talking about me even though I'm in the room.

Poppy gurgles, pulling my attention back to her, just as the door flies open and a scowling Roxanne bursts into the house.

"For fuck's sake, Mom, I can't even get on the driveway because that bitch's car is blocking it," Roxy cries, her puffed up lips drooping at the corners as she snarls bitterly.

"Roxanne," Chloe snaps.

"I'm not apologizing. This isn't her home, but her and her brat are taking over the place."

"Nice to see you too, Roxanne," Lulu says coolly.

"God you're such an uppity cunt, why are you even here? You decided to have the brat when you should have just gotten rid, now you expect my mom to look after her and let you live here rent free." Roxy glares daggers at Lulu, her eyes raking over my woman and dismissing her with a disgusted sneer. Shaking her head she turns to glance around the room, when her gaze lands on me the hatred melts from her face, replaced with a predatory gleam that she tries to hide with a wide smile.

"Penn," she shouts gleefully. "You're here. Oh, baby, I promise I was going to tell you, I was just mad at you."

Pushing up to my feet I narrow my eyes at Roxy, before cautiously glancing to Lulu. I still haven't told her that Roxy and I used to fuck. It's not exactly a conversation I was looking forward to having, but now that she's here I wish I had, because my woman is going to be so pissed if she hears it from Roxy.

"This is perfect, I knew you'd come back to me and just in time too," Roxy cries, rushing over to me and throwing her arms around my neck.

I freeze the moment she touches me, hating the way it feels to have her pressed against me. When I feel it, my eyes widen with shock as I carefully peel her arms from me and urge her backwards.

"Did you feel it?" she asks, biting her lip and lifting her shoulders, grinning at me excitedly.

"What's going on?" Lulu asks.

I turn and look at her, both Lulu and Chloe are standing up now, watching Roxy and I.

"Roxanne?" Chloe says slowly, her eyes wide, her face pale.

"Mom, I know I should have told you, but..." Roxy pauses for a second, then she unzips her jacket, pulling the fabric to the side and revealing her stomach and the round baby bump that was hidden inside.

"Oh my god," Chloe cries.

"Crazy, right!" Roxy gushes as she steps to my side and curls her fingers around my arm. "Penn and I are going to have a baby."

TWENTY

LULU

"Penn and I are going to have a baby."

I know I heard the words right, but my mind is struggling to process them.

"Penn and I are going to have a baby."

No. No, that doesn't make any sense. Roxanne and Penn. Roxanne and Penn?

He never told me he was in a relationship with the girl who is basically my cousin. She hasn't been here and she even told Chloe she was getting married to that guy who was in jail.

No, this must be wrong.

But she's there, next to him, touching him and she's

pregnant. Her bump doesn't look that big, but she's super skinny, so maybe she's just one of those lucky women who have tiny beach ball bumps. Not like me, I was huge.

Penn is having a baby with Roxanne.

My fingers reach out and grab hold of the couch, because suddenly my legs feel weak. Today I moved in with the guy who is having a baby with my pseudo cousin. Nausea rushes up my throat and I lift my hand to cover my mouth. Penn and I haven't been careful, he refused to wear a condom and because I was so caught up in him and this stupid love at first sight bullshit I just went along with it.

Oh my god, I've been having unprotected sex with him and I never even asked him if he was clean. Obviously the very pregnant woman whose rubbing all over my man is proof that Penn isn't very good at following the rules of safe sex. How many other women has he slept with? Could he have given me some nasty STI as well as the baby that could possibly be growing in my uterus right now.

Penn, Roxanne and Chloe are all speaking but I can't hear what's being said, because my thoughts are too loud. If I'm pregnant then my baby will share a daddy with Roxanne's baby. They'll be born in the same year, probably be in the same class at school.

Oh my god, I'll be the slut who slept with Penn while

his girlfriend was pregnant.

Suddenly the urge to run, to take Poppy and get the hell out of this house is all I can think of, so I move to where Poppy is sitting on the floor, pick her up, grab her change bag that's beside the couch and start to load her into her baby carrier.

I'm vaguely aware of the room going quiet, but I don't look up, I can't look at him or her, or her stomach right now. All I want to do is get out of here and away from them and this fucked up situation.

"Lulu."

Penn's behind me, his hands on my waist, his lips at my ear. "Let me do that, your hands are shaking."

"I'm fine," I say so quietly I can barely hear myself.

"No, you're not, I need to explain."

"I don't need to hear anything. She's pregnant with your kid. Which is pretty fucking funny because I think if you'd been in a relationship with my cousin, I'd have thought that might be something you mention."

"I'm sorry, I planned to tell you, but it's not exactly something that rolls off the tongue. Kitten, please look at me, I don't know who's that kid is, but I promise it's not mine."

"Are you fucking with me?" Roxanne shrieks. "This is your baby, Penn, we're in a relationship, we love one another and now we're having a family. Lulu, you need to back off, bitch, he's mine."

Penn's whole body tenses behind me and slowly his hold on me loosens. "Roxy, we had a friends with benefits thing for a little over a month and it ended a long time ago. That baby isn't mine."

"I'm seven months pregnant, Penn. Remember that night you were at the warehouse for Beau's bachelor party? You were steaming drunk and you dragged me into the bathroom stall." Her brows arch and she points down at her stomach. "Surprise."

Looking over my shoulder at Penn, I'm surprised to find him smirking. "Sorry honey, try again. Cody caught you trying to drag my drunk ass off and he told you to fuck off. That baby's not mine."

Roxanne shouts and Penn shouts back, while Chloe just stands stoically, shock etched across her face as she stares at her daughter's stomach. While they're all distracted, I grab my purse and Poppy's change bag, then quietly carry my daughter to the door and leave.

TWENTY-ONE

PENN

"That is not my kid, Roxanne," I snarl, shaking my head angrily.

"Yes, it is. Why are you lying, Penn?" Fake tears roll down her cheeks as she deliberately places her hands on her stomach, cradling her bump as she looks at me.

Closing my eyes, I will her to go away, to take her lies and her fucking pregnant belly and go ruin someone else's day. I saw the look of betrayal in Lulu's eyes, but I can fix this if I can get Roxy to admit she's talking shit, because we both know I haven't fucked her in over a year.

I turn to speak to Lulu, but she's gone and so is Poppy and her seat. "Fuck," I hiss, immediately turning my back on Roxy and heading for the front door.

"Where are you going?" she demands.

"To find my fucking woman and sort out this shit show you just created with all your bullshit and lies. That baby's not mine, we both know that."

"Penn, why are you saying all these awful things to me? We can be together now, we can be a family. I love you." Her voice is pleading, desperate, and if I wasn't so fucking furious I might feel sorry for her.

Stepping closer to her again, I reach out and take one of her hands in mine. "Roxy, honey, you need to get some help. I don't have any clue who your baby's daddy is, but we both know it isn't me. You don't love me and I've never loved you, we fucked a handful of times, that's all. Now it's time to get some self-respect and stop lying."

Snatching her hand away she straightens and places one hand on her belly. "This baby is yours, and you need to do your duty as a man and look after me and your child."

Shaking my head I sigh, glancing at Chloe before I turn my attention back to Roxy. "If this is the way you want to play it, then fine. I'll arrange for a DNA test, I'm pretty sure they can do them on unborn babies now."

"No," she cries.

"If this kid is mine, then I want to know. I'll schedule a test for as soon as possible."

"This is your child, Penn, you need to do the right thing, we need to get married."

I laugh, I can't fucking help it. "Roxanne, I don't know what kind of scam you think you're pulling here, but it isn't going to work. If by some fucking miracle that kid is mine, then I'll be a great fucking dad, I'll take care of my child, but you will never be a part of the equation. I'm in love with Lulu and if she won't forgive me for this, I'll be alone, because nothing and no one will ever be able to replace her."

"Her. You won't accept your child or me because of that… that fat bitch," Roxanne snarls, her teeth gnashing together as she speaks.

"Roxanne," Chloe admonishes.

"She's mine, Roxanne, so I suggest you keep your mouth shut."

"That fucking bitch, she strolls in here thinking she can steal my home, my mom and now you. I'll kill her, I hate her, she's always been jealous of me and now she's trying to take my life."

"Oh, for goodness sake, Roxanne, be quiet," Chloe snaps. "Lulu is family and lord knows she's tried to be friends with you. It's you who has always been jealous and I've never understood why. But this is enough now, it's time to grow up and stop behaving like a spoiled brat."

"Mom."

Roxanne's gasp of shock is almost enough to cause a smile, but then I remember that Lulu is gone. She's angry and upset and hurt and it's my fault. "Where would she go?" I ask Chloe.

"She doesn't really know anyone in town but you and your family, maybe back to Chicago?"

"That's a twenty-hour drive, she wouldn't do that, would she?" Panic starts to claw its way up my throat. She's upset, with Poppy in the car, and it's already evening. She'll have to drive an hour of country roads before she even hits the highway.

Grabbing my cell from my pocket I dial her number, but it rings three times before it goes to voicemail. "I have to find her," I say.

"What about me?" Roxanne shouts, actually stamping her foot.

"What about you?" I sneer. "I'll find a doctor in the morning to do a DNA test, and I'll send you the details."

"That's it, that's how you want to treat the mother of your child?"

"That's not my kid," I roar.

"Penn, you need to calm down," Chloe says, placing a hand on my arm and pulling me backward a few paces.

"How can I calm down when she's gone? I don't know where she is, Chloe." All of my anger drains in an instant and is replaced with an all-consuming fear. Chicago is a big city, it's hours away from here and she could be on her way there right now. I don't know her family, I don't know where they live or if she would even go to them.

Right now, all I know is that she's angry and upset and I need to be there for her, to take care of her and Poppy. I should be the one she turns to when she's feeling like this, not the person who caused all the anguish.

"Will you call me if she gets in touch?" I beg.

"Of course," Chloe nods.

Spinning, I lift my finger and point angrily at Roxanne. "You're having this DNA test, I'm going to prove that kid's not mine, then once I do, I never want to see you again, you won't come near me, Lulu or Poppy ever again."

With a sad nod to Chloe, I stride across the room, throw open the front door and leave. It's not until I step outside that I realize we planned to drive her car back home together. Pulling my cell from my back pocket I open up the family group chat and hit the video call.

One by one my family's faces appear on the screen, even Cora answers with Maverick resting over her shoulder while she rubs at his back.

"What's going on? Are you okay?" Beau asks.

Shaking my head, I tip my face back and look up at the night sky, inhaling deeply. "Roxanne showed up at Chloe's tonight. She's seven months pregnant and saying the kid's mine. I hadn't told Lulu about me and Roxanne hooking up. She's gone and I have no idea where."

"I take it you've tried calling her?" Cora asks.

"Yep, rang a couple of times then went to voicemail."

"Where does Chloe think she'll go?" Teddy asks.

"She's not sure, maybe back to Chicago." Sighing, I walk to the edge of the curb and sit down, my feet in the street.

"Is the kid yours?" Beau asks seriously.

"No. The last time I slept with her was right back before you and Bonnie got together."

"When is she saying it happened?" Granger asks, Alice beside him in the frame.

"She's saying we fucked in the bathrooms at the warehouse when we were there for Beau's bachelor party."

"Hell no, that didn't happen, I saw her with her skanky ass grinding all over you, but I put a stop to it, she disappeared after that," Cody says, his face stern.

"I said the same, she's still fucking adamant it's my kid. I'll sort a DNA test tomorrow, prove this baby isn't mine, but honestly that's the least of my worries right now. I need to find Lulu and Poppy."

TWENTY-TWO

LULU

Tears are streaming down my face, and no matter how many times I wipe them away they just won't stop. I know I shouldn't be driving, but I just don't know what else to do. Chloe's home is my sanctuary, or it was, but I can't go back there now, not with Roxanne there. All of my stuff is at Penn's but I can't go there either. The only other option is my parents' place, but honestly, I'd rather share a room with Roxanne than deal with my parents condemning me and my daughter again for my choices. I mean how the hell was I supposed to know that my boyfriend had a history of hooking up with my sort of cousin?

I've been driving now for thirty minutes with no real destination in mind. Montana is a sprawling state, and I know I've got a while before I even hit a highway and have to make a real decision about which direction I'm heading in. It's a full day's drive back to Chicago and it's already after 8pm, there's no way I can drive through the night so no matter where I'm going. I'm going to need to find a hotel to stay in tonight.

Thirty minutes later I finally hit the highway and when I see the sign for Buffalo, I hit my indicator and head in that direction. An ex of mine moved to Buffalo a few years ago, it's the only guy I've ever dated that I actually stayed friends with after we broke up. Bran is a great guy, and we dated for a few months in college, but it didn't last because when it came down to it, we both agreed that there wasn't enough spark between us to make either one of us want to fight for a relationship that was fizzling away.

Pulling up his number on my cell, I hit dial and listen as the line rings.

"Lulu?"

"Hey Bran," I say, hoping he can't hear the tears in my voice.

"Lulu, what's up? You sound upset."

"Err, I know this is out of the blue and it's been a really long time since we spoke, but I'm about two hours from

Buffalo."

"What the hell, I thought you were still living in Chicago?" he asks.

"I was until a few weeks back. A lot has happened since we last spoke. I have a daughter now, her name is Poppy, she's six months old. I moved to Montana to live with my godmother and I met a guy." My words become choked as I think about Penn.

"Lulu, Lulu. Did he hurt you? Are you okay?"

"No, he didn't hurt me. It's just… I can't go back to my godmother's and I saw a sign for Buffalo and just turned. Only now I'm driving and Poppy is in the back and I need to find somewhere to stay and organize a crib, because I left with just her bag with a few diapers and a bottle in." I'm rambling now, tears once again spilling down my face.

"Lulu, sweetie, I'm going to text you my address. I want you to come to me and you can stay here for the night, I have a spare room and I can borrow a crib from my neighbor, she has like four kids, she's bound to have something, okay?" Bran tells me, his voice calm and level.

"You don't have to do that, I just need to find a hotel."

"No hotel. Come to me, okay, it's all going to be okay, you just need to calm down and drive carefully. I don't want you to have an accident, so just take a deep breath and tell me about your daughter."

Bran spends the next two hours on the phone to me,

talking calmly while I drive. By the time we pull up to his townhouse I've at least stopped crying. The moment I put my car in park, he's beside me, opening my door and pulling me into a warm, familiar hug.

"Hey," he says, stroking down my hair with his hand.

"Thank you for this."

"You don't need to thank me, I'm just glad you're okay and that you made it here safe. Let's get you both inside, what can I carry?"

Grabbing Poppy's seat from the back of my car I hand Bran her diaper bag, pick up my purse and then follow him back toward the front door where a beautiful, petite woman is leaning against the doorframe.

"You must be Nina," I say holding out my hand to her.

"Hi Lulu, it's nice to finally meet you."

"You too, I'm so sorry for invading your home like this, I really can just get a hotel room," I tell Bran's wife.

"Don't be silly, come in. Let's get you a glass of wine and you can get your daughter settled." Nina waves me in, smiling down at Poppy as I step into their home.

"So do you think the baby's his?" Nina asks me half an hour later, once Poppy is asleep in the folding travel crib Bran borrowed from his neighbor.

"Why would she say it is if it's not?" I ask, hoping they have an answer because I can't think of reason why she'd claim Penn was the father if he isn't.

"Does he have money?" Bran asks, "Could that be a motivator?"

"He owns a garage with his brother, he's definitely comfortable but I don't think he's rich enough to be a target."

"You need to talk to him," Bran tells me as Nina nods.

"I agree, he's probably worried sick."

"I could be pregnant too," I whisper, focusing all my attention on the wine glass in my hand. "We haven't exactly been careful."

"Oh fuck," Nina gasps then giggles, slapping her hand over her mouth to cover it.

"Oh my god, it is funny isn't it," I half laugh, half sob. "I could end up sharing a baby daddy with my psycho almost cousin."

"Should you be drinking if you think you're pregnant?" Bran asks, his voice full of concern.

"You leave her alone, she deserves that drink and even if she is pregnant, it's too early to even show on a test yet," Nina scolds him.

"My period's due next week, I've been trying not to think about it, to be honest, because it's far too soon, but Penn, he's just so sure, so convinced that we're each other's future. He even mentioned adopting Poppy; he wants her to officially be his daughter."

Nina makes a soft noise as she tips her head to the

side and sighs dreamily. "He sounds almost too good to be true. You need to at least let him know you're okay."

Exhaling wearily, I nod. "You're right, I'll text him."

Nina nods, then pulls Bran up from the couch. "We'll leave you to it. Goodnight."

"Thank you both so much for letting me stay here, I really appreciate it."

"It's fine. Bran's told me all about you, it's nice to finally meet the woman who helped me get my happily ever after. He told me how you told him to man up and just ask me out," she laughs.

"All I did was give him the push; he was already completely in love with you," I tell her.

"Night," Bran calls as he follows his wife up the stairs.

Taking my wine glass to the kitchen, I wash it, then head for the guest room that's off the main living space. Checking on Poppy, I sit down on the bed and type out a text to Penn.

Me

Just wanted to let you know I'm okay.

I send the same message to Chloe too, although knowing Roxanne she's probably still in the midst of one of her epic meltdowns while her mom tries to calm her down. For the first time, I wonder if Chloe knew about Penn and Roxanne, I can't believe she did, because if she had she would have told me, she wouldn't have encouraged me to be with him.

My cell rings in my hand and I glance down at it, seeing Penn's name on the screen. Of course he's calling, he hasn't stopped calling. My head tells me to ignore it, to press the red button, but my heart is aching to hear his voice.

Hovering over the screen, I close my eyes a second before I hit the green button and the sound of his voice fills the silent air. "Lulu, kitten."

Slowly I lift the cell to my ear. "Hi."

"Oh, thank fuck, baby, where are you? Tell me and I'll come get you."

"I'm in Buffalo with friends, we're fine. I don't want you to come here."

"Lulu please, I need to come and get you both, I need my girls."

"I… I can't."

"It's not my baby, there's no way."

"But you had a relationship with her?" I say, my voice breaking.

"No."

"You had sex with her."

"I did. Rockhead Point is a small town, I knew who she was, but we weren't friends. One night she was in the bar, she came onto me. Told me she didn't want a relationship, that she just wanted a dick to ride. She suggested a friends with benefits deal and I agreed. Back then I didn't believe that you existed, it wasn't until I watched Beau and Huck, then Granger find their women that I truly believed you were out there, I just had to find you."

"I know you have a past, Penn, that's not the problem. The issue is that your past is here in my present, because it's someone I think of as a cousin."

"Kitten."

"She's pregnant."

"It's not mine, I haven't slept with her in over a year."

"Penn, I can't do this, I just text you to let you know I'm okay. I need some time to process this."

"Lulu, Kitten, don't you dare end this call. I swear to fucking god I will turn your ass red if you hang up on me."

"Bye Penn."

"Lulu," his angry roar is the last thing I hear before I pull the cell from my ear and hit the end button, closing my eyes and dropping the cell to my chest, gripping it tightly.

Sighing, I slowly open my eyes and glance around me. Bran's spare room is nice, cozy with warm colors and soft furnishings. "What the hell am I doing here?" I whisper aloud. "Jesus, Lulu."

I'm too old to be running away from my problems. I'm a mom, I have a child that relies on me to act like a grown up and be responsible, and here I am in an ex-boyfriend's house because I ran from my current boyfriend after I found out he used to have sex with my kind of cousin. My life sounds like the title of a Jerry Springer show.

Tomorrow I'll go home, back to Chloe's. I'm sure Roxanne is going to make my life a living hell, but that'll just give me more motivation to get my own place. Staying with Chloe was only ever supposed to be a short-term thing anyway, now it'll just be an even shorter, short term. And Penn, well, he was hers before he was mine and if she's saying that her baby is his, well then she must think it is and that's just not drama I want to get involved in right now.

A single tear rolls down my cheek and I don't try to brush it away, instead I swallow down the sob that's threatening to burst from my throat and squeeze my eyes tightly shut. Penn was a wonderful dream, but I won't get in the way of him and his child.

"But what if you're pregnant too?" the voice in the back of my head asks. My hand drops to my stomach and I allow another tear to fall. If I'm pregnant I'll cope, I've done it once, I can do it again. "But you love him," that pesky voice taunts me, and it's true, I do love him, I think. But how can I have a relationship with him if he has a kid with Roxanne? She hates me normally; she'll make both of our lives a living hell if I stay with him. She'll turn his kid against him and I can't be the reason he doesn't have a relationship with his child.

Stripping out of my clothes I slip under the sheet and lie staring up at the ceiling. How can I walk away from him? But how can I stay?

Penn sounded so sure the baby wasn't his, but why would Roxanne say it was, if it wasn't? Eventually I fall into a fitful sleep filled with nightmares about Penn holding his and Roxanne's baby while he looks at her the way he looks at me.

TWENTY-THREE

PENN

Staring down at the cell in my hands, I fight the urge to throw it across the room. She put the phone down on me. She put the fucking phone down on me after I warned her not to. My heart is beating at a million miles an hour, she ran, she's in fucking Buffalo, but at least I know where she is and it's a hell of a lot closer than Chicago.

"Is she okay?" Teddy asks, moving to sit beside me.

"I think so, she's in Buffalo. I could fucking kill Roxanne for causing this. I mean what the hell was she thinking saying that baby is mine?"

"Bro, that girl is crazy."

"I know," I say wearily.

"I hate to say it, but we warned you not to mess about with her."

"I know," I hiss, angry that he's pulling the 'I told you so' card right now.

"What are you going to do?"

Sighing, I let my head fall forward into my hands. "What the fuck can I do? I don't know where she is, Buffalo is a big place."

"Has she got Lojack on her car?" Teddy asks.

"No." Sitting up straighter I turn to look at him. "But she has got find my phone on her cell. She loses it all the time so she keeps it turned on. If I can get into her account, I could track her cell."

"Bro," he says warily. "You sure that's a good idea? Tracking her cell is kind of stalkery."

"I don't give a fuck, right now I wish I'd implanted a tracker in her fucking neck, then I wouldn't ever have to feel this way again. My girls are gone and I need them. When you meet your woman, you'll understand."

His eyes go cold for a minute, his face hardening, but in the blink of an eye his expression clears and it's just Teddy, my sweet baby brother again. "Do you know her passwords?"

"Don't need to, she signed in to her account from my cell the other day and I bet it did that automatic password save thing it does. It only takes me a minute to open the page and seconds later I'm watching a dot flash on a map showing me exactly where she is. "Got her," I say triumphantly, jumping up from the couch and stomping toward my boots by the door.

"Bro, seriously think this through. If you go banging on the door in the middle of the night you aren't going to get a warm welcome," he warns me.

"Then I'll sit my ass outside until it's morning. I'm not going to give her the chance to run again and if I have to haul her ass back over my shoulder, then that's what I'll do."

"Fuck," Teddy hisses. "Wait up, I'll come with, someone needs to keep a clear head and make sure you don't lose your shit."

Ten minutes later, we're on the road and with each mile closer I get to her, the better I feel. Lulu needs to learn that she can try and run, but I'll always fucking chase. It's the middle of the damn night by the time we pull down the quiet residential street and park behind Lulu's car outside a redbrick townhouse. The lights are all off inside, so despite my almost overwhelming desire to break down the door and get to my woman, I resist the urge and settle down in my seat to wait until the sun comes up.

Knowing she's close, my heart slows to a dull thud in my chest and I manage to close my eyes and get a couple of hours of fitful sleep. I wake every ten minutes to check her car is still here, that she hasn't run again. By the time 7.00 am rolls by I'm awake, leaning against the side of my car and waiting for any sign of life from inside the house. I don't know the friend she's staying with, she's never mentioned knowing anyone so close to Montana, but then she never really mentions any of her friends, so it's not surprising that I didn't know about whoever is harboring my runaway woman.

When the light turns on downstairs, I push off my car and stride to the front door, banging on it with as much restraint as I can muster.

The door opens and a guy stands before me. He's shorter and leaner than me and in an instant I decide I can take him if he's dared to lay even a finger on Lulu.

"Can I help you?" he asks me warily.

"I'm here for Lulu and Poppy," I growl, not even trying to tone down the possessive warning in my voice.

A smile spreads across his face. "Oh, you must be Penn."

"Yeah, that's me."

"Come on in," he says, opening the door a little wider and gesturing for me to go inside. "Does your friend want to come in too?"

Glancing over my shoulder I find my brother standing on the sidewalk, his body tense and ready to do whatever he needs to do to either support me or stop me from doing something really fucking stupid. "Teddy," I call motioning him forward.

"You good?" he asks, eyeing the guy at the door.

"Yeah, you coming in? This is…" I trail off waiting for him to fill in the blanks.

"Sorry," he laughs. "I'm Bran, I'm Lulu's friend."

My back straightens and I grind my teeth, this is the friend Lulu came to, a guy? What the fuck? I assumed he was the boyfriend or husband of the friend. My woman ran from me to another man. "This is my brother Teddy, and obviously you know I'm Penn, Lulu's man." I try to be polite, but I have to force the words out from behind gritted teeth.

"Coffee?" he asks cordially, either not noticing or not caring that I'm about ten seconds away from beating the shit out of him for being in the same space as my girls. Without a second glance he leads us both into the house and toward the kitchen. When I spot Lulu sitting at the dining table, all of my attention is drawn to her and my baby girl in her arms.

"Penn?" she gasps when she sees me, standing up from her seat at the kitchen table and eyeing me with confusion. "What are you doing here? How did you know where I was?"

"I came to bring you home," I say, my voice steely.

"What?"

"You don't get to run from me."

"Sounding like a bit of a psycho, bro," Teddy says quietly, stepping toward Lulu and pressing a kiss on her cheek as he reaches for Poppy. "Here, why don't I take Poppy so you guys can go talk."

Lulu makes a sound of annoyance when Poppy happily goes to my brother, but I don't give her a moment to protest, reaching for her arm and gripping her wrist tight enough to propel her forwards and away from the kitchen just as a woman appears on the stairs.

"Morning—" she starts. "Ohh." Her eyes widen a little as she sees me, then she relaxes and grins. "You must be Penn. I'm Nina, Bran's wife."

Some of the angry tension leaches from me at learning the guy has a wife, but I'm still furious Lulu ran from me to another man, regardless if he's single or not.

"Morning, nice to meet you. If you'll excuse us, we're going to step outside so we can talk," I tell her, before Lulu has a chance to speak.

"Oh, err, sure," Nina says, but I just keep on moving, towing Lulu along with me. Walking out of the front door, I close it behind us and steer her to my car, urging her into the passenger side before I get into the driver's seat, shutting and locking the doors once I'm inside.

"What the hell, Lulu?" I demand.

Closing her eyes, she lowers her chin and inhales slowly. "Why are you here?"

"What the fuck do you mean? Where else would I be?"

"I told you I needed time."

"I don't give a fuck what you need. You're my woman, did you seriously think I'd let you just fucking disappear and not chase after you?" I snarl angrily, wanting to force her face up and her eyes open, hating that she's refusing to look at me.

"You shouldn't be here."

"Then where the hell should I be?" I demand. "Did you expect me to go to work like a little bitch while you convince yourself you don't belong to me anymore?"

"You were hers first," she says so quietly I barely make out the words.

Grabbing her chin, I force her face up and turn her toward me gripping her in my fingers and squeezing. "Look at me."

When she keeps her eyes closed, I tighten my grip, I'd never hurt her, but I won't let her ignore me either. "Look at me, now, Lulu."

Her lids slowly part and her hurt filled gaze lands on me.

"I was never hers. I've never been anyone's until you. I'm yours, Kitten, just like you're mine."

Shaking her head she tries to close her eyes, but I give her chin a little pinch, warning her to keep her gaze on me.

"You're mine and I'm yours."

"You had sex with Roxanne."

"I've had sex with a lot of women, I've never belonged to any of them. But you own me, Kitten, just you."

"She's pregnant, Penn, I can't, I won't…" She trails off as if she just doesn't know what to say and I hate that this has hurt her, that my past is causing her pain. If I'd told her weeks ago about me and Roxanne, she'd know the truth and she wouldn't be doubting me like this. This is my own fucking fault, but I can fix it.

"It's not mine. I fucking swear it. There's no way it can be because I haven't touched her in over a year."

"It doesn't matter," she says, yanking her chin from my grip as her shoulders pull back and she straightens in the seat. "You fucked Roxanne, she's basically my family. This," she motions between us, "can't happen."

"Bullshit," I shout. "It's happening, it's been happening and you must have lost your mind somewhere between Montana and here if you think for a minute I'll ever let you go."

"You don't own me," she yells, her face flushed, her tits heaving up and down.

"Want to bet?" I ask a moment before I grab her

head and yank her onto my lips, forcing my tongue into her mouth and kissing her with a mix of anger and relief and desire. She fights me, batting ineffectually at my shoulders, trying to push me away, but I grab her hair and pull, warning her to behave, to kiss me back.

After a moment I feel her body melt and I start to relax. She can shout and scream and try to run, but her body knows who it belongs to, and no matter how much she tries to fight this, I'll always have this effect on her.

Reaching over, I part her thighs with my hand and cup her pussy over her pants. Grinding the heel of my palm over her clit, I smile against her mouth when her hips lift and tilt into my touch. "You belong to me, Kitten, and I won't allow anyone to come between us."

She freezes, her body tensing as I whisper the words against her lips. "No," she says, shaking her head and grabbing my wrist, trying to push me away.

I still, but keep my hand where it is cupping her sex. "Stop fighting me," I warn.

"I can't, it's not right, we can't do this."

"That's the biggest load of bull crap I ever heard, Lulu. Don't let her get in your head. Yes, I fucked her. Should I have told you about it? Yes, I should have, but she is so irrelevant to us I didn't want to rile up shit that didn't need to be riled. I fucked her six times, that's all, I fucked you more times than that the first week we met. Me and her were never a thing, we were never a couple, we weren't dating. She offered me no strings sex and I took her up on it, that's the extent of our involvement. We never went out to dinner, we never talked. We met up, we fucked, I left. That's it."

Lulu grimaces and I wish I could sugar coat things for her, but surely it's better for her to know Roxanne was nothing but a warm hole to fill than make it out to be romantic, when it wasn't. "I used protection every fucking time, then when I found her stabbing holes in the condom I told her I was done and that was it. I promise you there's no way that kid is mine."

"She's my family, Penn, would you want to be with a woman who had sex with one of your brothers?"

Wincing, I cup her cheek with my palm and nod. "I know, I should have told you, but it still wouldn't change anything. You're mine, Kitten, have been since the moment I laid eyes on you. I won't give you up because of her and her bullshit."

She shakes her head, denying my words. "Enough, Lulu, this is bullshit. I'm sorry I didn't tell you about her, but I am not the father of her kid and I fucking refuse to let you run from me. Get out the fucking car, pack up Poppy's stuff and let's go, I'm taking you home."

"Home to Chloe's," she says determinedly.

"Hell no, home to our home."

"I can't do that."

"Did I say I was giving you a choice?" My voice is barely more than an animalistic snarl but I don't try and tone it down, she needs to see and hear how fucking serious I am about this. She's coming home with me, nothing else is even an option.

"You're not giving me a choice?" Her spine goes ramrod straight, her eyes narrowing.

"No, I'm not. You're mine and you're coming home where you belong."

"You planning on locking me in the bedroom too? Because I'm not staying with you, I need to go back to Chloe's and see if I'm still welcome there."

"I'll keep you pinned to the bed filled with my cock if I have to. You're coming home with me and fucking staying there. I'm not playing with you here, Lulu."

Rolling her eyes, she tries to turn her face away, scoffing beneath her breath. "I cannot be with someone who is having a baby with my cousin, she will make all of our lives a living hell including the baby's. I will not be the cause of all of our misery."

"It's not mine."

"Are you one hundred percent sure? She's crazy enough to be stabbing holes in condoms, and you don't think she's capable of persuading you to go fuck her when you're drunk? She said it happened when you were blitzed at Beau's bachelor party. Cody might have run her off the first time that night but can you say without doubt that she didn't try again at some point when there was no one there to save your horny dick from her crazy pussy."

My lips part to tell her that yes I'm unequivocally sure I didn't do that, but the truth is that I was really fucking drunk that night. I remember her trying to persuade me to have sex with her, I remember Cody telling her to fuck off before I had a chance to, but there are parts of the night toward the end that are definitely hazy. Could she have tried again? Could Roxanne have taken advantage of my impaired drunken judgement and gotten me to fuck her?

No… no, even out of my mind I don't think I'd go near her again.

"I've already told her I want a paternity test, they can do them on unborn babies now. Come home with me and the test will either prove that baby's not mine or she'll confess she's lying about it. Either way, I'm sorry, Lulu, but I won't let you run from me. Wherever you go, I'll follow and I'll drag your ass back, that's just the way it is."

TWENTY-FOUR

LULU

His jaw is clenched tight, his eyes sparkling with that weird male intensity that I've never seen in real life before him. He's essentially threatening to keep me a prisoner and instead of being scared I just feel… relieved.

After tossing and turning all night, what I realized when I woke up this morning was that I'm in love with Penn Barnett. It makes no real sense, least of all to me, but I love him and even with noble intensions at heart, it would kill me to give him up.

I'm not sure how he figured out where I was, but he did and he came. He'll always come. I don't know how I know that for sure, but I do. He will always be here, he won't leave, he won't desert us, he won't turn his back. He will always be there for me and Poppy and despite all the drama that's surrounding us right now, something in my heart settles into place with the realization.

My body has always reacted to him, even though my mind had fought his possession at every turn. Now my heart is in the game, it would kill me to have to walk away from the future he's offering us. I want this man, I want to live with him, marry him, let him be the father he's promising to be for my daughter. But I need to know if that future is going to involve Roxanne and her child too.

"I was coming back to Rockhead Point today anyway."

"You were?" he asks.

"Yeah, last night I freaked out and I just needed some space. I saw the sign for Buffalo and remembered Bran lived here."

"Who is this guy anyway?"

"He's an ex," I say on a wince.

"You ran to your ex fucking boyfriend," Penn says, the calm in his tone not hiding the angry menace that's barely below the surface.

"Not him, just someone who knows the area, I asked if he could help me book a hotel so I didn't have to turn up somewhere late at night with Poppy and he offered to let us use his spare room. He calmed me down and stayed on the phone with me almost the whole drive here because I was upset."

His face reddens and he releases his grip on my me, lowering his hands to his lap as his fingers clench into fists. "Stay here."

"What are you going to do? He's married for god's sake, it's been years since we were together and we broke up because we realized we were better as friends," I say quickly as Penn opens the driver's door and climbs out.

"Get your ass back in the fucking car," he hisses as I open my own door and follow him out.

"No. What are you going to do? You need to calm down."

"I'm going to go and get my daughter, my brother and your stuff, then I'm going to thank your ex and his wife for taking care of you before I drive us home."

His words are polite, but the tension in his body and the anger that's clear on his face tell another story.

"No, I'll get Poppy, you stay here."

"Lulu, if you don't get in the fucking car right this second, I'm going to bend you over the hood, rip down your pants and fuck you right here out in the open so your ex can see exactly who you belong to now."

"You're being ridiculous."

A moment later my back hits the cold metal of my car, my legs spread wide with Penn's body pressed up against me. His finger collars my throat while his lips take mine in a claiming kiss that I can't help but respond to.

"You. Are. Mine," he taunts against my lips.

A moment later he releases me and turns, striding purposefully up to the front door as I sag back, glad for the support of my car behind me. By the time I've pulled myself together enough to move, the front door is reopening and a stern Penn is exiting, Poppy's baby carrier in one hand, her diaper bag in the other. Teddy follows behind him, chatting happily to a wide-eyed Bran and a smiling Nina.

"Go say goodbye," Penn grunts as he reaches me, opening the back door and clipping Poppy's seat into the car.

When I reach the front door, Teddy is just saying goodbye, and he reaches out and squeezes my shoulder as he heads back to Penn's car and slides into the driver's seat.

"Are you okay?" Bran asks, eyeing my crazy boyfriend behind me.

"Yeah, I'm fine. I was going to head back home this morning anyway."

"Penn is... intense."

A laugh bursts from me and I smile a little manically. "Yeah, he is. He has six brothers and they're all the same too, even Teddy, although he's a sweetheart."

"Are you sure you want to leave with him? He kind of

just told us you were going and marched out with Poppy. But if you don't want to go we can call the cops, you can stay with us as long as you need," Bran offers.

Nina snickers, curling herself around her husband's arm. "Honey, that man is crazy in love with Lulu."

"Oh he's definitely crazy," Bran says beneath his breath.

"I'm fine, I promise. He's organizing a DNA test for the baby, but he thinks Roxanne will admit she lied before it gets that far," I say with a shrug, looking down at my feet, not wanting to talk about all the tabloid style drama going on in my life right now.

"I'm glad he came for you," Nina whispers, "It's so romantic."

"I'll let you know what happens," I say with a smile, and she nods emphatically. "Thank you so much for letting us stay here last night, I'm so sorry I invaded with my drama and emotional meltdown."

"I'm just so glad I finally got to meet you. Poppy is an absolute darling and you guys are welcome any time. It'd be really nice to catch up over dinner or something once things settle down for you and Penn," Nina suggests, releasing Bran and pulling me into a hug.

"I'd really like that." Turning, I offer them a little wave, then let Penn guide me into my car, closing the door behind me with a firm thunk. I tense when he walks up the path to Bran, then relax a little when they shake hands. With a decisive nod, Penn walks around to the driver's seat and climbs in, starting the engine and pulling away from the curb a moment later.

An hour later, Penn speaks for the first time. "Can you text Teddy and tell him I'm going to pull off at the next

Penn

> Hi Teddy, Penn asked me to tell you he's pulling off at the next exit to find somewhere to eat.

Teddy

Okay, I'll follow.

The silence is so thick I can practically taste it. I'm not sure why he's not speaking, I can only assume it's the fact that I called Bran and he's my ex. "Surely you're not this pissed about me calling Bran?" I ask, unable to stay quiet anymore.

"Did you fuck him? Has his dick been in your pussy?"

"Are you serious? Do you know how hypocritical it is of you to even say that when the reason I was at his place was because you might have gotten Roxanne pregnant? You know I wasn't a virgin when we met, Bran and I had a short-lived thing in my freshman year of college, we both decided we were better as friends and broke up. You're being ridiculous and a massive hypocrite."

When he doesn't say anything, I turn and look at him.

His jaw is clenched tight, his knuckles white from his death grip on the steering wheel. "I'm not going to sit here and chat amicably about the men who've been inside you."

Rolling my eyes I shake my head and sit back in my seat, happy with the silence if he's going to be an asshole. We pull up outside a roadside diner and I open my door the moment the car stops, grabbing Poppy's seat from the back and striding toward the restaurant doors without looking back for Penn or Teddy.

Sliding Poppy's seat into the booth I follow her in and grab the menu, not looking up as the guys sit down on the other side of the table. I order when the waitress appears, then pointedly ignore Penn while I fuss over Poppy.

"Well this is fun," Teddy says, breaking the silence with a chuckle.

"Your brother is being a hypocritical asshole," I say, smiling at the waitress when she slides my food on to the table.

"Okay..." Teddy says, dragging out the word as he waits for either me or Penn to fill in the blanks.

"Bran is a friend, we also used to date."

Teddy whistles through his teeth. "You left town and went to your ex's?"

"I left town because I found out my boyfriend used to have sex with someone I consider family and got her pregnant."

"It's not my baby," Penn says through gritted teeth.

"Wow, you pair need to fuck all this tension out," Teddy laughs again.

Snapping my head up, I glare at him. "I can't wait to watch you find a girlfriend, I'll make that stupid suggestion to her when you're in the middle of an argument and you can tell me how funny it is then."

Smirking, he lifts his hands up in mock surrender. "I'll mind my own business. But I have no intention of having a girlfriend any time soon."

"You wait till you find your woman, it'll knock you on your ass and you'll be as fucking crazy as I am right now, you mark my words," Penn warns.

"Nope, that won't be happening to me."

"Why? I thought you all believed in the Barnett love at first sight myth?" I ask.

"Well, because I already found my woman," Teddy confesses a little sheepishly.

My eyes widen and I look up at him as Penn does the same.

"Who is it?" Penn asks. "Why the fuck haven't you claimed her?"

"Her name was Prudence."

"Prudence?" Penn questions.

"Yeah, she was Mrs. Hemmings' granddaughter, she came to stay with her for a while during my senior year of high school."

"What happened?" I ask.

"She was the most beautiful girl I've ever seen. Long, white blonde hair almost all the way down to her butt. First time I saw her I thought there was something wrong with me, I could barely breathe."

"So," I prompt.

"So, she was a freshman and I was a senior. Four years age difference might not seem like anything now, but when she was fourteen and I was eighteen that just wasn't okay. She was a kid and I was basically a man. By the time I decided I couldn't care less what anyone thought of the age difference, that I'd wait for her, she'd left, gone back home to her parents. I never saw her again," he says with a shrug. "I didn't believe what Dad said about there being just one woman out there destined to be mine. I had my chance and I blew it."

"You have to find her," I tell him.

Teddy scoffs lightly. "Lulu, it's been thirteen years and we weren't even friends. I'm sure she's married with a couple of kids by now."

"Bro, I'm sorry." Penn puts his arm around Teddy's shoulders and squeezes him, leaning down and resting their foreheads together in an oddly touching brotherly moment.

"Look, it is what it is, maybe fate will give me another

chance. But what you guys have is rare, don't let Roxanne's crazy ruin things between you."

The rest of the meal is still quiet, but the hostile tension between me and Penn dissolves and by the time we're climbing back into the car, I'm just sad that yesterday's revelations have caused this distance between us.

I must fall asleep because the next time I open my eyes, it's to the sound of gravel crunching beneath our tires as Penn drives us up to his house. "Why are we here? I need to go back to Chloe's."

"Not happening," he says, his voice low and gravelly.

"Penn," I exhale.

"Not fucking happening. Before Roxanne dropped the baby bombshell you were moving in, you're still moving in."

I open my mouth to speak, but he puts his hand over it silencing me.

"I'm not interested in arguments, Kitten. Now, are you walking in, or am I carrying you in over my shoulder? Either works for me."

"You're an asshole," I spit as I climb out of the car and move to get Poppy.

"I got her," he says, amusement lacing his words as he gently moves me out of the way and grabs her seat and bag, closing the door behind him. He surprises me when he locks my car.

"Why did you lock it?"

"Just making sure you can't run again," he says nonchalantly, like it's no big deal, as he slides the keys into his pants pocket and smirks.

"Asshole."

"Yep, an asshole that's going be all up in yours later on if you don't start minding your attitude."

I start to tell him he's going nowhere near my asshole, but shut up when we enter the house. His entire family is grouped together in the family room and they all turn and stare at us the moment we step inside. Cora, Bonnie and Alice all rush forward, pulling me away from Penn.

"Are you okay?" Bonnie asks, she's the youngest of the three, but you'd never know she's barely twenty-two.

Sighing, I reach up and run my hand through my hair. "Not really. I wanted to go back to Chloe's, but Penn—"

"Penn's a Barnett," Cora says, interrupting me. "He was never going to let you go."

"We can distract him if you want to make a run for it, but he's going to chase. The men in this family are relentless," Alice says quietly, glancing over her shoulder to where the guys are all sitting on the couch, Poppy in Penn's lap.

"What do I do if it is his baby?" I ask them, knowing that these women understand the caveman tendencies of the Barnett brothers better than anyone else.

"He swears it's not, and the guys all say there's no way it happened that night. When Beau and I first got together, she came to see Penn in the bar we were in and she was saying all sorts of crazy shit to him. I know she's Chloe's daughter, but she really is insane," Bonnie tells me with a rueful look.

"Oh, I know. She hates me, always has. Mainly because I'm so close to her mom and she's always had a tempestuous relationship with her. The thing is, even if this baby isn't his, she'll never let me forget that she's had sex with him. She'll torture me with it and honestly, I just don't know if I can cope with that. I know we both have pasts, I just wish his past wasn't someone I'm going to have to see every holiday."

The girls' wince, looking at me with sympathy. "I wish I could tell you what to do, but you're the only one who can decide if it's worth it. What I can tell you, and I think Cora and Alice will agree, is you'll never find anyone who will love you the way Penn will. These boys are big, crazy cavemen, but when they give their hearts to a woman, they give them wholeheartedly, forever, and once you've been a recipient of that kind of love, everything else will pale in comparison. Dealing with Roxanne and knowing she and Penn have a past might be hard, but living without Penn will be so much harder." Bonnie pats my shoulder and heads back toward the guys, pushing up onto her tiptoes to hug Penn and Poppy as she passes him.

"Come on, Kitten, we need to go talk," Penn says when he appears beside me.

"I—" I start.

"Walking or over my shoulder, pick."

Cora and Alice snigger as they scurry away. "Asshole," I snark, taking Poppy from him and walking away. Pushing open the door to Penn's mini apartment, I walk in expecting to find all of my boxes piled up in the living room, but there isn't a box in sight. "Where's my stuff?"

"I unpacked. I'm going to put her down for a nap."

"Didn't she sleep in the car?" I ask, pressing my lips to Poppy's head.

"No, she woke up not long after you fell asleep, she's been singing and cooing for the last couple of hours."

Holding out his hands for her, Poppy wiggles excitedly and I reluctantly let him take her, watching his back as he disappears into her room. Wandering into the living room, I glance around the space noticing the hints of me that are now dotted all around. Pictures of Poppy as a newborn, my books on the shelves, my knitted throw over the back of the couch. He hasn't just unpacked, he's moved me into every inch of his space.

I hear his footsteps a moment before his arm curls around my waist. "When did you do all this?"

"Last night after you ran out of Chloe's. I needed to

do something so I didn't lose my mind not knowing where you were."

His eyes are heated with a mixture of hurt and anger.

"I'm sorry," I tell him, lowering my gaze to where my hands are wringing together. "I shouldn't have just left, that wasn't fair of me."

"Fair," he scoffs. "Nothing about this is fucking fair. You ran, you were upset and you took Poppy. I had no idea where you were, if you were okay. You could have gotten hurt, I could have lost both of you." His voice cracks and he quiets, pursing his full lips as he inhales slowly like he's trying to calm himself.

"I needed some time, this is a fucked up situation that I shouldn't be in the middle of. I believe that you don't think the baby is yours, but Roxanne is crazy, I wouldn't put anything past her, including her doing whatever she can to deliberately get pregnant so she can trap a man."

"I found a place that does in vitro paternity tests, I'm going to call them and see how quickly they can fit Roxanne in. The results only take twenty-four hours, this will all be over by the end of the week."

Sighing, I close my eyes and let my head fall back for a moment. "It won't be over though. She'll always be my family, she's Chloe's daughter. I see her every holiday, we live in the same town now, she won't just disappear, regardless of the results of that test. She'll never let me forget that you've had sex and I just don't know if I can deal with that."

"So we move and I'll pay for Chloe to come visit us once a month, hell, once a fucking week if that's what you want."

"You can't move," I shriek. "Your life is here; your business and your family are here."

"You're my family," he says, closing the distance between us again and curling his arm around my back, pulling me to him. "You and Poppy are my whole fucking universe and without you I don't work anymore, you're a part of me."

Even though I know I should walk away, leave now while I can; moving out of his arms is impossible. "You can't move."

"Where you go, I go, even if that means moving in with the devil and standing in between you and Roxanne and all her hatefulness."

His hand lifts from his side and collars my throat as his eyes heat and darken. "I won't let you leave me and if you're really honest with yourself, you don't want to. You know you're mine. I own all of you heart, soul, cunt every fiber of your being belongs to me and you want that. I see the way your pupils dilate when I control you. I see the things you think you're hiding from me, the way your breathing shallows, how goosebumps coat your skin when I dominate your body. I see you, Kitten, the way no one ever has before and I hate that I made you sad, I hate that I made you cry. I fucking hate that you ran from me, when I only ever want to be the person you run toward. But if nothing else, all this shit that bitch has caused will only cement us together, because I refuse to let anyone, least of all her take you away from me."

"But–"

"No, Kitten, no excuses, no buts. We are forever, we're a family and I refuse to give that up."

Falling silent, he looks down at me, an impassioned flush filling his cheeks, his grip on my back and throat tight and unyielding.

All of a sudden it doesn't matter about Roxanne, it doesn't matter if she's lying or not, it doesn't matter that she'll never go away. This man, this crazy, ridiculous, brute of a man is standing here and owning me with his touch, his words and his very presence. I couldn't leave if I wanted to. "I love you," I blurt.

"What?"

"I love you. It's too soon and this is the worst possible moment to say it, but I love you. It's what I realized last night while I was lying in bed missing you and hating her for causing this rift between us."

"You love me?" he questions.

I nod.

"You love me."

I nod again. "You don't have to say it back, that's not why I told you. I just had to say it."

"Kitten, I've been in love with you since the moment I saw you. Love doesn't even begin to describe the depth of my feelings for you, but I suppose it's a good place to start. I adore you, admire you, covet you, crave you. I want to shield you, care for you, protect you. I want to own you, consume you, corrupt you. Love is only four letters that could never truly convey how my very being starts and ends with you."

Tears fill my eyes, but before they get a chance to fall he lifts me off the ground and carries me into the bedroom, placing me reverently down on the comforter. Our clothes seem to dissolve from us and it barely feels like a second has passed before his hands are caressing my naked skin. I cling to him, needing to feel him close and chase down the bliss our confessions have evoked. Soft lips find mine, kissing me quietly, slowly, not dominating me but controlling everything with a featherlight touch.

His hands feel like they're everywhere all at once, teasing my nipples, stroking my clit, filling my pussy up with his fingers and taunting my ass. My eyes roll back and I give myself over to him, holding him to me while he claims every inch of me and I bask in him. I'm soaked, the sound of my wetness surrounding us as he pushes me head long into an orgasm, pinching my clit and rubbing at the spot deep inside of me that makes me see stars.

"I love you," he whispers against my lips, as he guides his hard cock toward my core and slowly pushes inside of me. I've lost count of how many times he's fucked me, but the size of his dick still shocks me as he stretches me wide, easing his way into my pussy with shallow thrusts until he's sheathed inside of me, his hips pressed against mine.

"Jesus, Lulu, your cunt was made for my cock, so hot and wet and tight."

Moaning wantonly, I arch my back, closing my eyes as my heart beats so fast I can feel it in my chest.

"Open your eyes, baby, watch me fuck you, watch the way your cunt is gaping around my fat cock. You look so fucking hot, I can barely hold back from slamming into you and coating you in my cum. I want to fill you up and then watch it slowly drip out of your swollen slit."

His dirty words and the erotic sight of his cock glistening with my arousal almost has me erupting into an orgasm, but his hand at my throat stops me.

"No, you don't come until I tell you."

"I can't stop, I'm so close," I rasp, even more turned on by the weight of his hold on my neck.

"Fuck." Pulling his hips back he slams into me hard, setting a frantic pace that steals my breath and pushes me over the edge. I come on a cry, sinking my nails into his shoulders, holding on while he fucks me proprietorially until he stills, grunting out his release as he fills me.

We stay silent, holding each other tightly until our breaths return to normal. Pressing a kiss onto my neck, Penn lifts his head and looks down at me. "I love you, Lulu."

A slow smile spreads across my lips, I don't know how it happened, or why I was brought to this town, to this man, but lying here beneath him, somehow everything I've gone through in the last eighteen months makes sense. It was all just the path to him.

"I love you too, Penn."

TWENTY-FIVE

PENN

She loves me, she fucking loves me. Even though I'd felt it from her, hearing her say the words calms the panic that's filled my chest since Roxanne said that baby in her belly was mine. I can't lose Lulu and Poppy; I won't lose them. But knowing Lulu loves me makes everything more settled. I was never going to give her up, but at least now I know she feels the same way.

My dick's still inside of her, I only emptied my balls five minutes ago, but I'm already hardening again, eager to fuck the cum I just filled her with even deeper inside of her. Sliding my dick free, I sit back onto my haunches and stare at her gaping slit, the creamy evidence of my release coating her puffy pink folds.

When she moves to close her legs, I stop her, running my fingers up the inside of her thighs as I stare down at her. "Roll over, Kitten, hands and knees."

Her eyes widen fractionally, then a vixen smile spreads over her lips and she moves, rolling onto her stomach. Pushing her ass into the air, she pulls her knees upwards, putting her cunt and ass perfectly on display for me.

"Perfect," I whisper reverently, caressing her ass before sliding my fingers down to where my cum is dripping out of her. Using my fingers, I catch all of my release and push it back into her soaking core, fucking her with it as I force my seed high into her pussy, enjoying the way her muscles clench and flutter around me.

"Oh god, oh fuck," she cries, arching her back even further and sinking down onto my fingers as I slowly thrust in and out of her cunt.

Her hips follow me back when I drag my soaked fingers from her sex. Unable to resist, I slam my dick back inside her. The creamy mess of our releases coats her cunt, making it an effortless job to fill her completely with my cock until my stomach is pressed up against her back.

Grabbing her hip with one hand, I use the fingers still coated in wetness to press against her ass, coating the tight ring of muscle with my cum before I press one finger against the hole and ease it into her insanely tight ass.

"Oh god, oh my god," she chants as I slowly fuck her ass with my finger while her cunt is filled to capacity with my dick. Forcing a second finger alongside the first, I pump in and out, scissoring and stretching her ass as I slowly fuck her pussy with my dick in alternating thrusts.

A mewling growl comes from her and her fingers tighten and release in the sheet beneath us as I work both of her holes, overwhelming her senses. "How does it feel to have your cunt full of my dick and your ass full of my fingers?"

"So… oh Christ, so good," she pants.

"Who does this pussy belong to?"

"You."

"Who does this ass belong to?"

"Oh fuck. You, it belongs to you. Oh my god, Penn, I'm going to come."

Using a little more force, I pull back and slide straight back into her slit, filling her completely as I push a third finger into her naughty tight hole. "Come for me, Lulu, come on my dick while I fuck your ass and get it ready to take my cock."

Her core clamps down on me and she comes on a cry, her whole body tensing then convulsing as wave after wave of orgasm barrels through her.

"Good girl," I praise, "Good girl." Not waiting for her orgasm to subside, I pull my cock from her cunt and press it against her stretched ass hole.

"It hurts, it's too big," Lulu pants even as she pushes her ass back against my cock as I try to carefully ease the head inside.

There's no way I can fuck her ass with my whole dick, it'd tear her apart, but as her muscles relax and the head of my cock slips in to her tight ass hole, I wish I could plunge forward and slam in to her. Instead, I let the first few inches of my length fill her, then pull almost all the way out before carefully pushing back into her again.

The sight of her ass stretched around my dick is almost more than I can take and after three more measured thrusts... I'm done. I feel the first spurt of cum release inside of her and instead of pushing in deeper I pull all the way out, watching the beads of liquid coat her hole, her cheeks and pussy, branding her with my seed.

"Holy fuck," I growl as I keep her pinned in place with a firm hand on her back and enjoy the erotic sight before me. "That's the sexiest thing I've ever seen in my life. Your tight little asshole is red and loose, your cunt is puffy and swollen and they're both covered in my cum."

"Like in porn," she giggles.

"So much better than porn, because it was my cock that filled you, my cock that stretched and used you, and my cum that's dripping from both your holes."

"Wow, sweet nothings," she giggles again.

"Sometimes you want sweet words and sometimes you want to be owned, don't pretend otherwise," I whisper against her shoulder as I use my fingers to push my cum back into her ass.

A soft, contented sigh escapes her and she pushes down her knees and collapses onto her stomach, her arms falling to the comforter beside her. "What are we going to do?" she asks.

"Right now, we're going to lie here, naked and sated, and enjoy the moment. In a while we'll see what we can do to sort this mess out, but for right now we're just going to enjoy this, because no one gets to steal this joy from us."

I feel rather than see her nod of agreement, and as I settle in beside her and pull her into me, she leans back, twining her fingers with mine as we curl up together, messy, dirty and in love.

***

Poppy wakes us an hour later and I pull on some boxers and go get her, while Lulu heads for the shower to clean up. I'd rather she stay coated in my cum, but I let her go, hearing the shower turn on as I scoop Poppy from her crib and cuddle her tightly.

By the time I get back into our room and settle onto the bed with Poppy in my lap, Lulu is singing loudly in the shower. The tension from earlier is gone, replaced with the happiness that surrounded us before Roxanne the psycho bitch turned up and tried to shoot my life all to hell.

Grabbing my cell from the bedside table, I pull up the number for a clinic who offer the in vitro paternity tests and call them. Explaining my circumstances, I book an appointment for a few days' time for me and Roxanne to both get tested. While I'm finishing giving the nurse my details, Lulu appears from the bathroom, her skin pink, her hair wet. While I talk, she dries herself with a towel and pulls on comfy trackpants and a hoody, hiding her perfect body from my view.

"So, Friday, huh?" Lulu asks, when I end the call.

"Friday. It was the first appointment they had."

"You know she's going to lose her mind over this don't you?"

"I could give two fucks. She started all this bullshit, she can end it all by telling the fucking truth."

"Do you want to call her and tell her?"

"I don't have her number, I blocked her when she turned into a fucking psycho," I shrug, wishing I'd met Lulu in high school, that way I wouldn't have any ex fuck-buddies to come back and haunt me.

"I actually don't have it either, I could ask Chloe for it," she suggests with a grimace.

"We'll go see her tomorrow, but today I just want

to stay here in our bubble. You owe me a first night living together and I'm cashing it in right now. I want unadulterated us time, just me, you and the princess."

We spend the rest of the day lounging around and don't leave the apartment. I cook dinner and we eat around the small table in the kitchen, just the three of us. I love my huge, crazy family, but it's nice to spend time alone for once, to get used to being together and enjoying the easy domesticity we've had since day one.

Once Poppy is bathed, Lulu feeds her a bottle and we both take turns kissing her goodnight before I place her in her cot, the pink twinkle lights I hung from her ceiling illuminating her room in a pale pink glow. Slipping silently from her room, I close the door quietly behind us then follow Lulu into the living room.

"I'm exhausted," Lulu says, stifling a yawn.

"Marry me."

"What?" she chokes, turning with wild eyes to stare at me.

"Marry me," I say again.

"I think maybe we need to get the baby mama drama out of the way before we start thinking about weddings," she scoffs.

"Say yes. Marry me." Pulling the ring that I've been carrying around for weeks out of my pocket, I sink to one knee in front of her, grab her hand and slide the ring onto her finger. "Say yes."

"I…" she gasps. "What? How? You have a ring. How do you have a ring?"

"I picked it out the day after I met you. I knew right away that you were who I'd been waiting for so I took the day off, drove into the city and bought it. Do you like it?"

The ring is an oval cut diamond, mounted on a platinum band partially set with smaller round diamonds. It's a vintage style that instantly called to me the moment the lady in the shop bought out the tray of rings for me to look at.

"Of course I like it, it's beautiful," Lulu says reverently, her eyes fixated on the ring on her finger. "I…"

"Do you love me?"

"Yes," she confesses quietly.

"Do you trust me with Poppy?"

This time she takes a moment to consider my words before she nods.

A smile spreads wide across my lips. "Then say yes. I want us to be a family, I want us to all share the same name, to show the world that you're both mine. I want to be your husband and Poppy's dad, so say yes."

"But what about–"

"Nothing else matters, we can deal with the outside world and any shit that's thrown at us together. Just say–"

She cuts me off before I can finish my sentence.

"Yes."

"Yes," I parrot back, needing her to say it again.

"Yes, Penn. Yes, I'll marry you."

"And let me adopt Poppy?"

Tears fill her eyes and she nods again. "Yes, and let you adopt Poppy. I love you."

Jumping up from my spot on the floor, I grab her and lift her off the ground, spinning her around as I take her lips with mine. I kiss her until we're both breathless and a little dizzy. "Mine," I say with a smile as I carry her off to our bedroom.

TWENTY-SIX

LULU

I wake up surrounded by Penn, his front to my back, his arm banded around my waist, and face buried in my neck. It's early, the sun's just starting to rise and there's a pale glow filtering through the edges of the drapes, but I can still see the huge diamond ring that's adorning my finger.

Engaged. I'm engaged. The thought barely makes any sense but the proof is right here on my finger. Penn asked me to marry him. He asked me if he could adopt Poppy and I said yes. It makes no sense, it's rash and impulsive and so incredibly right that I smile even as my eyes close and I relax back into Penn.

Thoughts of Roxanne and the baby that's growing inside of her try to edge into the bubble of happiness we've created, but I push them away. I don't want to think about her. Honestly, I want to pretend like she doesn't exist, at least until I absolutely have to deal with her and all of the brutal reality that surrounds her.

If her baby is Penn's, then their child will be a part of my life. I'll be co-parenting he or she with Penn, and Roxanne will make all of our lives a living hell. Only yesterday I was questioning if I could handle that and the truth is that no, I don't think I can. But I'll deal with her vitriol and hatred every day for the rest of my life if my reward is getting to keep Penn. I love him, and now that I know he exists I don't think I could truly live without him. These past few weeks he's given me a glimpse into the future. Waking up with him, falling asleep with him, drowning in pleasure and passion and desire with him. Watching him care for me and Poppy, eating with his family, being happy and safe and cared for. He gave me all of that and now that I've had a taste of him and the life we could all have together, I want it... not just for me but for Poppy too.

I want my daughter to have a dad who loves her, who will take her to father daughter dances and teach her how she should expect to be treated by any boy that wants to go out with her; then chase off the boys that aren't good enough. She deserves a man like Penn to be her daddy and although I would have been mom and dad and whoever else she needs me to be, finding someone who will love her like she's his in every way, is more than I've ever dared to hope for both of us.

Hiding away yesterday was perfect, but it was only putting a band-aid on a festering wound and I know today we need to face her as a united front. Roxanne might be family, but she's never liked me and although in the past I've let her bad behavior slide to keep the peace, I won't let her ruin Penn and me because she's jealous.

I lie in Penn's arms as the sun rises in the sky, content just to be with him until Poppy wakes up and I'm forced to roll out of bed and grab my robe from beside Penn's on the back of the door. By the time I've collected her from her room, Penn is awake, sitting up in bed and waiting for us.

"Morning," he smiles.

"Hi." Climbing back into bed I sit Poppy between my legs, but it's only a matter of moments until she's cooing and holding her arms out to Penn for him to pick her up. He takes her from me and lifts her into the air, lowering her down and covering her face with kisses before he extends his arms and lifts her again.

"I need to go and see Roxanne to tell her about the paternity test, but you don't need to see her. I don't want to listen to her insult you and you shouldn't have to be verbally assaulted because she's bitter, jealous and crazy. I don't want to keep you from Chloe, but I'll bring her back with me, we could maybe even see if she wanted to stay the night, we have the room."

"Penn," I say, reaching out and laying my hand on his arm. "I can't hide from her. If this is your baby, I'm going to have to deal with her for the rest of our lives. She already hates me, avoiding her won't make it any better."

"She's lying," he says through gritted teeth.

"Then I want to be there when she has to admit it's all bullshit."

He nods, cradling Poppy into his chest, his eyes a mix of anger and desire.

"We should have breakfast, then we can head down to Chloe's, might as well get this over and done with so we can enjoy the rest of our Sunday."

Penn showers while I get Poppy dressed, then, for the first time, I head into the main house without Penn. We've spent every night here for the last couple of weeks, but I tend to stay in his apartment except when we eat with his family. Even then I only ever head into the main house with him, never alone.

It's still early considering it's a Sunday morning, but since Bonnie's announcement that she wants to have a baby, Beau convinced her to give up her job at Wake Up and Go Go. Something he's been apparently trying to get her to do since before they got married. She might not need to get up at 4.00 am for work, but she's still an early riser and she turns from where she's mixing something in a large bowl in the kitchen and smiles at me the moment I enter the room.

"Morning, how are you feeling? Did you and Penn get everything sorted out?"

"Morning Bonnie," I smile, resting my hip against the counter as I balance Poppy's tush on the granite surface. "We got things sorted more or less. I mean, until we know if Penn is the father, we can't really do much."

"Oh my god," she squeals, interrupting me as she grabs my hand and stares down at the huge ring on my finger. "Is that what I think it is? Oh my god, you got engaged?"

Smiling shyly, I nod. "Do you think I'm crazy? It's too soon, isn't it?"

Rushing around the counter she throws her arms around me. "No, it's not too soon, it's fantastic, I'm so happy for you both."

"Thanks," I say, hugging her back with one arm while I keep Poppy steady with the other.

"So when are you getting married? Is it going to be a city hall thing like Alice and Granger or you could have it here, or did you want to do it in Chicago with your family?"

Holding my hands up to stop her, I feel the panic creep into my expression. "This just happened last night, we haven't even discussed the actual getting married part yet."

"Of course, I'm sorry," she giggles, her cheeks heating to a pale pink color. "I'm just so glad you and Poppy are going to officially become part of the family. We need more women to even the numbers out, it's a total sausage fest in this place."

I grab myself a cup of coffee and chat to Bonnie until Penn appears freshly showered and smelling of mint and lemon. His eyes warm as he walks toward us, taking Poppy from me as soon as he's close enough and then leaning down and pressing a lust drenched kiss against my lips. "Hey."

"Hey," I smile.

"Congratulations," Bonnie shrieks, bouncing over to him and hugging him tightly.

"You told her?"

"I saw the rock, it's beautiful," Bonnie tells him, grabbing my hand and lifting it so she can admire the stunning ring on my finger again.

"What are we congratulating?" a sleep rumpled Cody asks as he emerges from his door shirtless, in just sleep pants with multicolored donuts all over them.

"Lulu agreed to marry me and let me adopt Poppy,"

Penn says proudly.

All the sleepy distraction clears from Cody's expression in an instant, replaced with pure happiness. "That's amazing, congratulations."

I'm pulled from hug to hug as the rest of the Barnett clan hear the news and offer their congratulations. Bonnie sets three platters piled high with freshly made waffles and bacon down onto the table and we all sit down and eat together, one huge, rowdy, wonderful family.

My good mood lasts until we turn onto Chloe's street and I see Roxanne's red two-seater sports car parked in the driveway. "You don't have to come in with me if you don't want to," Penn offers, reaching over and taking my hand in his.

Inhaling a fortifying breath, I shake my head. "No, we're in this together, right?"

"Absolutely."

"So, we need to show a united front. We go in there, tell her about the appointment, I talk to Chloe, then we leave. I don't want to be away from Poppy any longer than we have to be."

"Poppy has six uncles and three aunts taking care of her, she'll be fine," he assures me.

"I know she will, but weekends are my only real time with her, I don't want to miss out on more than we absolutely have to, especially because of Roxy."

"Agreed," Penn says squeezing my hand as he parks at the curb and kills the engine. "You ready?"

"Not even slightly, but let's do it anyway."

Penn keeps hold of my hand as we walk up to the front of the house, his finger twisting my engagement ring from side to side. I contemplate knocking when we get to the door, but damn it, I refuse to let Roxanne make me feel like a stranger in the place I called home until two days ago. Turning the handle, Penn opens the door and leads me inside, closing it behind us. Chloe is sitting on the couch, nursing a mug as she smiles wearily at us.

"Morning."

"Morning, you look tired," I tell her, pulling my hand free from Penn's and sitting down next to her on the couch.

"My daughter is enough to make anyone exhausted," she says with a wan smile. "There's coffee in the pot."

Penn nods and moves to the kitchen, pulling out mugs and pouring coffee with a practiced ease that shows how much time he's spent here the last few weeks.

"Where is she?" I ask, taking the coffee from Penn.

"In bed, being as self-absorbed and self-righteous as she is takes it out of a girl," Chloe snarks, rolling her eyes.

"We've booked an appointment for a paternity test on Friday," Penn tells her.

"I'm not taking a damn paternity test," Roxanne screeches, stomping down the stairs, her boobs practically falling out of a bralette, her ass barely covered by tiny booty shorts, her bulging stomach completely on display.

Of course she doesn't appear to have a single stretch mark marring her taut skin, her belly a perfect beach ball shape, nothing at all like my whale-like appearance when I was carrying Poppy.

"Is that because you're ready to admit the baby's not mine?" Penn asks.

"We had sex, Penn. Babies are what happen when you're not careful," she says, a malicious grin etched across her lips.

"I was careful and thank god I was, seeing as I found you stabbing holes in the condom you tried to get me to use and I haven't touched you in over a year. Please just be honest and stop living in this fantasy world you've created in your warped head."

Instead of acknowledging Penn's words, she narrows her eyes and turns a hateful glare in my direction. "Why are you here? Penn and me have absolutely nothing to do with you. This is *our* baby, the three of us are going to be a family. You need to take your fat, used up, jealous ass and leave, take that reject brat with you."

I open my mouth to tell her how much of an evil bitch she is at the same time that both Chloe and Penn start to shout. In the end, Penn's tirade is louder and angrier than both mine and Chloe's and we fall silent.

"Do not speak to my fucking wife like that ever again," he growls. "If by some miracle that kid is mine, I'll take care of the baby, I'll be a good dad, but you will only ever be that child's mother to me and nothing more. I love Lulu, she's mine and Poppy is our daughter so you can keep your bitter, vile delusions to yourself. Now you will be having this paternity test on Friday and if you don't attend, I'll get a lawyer and drag you through court until a judge orders you to get one."

"You're an asshole, you led me on, told me you loved me and got me pregnant. We had a future planned and now she's ruining everything." Tears roll down her cheeks as she points at me like I'm the scarlet woman who's stolen her happiness away. What the actual hell is going on here?

"Roxanne, three weeks ago you were engaged to a felon and asking me for ten thousand dollars for a dress and a honeymoon. Baby, I love you, but this has to stop," Chloe says, her tone imploring as she moves toward her daughter.

"This is all because of her," Roxy hisses, pointing menacingly at me. "You've always loved her more than me, your real daughter. Now she's here and trying to steal my man and you're taking her side."

"Roxanne," Chloe sighs.

"No, fuck you, all of you," she cries, then turns and leaves, stomping up the stairs in dramatic fashion.

For a moment the three of us just stand there and stare at each other. I believed Penn when he said the baby wasn't his, but I think even he had an inkling of doubt. Roxanne is more than calculating enough to take advantage of him when he's drunk and his judgement is impaired. But the performance she's putting on is most definitely overkill. A drunken mistake would have been more believable than the song and dance she just put on about her and Penn being in love.

"She's lying," Chloe says, breaking the silence.

"I know," I agree.

"I'm sorry, Chloe, I know she's your daughter, but fuck, that bitch is certifiable." Penn exhales, running his fingers through his hair agitatedly.

Slumping back down onto the couch, Chloe shakes her head. "I just don't know why she's like this. I don't understand her animosity toward you, Lulu, you're practically the same age, we're family, as good as cousins. You should be close like you and James are, there's no reason for her to hate you."

"I'm so sorry, she's your daughter and she's obviously upset that I'm here, that must be why she's acting out like this," I cringe, feeling awful that she's having to deal with all this drama.

"Don't apologize, Kitten, this is all on Roxy not you, she's a god damn adult it's time she started acting like one."

"Penn's right, honey," Chloe agrees. "Send me the details for the appointment and I'll make sure she's there. Once the results prove this isn't Penn's baby, you can put this behind you and I can try and get her some help."

As much as I hate to do it, for the rest of the week I keep Poppy away and avoid Chloe's house and Roxanne like the plague. I know Chloe would never let anything happen to Poppy, but I don't want her in a house with Roxanne. After explaining the situation to Taylor, he agreed that I could work from home for a week until I can sort alternative childcare for Poppy. I'm not sure Janet even realizes I'm not in the office, as the menial tasks she's still having me do keep arriving in my email.

When Friday arrives I'm a mess of nerves, my stomach threatening to revolt when I sip the coffee Bay hands me.

"You okay?" he asks.

"Not even slightly, I just want this over with."

"I get it," he says with a sad smile. "It'll be okay, sis, whatever happens."

I nod, leaning into him when he pulls me in for a brotherly hug. I'm not sure when it happened or if it's been this way since the first time Penn bought me back here, but this feels like home and the Barnett clan feel like family. Spending all my time here in the last week, I've had the chance to do more than just eat with them. I've watched films with Teddy, visited the ranch with Bonnie, helped out Cora with Maverick. None of this is big or special, but I think that almost makes it more important. Since I told my family about Poppy I've been completely alone except for Chloe, but I'm not alone anymore. I have brothers and sisters, Poppy has aunts and uncles and I have Penn. My man, my love, my heart, Poppy's daddy.

Bay's right, whatever happens today it'll be okay, Penn and I will be okay.

The drive to the clinic seems to take forever, even though it's only about an hour from Rockhead Point. We arrive first and Penn is taken back by a nurse in blue scrubs just before Chloe and a pissed looking Roxanne push through the entrance.

"God, you're like a bad smell, you just won't go away," she sneers to me.

"Go check in," Chloe says, offering me a sad smile as she herds Roxy to the desk, waiting for the nurse to escort her away before she sinks down into the chair beside me.

"I never even got to say congratulations or tell you how sorry I am for not telling you about Penn and Roxy," Chloe says, her expression stricken.

"That's okay."

"No, it's not. It's not okay at all. I knew they had a dalliance, but it was so long ago and all I heard was that they'd been seen together a couple of times at a bar."

"It doesn't matter now, neither of us were virgins before we met."

"I should have said something, but I just wanted you and Poppy to have the happiness I knew Penn could give you so bad that I kept it to myself."

"I might have been a little more prepared, but really, knowing about them wouldn't have changed anything. I might have fought a little harder, but we'd still end up in the same place."

"When did he ask you to marry him?

I tell her about Penn asking, how he just blurted it out completely out of the blue.

"Have you told your parents?" she asks.

I shake my head, "Not yet, I will. We check in every couple of months so I'll tell them then."

"How's Poppy?"

"She's fine, being spoilt rotten having me, Penn, six uncles and three aunts all doting on her, I've no idea how she's going to cope when I go back to work," I laugh, although it sounds as strained as it feels.

"I miss her. Maybe I could come to the Barnetts' and watch her there if Roxanne is still here next week?" She sounds so hopeful that I take her hand in mine and squeeze it. "Of course you can, if that's what you want, she misses her aunt Chloe."

The nurse reappears at the reception desk and the sight of her brings back the reason we're here. Nausea leaps up my throat and suddenly I know I'm going to be sick. Jumping up, I clamp my hand over my mouth and surge toward the desk. The nurse eyes me and calmly points down the corridor. "Bathroom is the third door on the left."

Without pausing to thank her, I run for the bathroom, barely making it to the toilet before the coffee and toast I ate this morning make a reappearance. Once I clean up and splash cool water on my sweaty face, I open the door, pausing when I hear the familiar sound of Roxanne's voice coming from the room on the opposite side of the corridor.

"Dr. Connor, I need this test to show that Penn is this baby's daddy, maybe we can work something out between us to make that happen. I've been told I can make a man feel really good and this pregnancy is making me all hot and bothered all of the time. My pussy is so wet, I'd bet you'd just slide right inside of me."

"Miss Mason, this is completely inappropriate," a male voice says.

"No one would ever have to know, this could be all our little secret," she says seductively, her voice breathy and sexified.

"Miss Mason, I'm going to have to ask you to leave my office. I am a doctor, a professional and I would never fabricate results."

"I'm sure there's something you want, something your wife would never let you do, a fantasy you've never confessed to her. If you help me, I could help you. Anything you want, I'm incredibly..." she pauses for a minute. "Open-minded."

"Miss Mason, is the father of your baby Mr. Barnett?" the doctor asks in a no-nonsense tone.

"Of course it isn't, but that's why we need to come to some kind of arrangement," she purrs, like a sexed up porn star.

I can't help it, my feet move without thought and I push the half open door wide and step into the office. "Do you even know who the father is?" I demand

"What are you doing, you can't be in here, this is a private meeting between me and my doctor. Get out," Roxanne yells, actually lifting her hand and pointing in the direction of the door as if that's going to make me leave and forget what I just heard.

"I heard you. I heard you try to offer this doctor sexual favors in exchange for him faking the results of the paternity test."

"You're crazy," she says with a flounce.

"There's only one crazy person in this room and it isn't me."

"Miss Morgan, you just confessed that you know that Mr. Barnett isn't the biological father of your baby. You attempted to bribe me to doctor the results. I think it would be best if we bring in Mr. Barnett and inform him of what you have just advised me," the doctor says calmly.

"I'll go and get him," I tell them both, my stomach still rolling, my legs unsteady. Penn jumps up from his seat the moment I step into the waiting room. "Are you okay? Chloe said you got sick."

"It's all a lie."

"What is?" he asks, taking my hands and trying to lead me over to a chair.

"We need to go back there, I came to get you."

"Why?" His brows are furrowed with concern and I reach out and smooth a finger across his face.

"It's all a lie, I was coming out of the bathroom and I heard her speaking in the opposite room. She was offering to fuck the doctor if he falsified the paternity test results. She knows this baby isn't yours but she wanted him to fake the results so you'd think it was."

"Fuck," Penn hisses through gritted teeth.

"The doctor wants us to go back there."

Linking our fingers together, Penn's gaze locks with mine as he lifts my hand to his lips and presses a kiss just above where my ring sits.

"I'm so sorry," Chloe says, her voice shattering the intensity of the moment Penn and I were sharing.

"You have nothing to be sorry about," Penn says. "Roxanne's an adult, she knew exactly what she was doing, don't try to take responsibility for her actions."

Chloe nods, swallowing visibly. "If Lulu hadn't heard, if she'd managed to convince that doctor to help her. She could have ruined yours and that poor child's lives, she'd have taken your money and let you think that baby was your son or daughter." Covering her mouth with her palm, she shakes her head again as if the words she's saying are just too horrible to say aloud.

"Come on, let's go back there, I want to get this over and done with and go home," Penn says firmly, guiding me in front of him as he reaches out and gently squeezes Chloe's arm.

As we file into the doctor's office, I avoid making eye contact with a sullen looking Roxanne who is playing with her cell, looking for all intent and purposes like she hasn't got a care in the world.

"Please sit," the doctor says, motioning to the chairs positioned in front of his desk. "Mr. Barnett, I presume?"

"Yes," Penn confirms, leaning forward to offer the doctor his hand to shake. "This is my fiancé Lulu and Chloe, Roxanne's mother."

"Ahhh, yes," the doctor says, glancing between Chloe and Roxanne. "I'm Dr Connor and I'm afraid to inform you that there has been an incident this afternoon, whereby Miss Mason attempted to bribe me to change the results of the paternity test you are here today to perform."

"For fuck's sake," Roxanne snaps. "Kid's not yours, Penn, I'm sure that bitch has already told you. I lied, okay? You pair can live your disgusting little happy ever after, you, her and the brat. Can we all go now?"

"Mr. Barnett, although the choice is of course yours I would suggest we perform the paternity test anyway. I personally took the sample from Miss Mason so I know it hasn't been exposed to any kind of fraudulent behavior and I will oversee the testing and results. Normally you'd receive the result within twenty-four hours, but as we test onsite, if you can wait, I can have a definitive answer about the paternity of Miss Mason's baby within the hour.

"I appreciate that, Dr Connor, I'm happy to wait."

"Well I'm not," Roxanne says, pushing up from her chair and moving toward the door. "I already told you, kid's not yours. I'm leaving."

"Miss Mason, the police have been called and they're on their way, attempting to defraud medical records is a criminal offense, so if I were you, I would sit back down until they get here," Dr Connor says, turning a steely glare in Roxanne's direction.

Roxanne's face pales and she looks to Chloe who just shakes her head, disgust at her daughter's behavior clear on her face.

The next hour is the longest of my life. The police arrive and take Roxanne and Chloe into another room while Penn and I stay in the doctor's office. The nausea I'm feeling doesn't fade until Dr Connor enters the room, a file in his hand.

"I have the results of the test here, Miss Mason and her mother will be rejoining us shortly."

Penn nods, gripping my hand tighter as Roxy and Chloe walk back in. My godmother's eyes are red and puffy, it's clear she's been crying and I hate that in this moment I can't go to her. I can't make this any better, all we can do now is hear the truth and then go home.

"With regard to the unborn baby of Miss Roxanne Lillian Mason, the alleged father Mr. Penn Hanlin Barnett is excluded as the biological father based on DNA samples taken."

He carries on speaking using technical jargon, but I barely hear him, because I'm stuck on the most important thing he said. Penn isn't the father of Roxanne's baby.

TWENTY-SEVEN

PENN

I'm not that kid's dad. I know the doc is speaking, but all I can hear on repeat in my mind is that I'm not that kid's dad. I already knew it wasn't mine, but knowing and *knowing* are two very different things.

A shaky exhale falls from me and I grip Lulu's hand just a little bit tighter. I love her so fucking much. If by some fucked up twist of fate the kid had been mine, Lulu and I would have been okay, but this is so much better and all I want to do now is grab my woman and go home and bind her to me so everyone in the whole fucking world knows she's mine.

I nod and thank the doctor, then pull Lulu to her feet

and lead her to the door, eager to get the hell away from this office and Roxanne. The police are waiting for Roxy when we come out and they escort her to a waiting cop car, carefully loading her into it as Chloe looks on with watery eyes.

"Are you okay?" Lulu asks Chloe.

"They ran her name when they came to question her, she has an outstanding warrant for identity fraud so they're taking her to the station to be arraigned."

"Do you need me to help you find a lawyer?" Lulu asks. "I have a few friends that are practicing now, a couple of them specialize in criminal law."

"Why would you want to help her after what she's done to the both of you?" she asks incredulous.

"I don't want to help her, I want to help you," my woman says simply, pulling her hand free from my hold so she can tug Chloe into a tight hug.

Their hug lasts a long time and when they separate, both women have tears pouring down their faces and watery smiles.

"You should get home, I have to call Wade and tell him his daughter has been arrested."

They hug again, then separate as Chloe heads to her car and I lead Lulu to mine. "I love you," I tell her, turning her and backing her into the side of my car.

"I love you too."

"I'm sorry you've had to deal with all this bullshit."

"Me too, but at least it's over now."

"Now we can look forward to the future. Weddings to plan, babies to make." I wink at her and she laughs, slapping lightly at my chest before she wraps her arms around me and hugs me tightly. "Let's go home."

"Home," she agrees with a smile.

We celebrate that night with champagne, Chinese food and a healthy dose of family. By the time I follow Lulu through the door into our rooms, it's well past midnight and I'm desperate to strip her naked and lose myself in her lush curves and warm pussy.

"I love you so damn much," I confess, lifting her up and encouraging her to wrap her legs around my waist.

"I love you too," she says, pressing her lips to mine and kissing me roughly.

I never thought I'd find a woman I could see myself settling down with, not until the moment Lulu literally fell into my orbit. She's everything I could ever want and not only did she give me herself, she gave me Poppy too.

I have a woman, I have a daughter. I'm the luckiest man alive and as I strip Lulu's clothes from her body and sink into her heat, I know that my fiancé and my baby girl have claimed me, heart, body and soul.

The End

EPILOGUE

LULU

Remember that time I threw up at the paternity test place? Yeah, that wasn't just nerves, that was the baby that's growing in my belly attempting at saying hello. I'm pregnant. I'm a pregnant bride, because Penn convinced me he couldn't wait, so here we are on our two-month anniversary getting married in the beautiful meadow behind our house.

My parents have chosen not to be a part of our day. Yet again they disapprove of my decisions and that's okay, I don't need them here. We have plenty of people who want to help us celebrate the new life Penn, Poppy and I are starting here together. My six new brothers, three new sisters and one new nephew are all here, as well as my new adopted sort of in-laws in the form of Bonnie's dad and Cora's parents who are all part of the Barnett Clan.

Chloe's hand is tightly gripping mine as she walks me down the makeshift aisle to where Penn and Poppy are waiting for me beneath an archway of flowers. Despite everything that's happened, Chloe is my godmother, my pseudo mom and biggest supporter, there's no one else I'd rather have give me away.

After the police arrested Roxanne, she was arraigned, bailed and then convicted of identity fraud, the judge gave her a suspended sentence and ordered her to undertake a mandatory psych evaluation. According to Chloe, Roxanne has a lot of issues, and although I'm not unsympathetic, I was still very glad to hear that she's moving to Wyoming to be closer to her dad. Turns out the baby's father was a one night stand she met in a bar in New York. She doesn't know his surname and never bothered to ask for his cell number before she left the alley they fucked in.

When we reach Penn, Chloe hugs me, then steps away, taking a seat beside Bay as the justice of the peace starts to talk. Penn offered to give me a big elaborate wedding, but when I really thought about it, all I wanted was to marry him, in this beautiful setting, surrounded by people who care for us.

My dress is simple, white satin that hugs my curves, falling to the floor and into a small fishtail at the back. My hair is loose, falling in waves over my shoulders, and I'm wearing the most obscenely ridiculous sparkly shoes that I fell in love with the moment I laid eyes on and simply had to have. Penn is wearing a white button down, the sleeves rolled up to his elbows and navy-blue pants. Cradled to his chest is Poppy. Her dress is white with a navy-blue sash and a matching bow for her hair.

The service starts and words are spoken, but I don't really hear them. The world narrows to just me, Penn and Poppy, we're a family.

Reaching out, I take Penn's hand and pull it toward me, spreading his palm over my stomach and making our baby a part of this ceremony too. His eyes widen, his lips falling apart as he glances down at my stomach and then back up to my face. When he smiles it's like the world gets brighter, the sun gets warmer and each perfect moment lasts forever.

Before Penn, I never believed in fate or myths about love at first sight. I was determined to make a life for me and my daughter, no matter how sad and jaded and alone I felt. The path to here and now hasn't been straightforward, and despite Penn's enduring belief that we were always meant to be, it's taken him proving to me over and over again that I am his and he is mine to truly believe.

Destiny, chance, luck, call it what you will, Penn is my love, my heart, my soul, my daughter's father in all the ways that matter, he's my family and my happy ever after.

ACKNOWLEDGEMENTS

Wow this book seems to have taken FOREVER to write.

Turns out writing a romance novel while you're pregnant can be a pretty crazy experience and apparently while I was busy growing a baby, my hormone addled brain decided this book needed to have plenty of bouncing bundles of joy too.

So I had another kid, her name is Violet and she's the person I had no idea we were all waiting for to make our family complete. She's the most beautiful little girl in the world and the reason this book is so late is because I just couldn't stop staring at her.

Right now I'm so high on baby smiles and cuddles that I love everyone and everything and I'm crying while I write this because I just feel so lucky.

Sarah my wonderful bestie, you have as always been my rock, you've held my hand, kicked my ass and during this book, listened to me moan about how old I felt being pregnant in my late thirties.

To my fabulous publishers Hudson Indie Ink, thank you for letting me do my thing, you guys rock and I'm so grateful that being a part of this team lets me write books about babies and sexy mountain men when I'm hocked up on mama crazy juice.

Special thanks to my wonderful editor Sarah, this book is either awesome or insane, honestly I'm not sure which it is yet. Aren't you glad that you get to be the one to tell me lol. You polish my word and make them shine, I couldn't do this without you.

Let's give a shout out to all my wonderful readers, thank you for sticking with me, even though Penn's book has taken a little longer than expected. I've had so many messages begging for the next mountain man and I love that I'm dragging you all into this fantasy world with me.

Finally, and he's never going to read this, because he's never made it past the first page on any of my books, I'm going to mention my husband Martin. You got me pregnant AGAIN! Then you got me a cleaner, it's the best gift ever. I love you and I promise one day you can retire and I'll buy you all the pretty things and if we're really rich maybe even that yacht you keep talking about.

ABOUT THE AUTHOR

Gemma Weir is a half crazed stay at home mom to three kids, one man child and a hell hound. She has lived in the midlands, in the UK her whole life and has wanted to write a book since she was a child. Gemma has a ridiculously dirty mind and loves her book boyfriends to be big, tattooed alpha males. She's a reader first and foremost and she loves her romance to come with a happy ending and lots of sexy sex.

For updates on future releases check out my social media links.

ALSO BY GEMMA WEIR

The Archers Creek Series
Echo (Archer's Creek #1)

Daisy (Archer's Creek #2)

Blade (Archer's Creek #3)

Echo & Liv (Archer's Creek #3.5)

Park (Archer's Creek #4)

Smoke (Archer's Creek #5)

*

The Scions Series
Hidden (The Scions #1)

Found (The Scions #2)

Wings & Roots (The Scions #3)

*

The Kings & Queens of St Augustus Series
The Spare - Part One

(The Kings & Queens of St Augustus #1)

The Spare - Part Two

(The Kings & Queens of St Augustus #2)

The Heir - Part One

(The Kings & Queens of St Augustus #3)

The Heir - Part Two

(The Kings & Queens of St Augustus #4)

*

The Montanna Mountain Men

Property the Mountain Man
Owned by the Mountain Man
Kept by the Mountain Man
Claimed by the Mountain Man

OTHER AUTHORS AT HUDSON INDIE INK

Paranormal Romance/Urban Fantasy

Stephanie Hudson

Sloane Murphy

Xen Randell

Sorcha Dawn

C L Monoghan

Sci-Fi/Fantasy

Devin Hanson

Crime/Action

Blake Hudson

Mike Gomes

Contemporary Romance

Gemma Weir

Lightning Source UK Ltd.
Milton Keynes UK
UKHW011827190622
404644UK00001B/9

9 781913 769741